THE HEALING

LYNN L. SAUNDERS

DISCLAIMER

This book is a work of fiction and a product of my own imagination. Nick Curtis and all the other characters in this book are fictitious. There is no Rose Briar Cottage or village. All the people, places, businesses, TV shows, organisations, and police incidents (both in the UK and USA) portrayed in this book are made up by me and any resemblance to actual incidents or persons, living or deceased is entirely incidental. References to real organisations and places are only intended to provide a sense of authenticity.

Text and Photograph Copyright Lynn Saunders, who asserts the moral right to be identified as the author of this book.
2023

Books by Lynn Saunders

The Bay View Trilogy:

FOR MY FAMILY,
AND
FOR WOMEN EVERYWHERE – STAY STRONG

PROLOGUE

Ten years previous - JOE

The smell of cooked cabbage filled the corridor. Further along, behind closed doors, a young child was bawling. Home after finishing a hectic early shift, Joe rummaged for his door key to let himself into the flat where he and Ally now lived. The place served its purpose and would do them for now but, never, in a million years, would he ever be happy to call it his proper home. As he neared the door to their flat, he could hear the couple across the corridor having a very loud and angry slanging match. He cursed under his breath, realising that his plan for an afternoon of peace and quiet had vanished. Slipping the key into the lock, he wondered if the noise from his neighbours would ever stop. Their rows seemed to be getting more frequent, and he would need to keep an eye on the situation.

He absently threw his keys down on the hallway table, where they landed with a dull clatter. As he looked up, he caught the reflection of his tired pale face in the mirror. Long gone was his usual healthy glow gained from a summer of sailing his dinghy off the Cornish coast. He had traded sea and fresh air for the busy and grey streets of London.

It was almost two years ago that he had given up his job with the Cornish police and followed Ally to the capital city. They had searched long and hard for somewhere to set up home together, and this little rented flat, in this not so nice part of London, had been all they could afford. When they had first moved in, the state of the flat had not bothered them, for they had been completely loved-up and life was one big adventure. They had taken great pleasure in buying a few bits of furniture and some colourful rugs and cushions from budget stores to brighten the place up. He glanced at the mirror again, it had been one of the first things they had chosen together. He thought back to how excited they'd been when they'd hung it above the shabby half-moon table. Neither of them had two pennies to rub together and this mirror, bought at the local flea market, had been a major purchase.

It was only after a few months that he and Ally began to realise the flat's shortcomings. Although things weren't perfect, they had both agreed to stick with it so that Ally could further her acting career. The past two years had not been easy, but he still stood by his decision to support his girlfriend because he loved her and couldn't imagine life without her.

Even though it was only mid-afternoon, the tiny kitchen of the flat, which Ally had labelled the shoe box, was gloomy. Reaching for the switch, the fluorescent strip blinked sluggishly into action. With its worn 1970s vinyl floor, sludge green walls, and the repetitive dull thud of water on steel from the dripping tap, the cold north facing kitchen felt damp and unwelcoming no matter what time of year.

Unzipping his holdall, he pulled out his grubby police officer shirts and loaded them into the washer. He was so looking forward to his couple of days off shift, work had been so busy. Reaching over to switch on the kettle, he noticed a scribbled note from Ally.

Pl can you get some food for dinner tonight, fridge empty.

He frowned. Lately they were like ships passing in the night. He checked his phone for the umpteenth time, there was nothing from Ally. He knew that she had gone for another audition today and he was desperate to know how she had got on. He really hoped she had managed to nail this one, for it was a biggie, being a leading role in a new soap, or continuing drama as they called them these days. As far as he was concerned, Ally was well overdue her big break because she was amazing.

The clock on the ancient cooker told him that if he hurried, he would be able to pick up some food at the local mini mart before it closed.

Grabbing his jacket and keys, he ran down the communal stairs. Stepping out onto the busy street, he glanced up at the leaden sky. It was just starting to rain, hopefully he'd be there and back before it started pouring down. Yanking the collar of his jacket up around his ears, he strode purposely down the road towards the mini mart. The rain had now turned into a full-on downpour, the driving torrent was slanting towards him, turning the pavement from a dull grey to a shiny black and coating the front of his jeans. London in the rain seemed even more miserable than when it rained back home. Apart from the local park and the bright red London buses, everything else seemed to lack colour. There were rows and rows of rain-soaked shiny roofed terraced houses, each one blessed with a tiny front garden with just enough room to squeeze in a couple of wheelie bins.

As he turned the corner, he glanced up and caught a glimpse of the sky between the high-rise flats. It was obvious that the rain was set to stay, for all he could see was a blanket of grey with no sign of a break in the cloud. How he yearned for the sound and smell of the ocean instead of the honking of horns, vehicle sirens and fumes from the noisy London traffic. He knew he was homesick because he even missed the frustration of getting caught behind a slow-moving farm vehicle on Cornwall's narrow twisty lanes. Anything was better than the endless kebab and fried chicken shops and other takeaways which lined the high street and the smelly food cartons people left behind littering the pavements.

Grabbing a bag of salad and a pizza from the mini mart's chilled cabinet, he did a de-tour to the wine section and grabbed a bottle of Ally's favourite. He hoped there would be something to celebrate, because his girlfriend had put her heart and soul into chasing work. A few small parts had come her way, mainly television ads and voiceovers, but nothing major had come along, and it was about time her luck changed.

The excitement of moving to the big city had long worn off; not only for him but for Ally too. It hadn't been quite what they had envisaged; not quite the romantic idyll they had imagined. There had been a few niggling worries about Ally too. She had been snappy and tense lately and he had to seriously bite his tongue to stop himself snapping back. She was often moody and uncommunicative and at times he could tell that he was being shut out. More and more he was having to tread on eggshells to appease her and would get his head bitten off if he broached the subject. He had put it down to her not being able to find any decent acting work and he told himself that things would get better. He loved Ally, and even though things were not great, he knew he wouldn't change a thing.

As he joined the long slow queue to pay for his shopping, he first checked his phone for any messages, then clicked on his weather app. He wasn't surprised when he saw that for the rest of the day, under every hour, there was a black cloud icon with two raindrops. Scrolling down further, he looked to see what the weather was like back home and couldn't help feeling a pang of envy on seeing that the weather in Cornwall was bright and sunny. He checked out the wind direction, it was a habit he couldn't kick, for once a sailing geek, always a sailing geek. He thought about his little dinghy, unused and still covered in tarpaulin, he would probably need to do a bit of maintenance on it when he next went home. A trip home was long overdue. It had been quite a while since he'd seen his parents and younger brother Tom, and he missed them. He knew Ally missed her parents too. Conveniently for them, both sets of parents lived in the same harbour village, something he and Ally were very grateful for.

As he shifted slowly along the queue, his phone pinged with an e-mail, a utility bill was overdue. Thank goodness he had enough money in his account. His salary, with overtime, was just enough to cover the bills. He thought back to when he had first left Cornwall to join the police here in London. At first it had been hard settling in. The place had seemed hostile, like a concrete jungle. Even his colleagues at the police station didn't seem that friendly. He had hoped it was just a new kid on the block thing and that they would soon accept him, but two years on he still felt like he didn't fit in. It was a bit like dog eat dog in the office they all shared at the police station. He was glad to get out on the beat, at least that got him away from the office politics, and the sergeant, who didn't seem to have a good word to say to anyone, especially to him.

'Yes?'

He was snapped out of his thoughts by the shopkeeper looking quizzically at him while impatiently drumming his fingers on the counter.

'Oh. Sorry, how much?' Joe fumbled for his card to pay, trying to ignore the man's obvious irritation. After paying, he beat a hasty retreat.

Soaked through, he let himself back into the tiny, third floor flat. He sighed as he glanced around at their cramped living conditions. Pushing any negative thoughts aside, blaming them on the weather, he pulled open the fridge door to put away the shopping he'd just bought.

The wine was cooling, the table laid, salad in a bowl, and the oven was on. He'd changed out of his soaked clothes and their favourite music was ready to go. All he needed now was Ally. He switched on the kettle to make himself a cup of coffee.

Two coffees later, he heard the key in the lock. Ally came in beaming from ear to ear - she had got the part. After celebrating over wine and pizza, he knew he had his old Ally back.

Life continued to bubble along. Ally was in her element, every night she came home relating tales of her new role and how happy she was. He was happy for her, after all that's what they had moved to London for, and they now had more money to spend too, which was a bonus.

There was a fly in the ointment though. He was starting to become aware of a change in his girlfriend. The chattiness over her new job had stopped and she was often home late. When she did eventually arrive home, she was vague and even more distant. He had caught her checking her mobile phone when she thought he wasn't looking and she no longer left it lying about, which was unusual because she'd never done that before.

Ally was late home again. He switched off the oven and plated up her dinner.

He heard the house phone ringing in the hallway. Thinking it was Ally calling to let him know that she was on her way home, he went to answer it. Not stopping to wonder why she was using that number instead of his mobile, he was totally unprepared for what was to follow. On the line was a total stranger. The lecherous silky-voiced guy who was wanting to speak to Ally obviously hadn't a clue who he was. Joe didn't think he would ever forget the insinuation in the bloke's voice.

'Hi, is Ally there?'

'No, she's not here, she'll be back later. Can I help instead?'

'Are you her flat mate? Can you give her a message? It's Nick from the TV studio. She gave me her mobile number, but I've stupidly mislaid it.'

As Joe listened, he knew the creep's exact words and the snigger in his upper-class voice would be etched in his memory for ever.

'Tell her she's one very hot, sexy babe and I can't wait to get up close and personal with her again very soon. In fact, please can you tell her I've already booked a table for us at The Ivy for tomorrow night.'

The bottom had fallen out of his world, still dazed, he numbly put the phone down. Then the anger came, he crashed his fist several times against the wall. What a fool he'd been. He'd seen the signs and stupidly ignored them. He put on his coat and stormed down the road to find the nearest pub to drown his sorrows. There was no going back from this, when she eventually showed her face, he was going to have it out with her. She was not going to play him about after the sacrifices he'd made for her.

When Ally arrived home that night, they had a blazing row when she admitted falling for the guy who was a TV executive on the production she was working on. Shortly after that, she moved out and not long after, he had handed the keys to the flat back to the landlord and headed home to Cornwall, where he re-joined the Cornish police.

CHAPTER 1 - Ten Years Later

JOE

The Cornish weather was at its best today and he had booked a week's annual leave and was determined to make the most of it. Here he was, out on his boat with the sun warming his back, as he contentedly sailed his dinghy towards Gribbin Head.

His thoughts began to wander. Why it popped into his head he didn't know, but it was ten years ago, almost to the day, that he had picked up the phone and realised Ally had been cheating on him. He thought back to the massive argument that had followed, which had led to their break-up and him moving back home to Cornwall.

Even now, all these years later, it stayed with him. Although he had moved on, he still thought about Ally. It was bitter-sweet, even though he'd been hurt, he knew he hadn't lost all feelings for her. There was still something there, despite the way she had treated him. They hadn't stayed in contact with each other, but he had followed her career. She was doing very well for herself and was quite a famous actress now on a hospital tv drama.

Out of his old group of school friends, Ally was the only one of them who he didn't see anymore. Kat saw her though. She and Ally were still quite close and saw each other when Ally came home to Cornwall to visit her parents. It was funny how things had turned out. Always the sensible one, Kat had married their trouble-prone friend CJ. Kat was now a teacher at the local school and CJ, despite being a bit of a disaster at school, had turned it around was now a fat cat businessman, who owned a company that built houses. It was CJ's building firm who had built the little two-bedroom terraced house on the edge of the village that he now rented. His other great friend, Kat's twin brother Marco, had moved away. He never came home after graduating from Southampton Uni. Marco now lived in Plymouth and worked for a multi-media company. All of them regularly met up, except Ally; she was like the elephant in the room and his friends never mentioned her while he was about.

He felt the wind against his face and the salty water spray his lips and felt good. There would be no more London living for him ever again. His roots were here. His career was going well, he had taken his exams and was now a sergeant. He had a girlfriend too, Maxine, a fellow police officer. He liked her, she'd even moved in with him, but despite her best efforts to get him to put a ring on her finger, he had resisted. There had only ever been one woman for him, and she had dumped him for some high flying tv executive. Never again would he get caught - once bitten, twice shy as the saying goes. He tightened his grip on the dinghy's rudder.

ALLY

It was still dark outside, but she knew she needed to get an early start to avoid the traffic. Ally looked around the spacious flat overlooking the Thames for one last time to make sure that she had left nothing behind. The flat was a world apart from the tiny, shabby but cosy place she had rented all those years ago with Joe. This one was expensively furnished. All glass and metal furniture; high-end designer but certainly not comfortable. Nick, her partner - but as of now her ex-partner - had purchased the flat years ago, long before she had moved in with him. The few bits of her own that she had bought to make the place feel more homely had already been transported down to Cornwall for her parents to store in one of their outbuildings. Along with most of her other possessions, they would be kept safe until she knew what she was going to do with her life.

After leaving her set of keys on the glass console table, she took a deep breath as she walked out of the door for the very last time. Pulling the door firmly shut behind her, she felt no emotion. It was ten years of her life gone, most of them unhappy. She hadn't seen Nick for nigh on a fortnight. She didn't know where he was and didn't really care either. They had not parted on the best of terms having had a massive row, which had resulted in a nasty bruise on her back where Nick had pushed her into the corner of their dining table. Feeling no sadness or regret, she found there was a spring in her step as she walked away from a part of her life that she wished she could erase from her memory forever.

Dawn was only just breaking as the elevator doors opened onto the private underground car park. The place was deserted, the nightlights still on, throwing their gloomy light around the rows of luxury cars. Her car was already loaded to the hilt, and she was ready for the long drive to Cornwall. She thought back to the first time Nick had brought her to the penthouse flat. Then everything had been exciting, that was before her life started to fall apart. She wished she could turn back the clock. She never wanted to see Nick again and hoped he would leave her alone.

It had been a long journey, and despite stopping at the services at Exeter for a strong coffee and pack of sandwiches, she could feel her stomach rumbling. Wearily, she glanced at the Satnav; it was telling her that she had reached her destination. She kind of knew the area because she was not a million miles away from her parents' house, six miles to be exact. She couldn't remember the last time she had visited this bustling village nestled on the banks of the river. It would have been a long time ago, when she and her parents had first moved down to Cornwall. She wondered how far away the cottage that she'd taken a long let on was. The letting agent's photo showing the amazing view of the river from the bedroom and the roses climbing around the front of the cottage had sold it to her. The location of the cottage would provide her with a sanctuary, while also having the advantage of being near her parents. She had telephoned the letting agency from the London flat and taken the lease on the cottage without even seeing it, so desperate was she to get away.

She studied the details from the letting agency to look for clues of where to find the cottage. She had driven up the main street three times and still had not found it. It was late afternoon, and it wouldn't be too many hours before the daylight started to fade. The long drive had made her tired and she was anxious to get the contents of her car unloaded and into her new home as soon as possible to familiarise herself with it while it was still light. There was no choice, she would have to ask someone where the cottage was. After parking up the kerb of the narrow road, she headed into what looked like the local newsagent shop. The bell jangled. An elderly Asian man was reading a newspaper behind the counter.

She tentatively smiled at the man who was looking at her curiously. 'Um, please can you help? I'm looking for Rose Briar Cottage.'

'Ah. Not many people around here go near that place anymore, but if you follow the road down, past the church, you will see a narrow road off to the left. Go down half a mile and you will come to two cottages, the one you want is the one on the right. The other cottage belongs to old Edna, she's lived there for years.' His eyes narrowing, he looked at her. 'Mind how you go now.'

Driving slowly down the uneven gravel track, she peered through the car windscreen looking for her new home.

There it was. Even in the late afternoon light, the cottage looked just like the photo she'd received from the letting agent. She pulled the car in close to the gate and turned off the ignition. Winding the car window down, she read the name engraved on the slate sign. 'Rose Briar Cottage' lived up to its name, for pale pink roses clung to the walls and trailed over the front door. The gate and picket fence had been painted the same light blue as the cottage's windows and front door. She felt a thrill of anticipation run through her. Even though the gate could do with a lick of paint, she hoped the inside of the cottage was as lovely as the outside.

Opening the back of her car, she grimaced at the mountain of stuff she had crammed into it. Even though she felt tired, she knew there was no point in delaying, for the car wouldn't unpack itself. Heaving the first of the extremely heavy plastic sacks off the top of the pile, she bumped it along the pathway to the front door of the cottage. After setting the bag aside, she inserted the key into the lock. As the lock clicked, an overwhelming feeling of excitement swept over her. Her new home, new beginnings and all that stuff, a cliché she knew but it was true.

Pushing against the door with her foot, she hoped it would open easily, but something was stopping it. The bottom of the heavy wooden door seemed to be dragging against the coir doormat. Quickly realising that she would need all her strength to open the door, she used both her hands to give the door a jolly hard shove. The door sprung open. She wrinkled her nose at the damp, musty smell. She would have to give the cottage a good airing.

The curtains were closed, making the place look dark. After switching on the light, she looked all around her. The square shaped living room was a decent size, certainly large enough for her. Taking up the far wall was a brick inglenook fireplace. There was a rusty grate in the open hearth, complete with traces of ash from a long-ago fire. She shivered, despite being warm outside, the room felt icy cold. Facing towards the fireplace, a shabby but comfortable looking dark red sofa was the centrepiece of the room. A well-worn Persian style rug had been placed on the floor in front of the sofa, covering the stone flags. Someone had obviously tried to make the room look cosy. Her eyes quickly travelled around the room, taking in the steep narrow stairs in the far corner. Tucked under the rise of the stairs was a small dark wood table and two dining chairs.

A door off the living area revealed a small kitchen with narrow wooden floorboards. Glancing around, she guessed the tiny room had once been an outbuilding but over time had been re-built as part of the cottage. This must have been quite a few years ago, judging by the dated electric cooker. A door at the far end of the kitchen opened to reveal a bathroom with a pale pink bathroom suite, with the bonus of a shower over the bath. She glanced around, everything was basic, but it suited her needs. The kitchen had seen better days, but it had a sink, cooker and fridge and there was an adequate bathroom too, that's all she needed, that and solitude. It would do her fine for the time being.

The soft cushioned sofa looked so tempting. She had hardly slept a wink the previous night as everything had been racing through her mind. Even though she wanted to, she couldn't afford the luxury of sitting down. There was no time to waste. She had to unload the car, and the sooner she got it done, the sooner she could relax. First though, she needed to get some light into this gloomy room.

After pulling open the curtains, the light flooded in. Smiling, she looked around her; it was already looking better. She headed back to her car to grab a couple more bulging plastic sacks.

Slightly out of breath and with aching arms, she deposited her expensive duvet and matching pillows, which she had impulsively snatched from her London bed, on the sofa. She would take them upstairs after she'd emptied the car. Reasoning that if she got too tired, all she had to do was fling her duvet and a couple of pillows on the bed and get her head down. Anything else could wait until tomorrow.

With her car now mostly empty, its contents piled up in the corner of the living room, Ally scooped up her duvet and pillow. Peering over the top of the squashy bundle, she struggled up the stairs onto the small windowless landing.

The bedroom door creaked as she pushed it open. The room appeared quite dark, apart from a small chink of light coming through a gap in the heavy brocade curtains. Finding the light switch, she stood on the threshold for a moment. The first thing she noticed was the old-fashioned bedside cabinet and matching triple mirrored dressing table. Quickly looking around the rest of the room, she took in the other bits of furniture, which looked to be from a hodgepodge of different eras. Throwing her bedding down onto the blue and white ticking mattress, she nodded to herself. It was old but clean. All good so far. She reached for the switch on the barley twist bedside lamp. Instantly it gave the room a cosy hue, highlighting the pink cabbage rose wallpaper. She wondered who had previously occupied the room and how long ago, as it dawned on her that the whole cottage was in a time warp, possibly pre-second world war. There were two other bedrooms. She quickly opened the doors and looked in. One was a tiny box room and unfurnished, which would do for storage, the other room was a good size and had a bed.

Although she had been sorely tempted to lay down on the bed and curl up beneath her duvet, she decided to go back downstairs and continue unpacking. Eventually, the tiredness got the better of her. Sinking into the soft sofa cushions, it wasn't long before she had drifted off to sleep.

Waking with a start, Ally looked around her. The dim ceiling light threw shadows around the room. She stared for a moment at the fireplace just a few feet in front of her before remembering where she was. She didn't know what had woken her, but hearing her stomach rumble, quickly realised that she hadn't eaten since Exeter. She checked the time on her phone, it was too late to buy anything, the shops would be shut by now. Remembering the big bag of root vegetable crisps and bottled water that she'd bought earlier, she dug them out of her backpack. Not ideal but would do for now – part of her five a day she thought wryly. Tomorrow she would unpack properly then explore the village and find the nearest supermarket.

Wearily, she carried her heavy suitcase up the stairs, then began hanging her clothes in the mothball scented wardrobe. Placing her toiletries on the dressing table, she rummaged around in her bag for the small tub of pills that she took everywhere. The pills, which had been prescribed by her London doctor, had been to help her live her life without anyone noticing the turmoil inside of her. Holding the almost empty white plastic tub in her hands, she stared at what was left of her three times daily life support system that had kept her going for the past few years. That and the bottle of wine she seemed to get through almost daily. Well, things were going to change. That's what she was here for – a complete lifestyle overhaul. Before she left London she had, with the full support of her doctor, started to slowly wean herself off the mind-numbing pills. There were only a couple of pills left and she hoped she wouldn't have to take them, for she desperately wanted them to be gone from her life for good. The bottles of wine would go too, she would drink squash or water and lots of tea and coffee instead. A fresh start, a new home, new people. She was determined to start over and put the last few years behind her.

CHAPTER 2

The next morning, She woke for the first time feeling better than she had for a while. It was good to have had a decent night's sleep for once, it had been well overdue. She had been so tired from the drive that she had gone off like a light as soon as her head had hit her pillow.

Kicking off the duvet, she swung her legs over the side of the bed and walked over to the window. Pulling back the curtains, she blinked as the bright sunlight streamed in. What she saw caught her breath, the view was amazing. The cottage had been built on a hill, and she looked down in awe at the stretch of twinkling blue water which was dotted with colourful boats. Her gaze travelled over to the far side of the river where she took in the tall white houses on the opposite bank which dazzled in the morning sun. It was busy; she could see people on the jetty queuing for the ferry. She felt a ripple of excitement shoot through her; it was so good to be back in her home county, she hadn't realised how much she had missed it until now.

Reaching for her phone, she checked the time. It was later than she wanted it to be. Cornwall must already be working its magic, because it was unusual for her to get up this late. She headed down the stairs, thankful that she had switched on the immersion heater. Throwing the last of her expensive bath bombs that she'd brought with her into the warm water, she climbed into the deep tub. Wallowing in her newly gained independence, she started to plan the first day of her new life.

Later, dressed in her comfiest clothes, with her hair tucked under a baseball cap and not a scrap of makeup on her face, she headed out to get some shopping, hopeful that nobody would recognise her. Locking the door, she slipped the keys into the wicker shopping basket she'd found in the kitchen. She needed supplies, so her first port of call would be the little shop on the corner that she'd noticed last night. It looked like it sold everything. She would buy a few essentials to keep her going until she did a big supermarket shop in the town.

The bell above the door of Mort's Mini-Mart jangled as Ally walked in. The teenage girl behind the counter, wearing heavy makeup and her hair dyed a vivid purple, looked at her with undisguised interest.

She decided to put her out of her misery. 'Good morning, I'm renting nearby and need to buy a few bits.'

The girl nodded. 'The bread and cakes and everything else be just over there, but if you want milk and stuff, the fridge and freezers be at the back of the shop,' she said, pointing.

She was just reaching for a carton of milk, when she became aware of someone standing close to her. She turned to see who it was and saw the young shop assistant had followed her.

'You be stayin' long then?' the girl asked searchingly.

She was just about to answer when a middle-aged woman wearing a pink overall entered the shop through a doorway behind the counter.

'Ay, Kirsten, don't be vexing the lady. She won't be wanting twenty questions from you.'

Smiling, she turned to the young girl whose face had now pinkened. 'It's okay. I've taken a long let on Rose Briar Cottage, so I'll be here for a while.'

'Rose Briar Cottage?' The woman behind the counter looked surprised. 'Not heard of anyone being there for a while. It has history that place, did you know?'

'No, but I realise that the cottage must be very old.' Her curiosity was aroused. She looked expectantly at the shopkeeper. 'What sort of history?'

'Well, a long time ago, well before my time I might add, the place used to be called Crow Cottage, but over the years the name got changed, probably to fancy it up. I haven't got time to tell you all of it, for it be a bit of a long story, but some of it is in that book over there.' The shopkeeper bustled over to the rack of tourist information books and pulled out a dog-eared copy of a paperback book from the back of the stand. 'This one.' She held the book out for Ally to see. 'Written by a local author it was, he be long-dead now. The book is quite old, had it for years, was going to bin it, can't stand clutter.'

'Oh wow, thank you.' Ally read the book's cover. 'Can I buy it? I would love to have a read of it later.'

'Ay, don't want any money for it, it's just been sitting there gathering dust.'

Her face lit up. 'Thank you, that's very kind of you.'

The shopkeeper smiled. 'Mind how you go dear,' she said, before scuttling back through the doorway.

Kirsten, who had now moved behind the counter, was busy inspecting her neon painted nails. Ally waited patiently to pay for her shopping. The girl suddenly looked up. She studied Ally's face long and hard. 'Have I seen you somewhere before?'

'Er.' Ally could feel the panic beginning to rise within her. No way did she want to be recognised. Holding herself tall, she looked Kirsten square in the eye. 'No, sorry, I've not been here before. Thank you.' Giving the girl a quick nod, she quickly gathered her shopping and hurried out of the shop, wishing she had worn her sunglasses as an extra layer of disguise.

Back at the cottage, she unpacked her shopping. Her next job would be to set up the wi-fi as per the instructions in the little book left on the worktop. Then she would make herself a coffee to go with one of the saffron buns that she'd just bought and take them into the garden to sit and relax. There was a wooden bench just outside the back door that she'd noticed earlier. A feeling of contentment swept over her. It was so good to be free.

Unlocking the door, she stepped into the garden. Stacked against the cottage wall she noticed several terracotta pots, empty and just begging to be filled. She smiled, she loved colourful pots and would take great pleasure in planting them up, but more importantly, it would give her something to do. She sat down on the weathered bench and let the warm sun caress her face. For once she couldn't give a fig about catching the sun, knowing there was no longer any production crew to chide her. After sipping her coffee and nibbling on the bun, she closed her eyes and tried to relax. All she could hear was the sound of birds in the trees at the far end of the garden. The heady fragrance from a nearby rose bush filled the air. She could feel herself nodding off.

Bzzz, bzzzz, it was her phone vibrating. Her eyes sprang open. She'd forgotten that she now had wi-fi. Picking it up, she saw it was a message from her mother, wanting to know if she was alright. Instantly she felt mean because she hadn't let her parents know she had arrived. Tapping out a message, she promised her that she would phone her later. Stretching her arms out wide to wake herself up, she gathered her thoughts.

She must have been asleep for quite a while because the sun had clouded over. Looking around her, she decided it was time to explore the grassy rectangle with its weedy borders that was the garden. What was left of the sun had now settled over the overgrown laurel hedge at the far end. A sudden break in the cloud delivered a shaft of sunlight and she caught sight of something wooden peeping through the hedge. Within seconds the clouds had moved, putting whatever it was back in the shade. Not sure if it was a fence or a gate, she headed down the garden to have a look.

Tugging at the laurel, Ally looked through the gap she had made. At first, she thought it was just a wooden fence that she had found, but on further probing, she saw what looked like a rusty bolt. Continuing to pull away the laurel, she realised that she had unearthed a gate. Where did it lead to? Even by standing on her tiptoes, she still couldn't see what was on the other side of the gate.

Brambles and other vegetation had obviously taken hold. It looked lethal and she would need something other than her bare hands to cut through the thick stems and prickly brambles. Accepting defeat, she realised that it would have to be a job for another day. It was now early evening, and there was no way she was going to be a meal for the midges which were starting to hover.

It was approaching 10pm, but having fallen asleep while sitting on the bench, she didn't feel at all tired. She wandered into the kitchen to find something to eat and pulled open the fridge to see what took her fancy. Nothing did. Having eaten earlier, she wasn't hungry, just fanciful. She helped herself to a glass of apple juice and opened a pack of cream crackers, slicing some cheese to go with them. Back in London, she would have been on her second glass of wine by now, but that was all in the past. From now on she would look to the future. She was absolutely determined to knock the drinking and the pills on the head, no matter how much it hurt. She had taken advice from her London doctor and would follow it to the letter and was hopeful that she could put the trauma of the last few years behind her and start getting her life back on track. There were no immediate worries about money either, she had enough saved to enable her to have a decent time off. Pulling out one of the old wooden dining chairs, she sat down at the tiny table to eat her cheese and crackers.

Taking her empty plate into the kitchen, she noticed the pile of dirty dishes she had left stacked on the worktop earlier. The only dishwasher in this place was herself but she didn't mind. Her time was her own and she could do whatever she liked with it. As she stood at the sink rinsing the suds off the dishes, it brought back fond memories of the time when she and Joe had first set up home together in their pokey London flat. It had all started off so well, they had been so loved up. Joe had been her soul mate. He was a good person, one of the best, and she'd let him down. She had no excuses for why she had stupidly gone and ruined everything. He hadn't deserved to be treated so awfully by her. She had acted like a spoilt brat back then and was surprised he had put up with her for so long. She wondered how he was. There was no way she could ever face him again after what she'd done to him. It was her loss and she had to get over it. Kat had told her he was back in Cornwall and had a girlfriend, but other than that none of her friends talked about him in front of her. She knew they saw him regularly. After all these years, it was still a taboo subject that everyone skirted around.

The next day was spent shopping. Her father had an important Law Society dinner coming up and her mother wanted to buy a new outfit to wear to it. They had gone shopping in Plymouth. It was late that evening that she remembered the book. Her half empty shopping bag was still on the kitchen worktop. Taking the book out, she noticed the bag of chocolate raisins which she had impulsively grabbed while shopping. Now, more than ever, she needed to take her mind off her cravings and self-doubt. The plump, chewiness of the raisins, combined with the sweet chocolate would certainly hit the spot. Tearing the bag open, she tucked the book under her arm and headed back to the sofa.

Once she started to read, she didn't stop until she'd finished the chapter on Rose Briar Cottage. She had no idea the cottage had such a history and was that old. Built in the early 1600s, it had indeed been called Crow Cottage by the village locals. The cottage gained notoriety when it was inhabited by a woman named Mary. She shuddered as she read that Mary, loudly protesting her innocence, had been hanged in Launceston for being a witch in the mid-1600s. Her crimes being that she kept a crow as a familiar, which in Western demonology was a small animal or imp, believed by many to be a witch's attendant, allegedly given to her by the devil or inherited from another witch. Mary had made potions from herbs to sell. The local farmer accused her of causing the failure of his milk to churn and giving his crops blight, and even worse, after taking a potion supplied by Mary, the farmer's child had got sick and died. It was all fascinating stuff, and even more so because Mary had lived in this very cottage.

She eagerly turned the page. The author's words sent a bit of a chill through her. 'Over the years Mary has made her presence felt. Scores of people had been documented as having seen what they believed to be her ghost and there have been several sightings of Mary's pet crow flying around inside the cottage. To this day it was said that traces of Mary's herbs could be found growing at the bottom of the garden.'

After reading the book she felt spooked. Was the cottage really that old? Parts of it appeared ancient, especially the roof. She glanced around the room. She could see that the cottage had had bits built on to it over the years and was now probably unrecognisable from when Mary lived here. Did Mary deserve to hang though? Surely, she wasn't responsible for all the stuff she was accused of. Was the poor woman hanged as a witch just because she kept a crow in a cage and gave out herbal potions?

Putting the thought of Mary's unfortunate demise out of her head, she switched on the television. It was showing the hospital drama which had been such a huge part of her life until recently. Seeing herself and her co-stars on the screen was bitter-sweet. Although glad she had got away from it all, a small part of her really missed her small group of friends on set. As far as she was aware, none of them had any idea what had been going on in her life or the cruel abuse she'd been suffering and the toll it was taking on her. She had tried very hard to keep her personal life private, always covering up any bruises with makeup and wearing a cheerful smile. She'd done this more out of shame than anything else. No one likes to admit their relationship is a car crash. Feeling tears starting to prick her eyes, she quickly pressed the menu button. After frantically scrolling down, she chose a less painful but slightly boring nature programme to watch instead. So desperate was she to stem the tide of emotion that was threatening to engulf her.

CHAPTER 3

The next day, while sipping her mug of tea, she gazed through the front window of the cottage. There wasn't much to look at, only a couple of blue hydrangea bushes and a small lawned area with a narrow path leading down to the painted gate. The gate, flanked on both sides by a picket fence, led out to a gravel road, whose only purpose was to service this cottage and the one next door, and was effectively a dead end. Beyond the road were the backs of more old houses, which obscured any view of the river below.

There had been no sign of her neighbour, who she thought was named Edna. Those early days were a bit of a blur after her long journey and lack of sleep. She had been here a few days now and was starting to feel more settled and rested. Aware that she hadn't spoken to a soul since she had arrived, other than her parents and the people in the corner shop, she was rapidly coming around to the idea that she needed to do something different other than sit around. Finishing her tea, she decided to go for a potter around the garden.

Pulling open the back door, she stood on the step for a moment watching a large black bird pecking away at the grass. Not knowing too much about birds, she guessed that it couldn't be a blackbird because blackbirds had yellow beaks. It was probably a crow or something similar. The bird looked up from its pecking and appeared to be staring at her long and hard, like it was assessing whether she was a friend or foe. She shivered; she'd never been stared at by a bird before, especially a huge brazen black one with a mean look in its eye. Standing very still, she waited until the bird had decided it had had enough of scrutinizing her. She watched it fly away, disappearing over the hedge at the bottom of the garden. It was then she remembered the gate she'd seen previously, the one hidden behind the overgrown hedge.

She headed down to the bottom of the garden and, as she had done previously, pulled back the branches. Feeling a sharp stab on the back of her hand, she knew she had scratched herself, soon confirmed by the specks of blood appearing. She stared in dismay at the thick thorny stems. She'd clean forgotten about the brambles hidden within the hedge. They weren't going to stop her though, after all, she had nothing better to do. Running back into the kitchen, she washed the scratch, stuck a plaster on it then grabbed a sturdy pair of scissors and a carving knife from the kitchen drawer.

'Ouch! The brambles were certainly proving to be vicious. She continued cutting through the thorny stems. It was much harder than she had imagined, and she knew that she was only one step away from giving up. It was only her deep curiosity that drove her on. A while later, she looked down at her handiwork and was satisfied that she had now revealed enough of the gate to maybe get it open. Setting aside the scissors and knife, she used both her hands, and as much strength as she could muster, to jiggle the rusty bolt. After a lot of effort and sore fingers, she eventually managed to slide the bolt across. Now she had to get the gate open. Using her body weight to barge against it, she was disappointed when it didn't move. After several failed attempts, she noticed that the bottom of the gate was caught up in the long grassy weeds. Bending down, she began pulling them out of the ground, not stopping until she had cleared beneath the gate.

She stared through the open gate at the wilderness before her. Neglected and overgrown, Tall self-seeded saplings had sprung up between the weeds. The grass was almost up to her knees. Something caught her eye. Through a gap in the vegetation, she saw what looked like a brick wall. She waded further through the long grass to get a better look. The structure, whatever it was, could only be a few feet away and she had to see what it was. It was obvious that no one had been here for a very long time. Pulling and cutting the overgrowth as she walked, it soon became clear that the wall was part of a brick-built hut with a pitched roof. She wondered if there was an easier way to reach it without thrashing through the long weedy grass, full of goodness knows what. Kicking at the grass, she thought she felt a hard surface underfoot. Maybe there was a path beneath, she started to tug away at the dry grass.

'*Kraa, kraa.*' She looked up. Sitting on top of the roof of the hut was a big black bird who was looking down at her. Could it be the same one she had seen earlier? She felt slightly spooked as she stared at the black feathered creature who seemed to be talking to her. She thought about Mary's crow. Her imagination was getting the better of her.

Hearing the faint sound of a phone ringing, she recognised her own ringtone, remembering that she had left her phone on the bench. The sound of it brought back a sense of normality. Gathering up her makeshift gardening tools, she headed back to the cottage to see who was calling her. There were four missed calls from a number she didn't recognise. Who could be calling her? She slipped the phone in her pocket. It was probably a junk sales call. Tired and hot, she couldn't be bothered to go back down the garden. It would keep for another day. Now she needed a cold drink. She headed to the fridge for some more apple juice and a stale saffron bun.

It was Saturday morning, and she raked through the limited amount of clothing that she had brought with her, wondering what to put on. This was her first bit of socialising since coming back to Cornwall. So far, the only people she had spoken to had been her parents, apart from the passing of small talk with the local shopkeepers that is. She had arranged to meet up with her old schoolfriend Kat in the fishing village where they had been brought up. After pulling on her jeans, she grabbed one of her expensive white shirts from the hanger and slipped it on. She surveyed her pale face in the mirror; she looked tired and wondered what Kat would think when she set eyes on her. Although she was starting to feel a bit better, she knew she was not looking her best and was no longer the bright young thing that Kat had once envied. There were now a few wrinkles on show and even her recently improved sleep hadn't quite got rid of the dark shadows under her eyes. There wasn't going to be any makeup artist on hand to hide her imperfections now. After scooping her blonde hair up into a scrunchie, she put on some lippy and checked herself in the mirror. She shrugged her shoulders. 'It is what it is,' she muttered to herself, as she grabbed her purse and car keys and headed out the door.

After parking her car, she walked down towards the quay. It had been a long time since she'd been here. Even though she had frequently visited her parents who lived nearby, she had always been very careful to avoid bumping into Joe's parents, more because of her own shame and embarrassment than anything else. According to Kat, Joe's parents still lived in the same cottage overlooking the harbour.

She felt a lump forming in her throat. This village, especially the cottage where Joe and Tom had lived and the harbour with its adjoining beaches, held so many memories; memories so wonderful that it almost hurt to think about them. She wished that she could go back in time and live them all over again. Glancing around her, she could see that the pub still looked the same but there had been other changes, and not for the better in her view. The harbour was no longer the place it once was. It was all much more commercial. Eating outlets now lined the far side of the quay with adjacent tables and there was a stall selling all kinds of souvenirs and branded alcohol, all of which was targeted at the tourist trade. She looked over to Joe's childhood home and wondered what his parents thought of all the changes and doubted they approved, for Joe's dad was born in that cottage and had lived and worked all his life here in the village. He and Joe's mother were old school Cornish through and through.

Crossing the swing bridge, she walked to the end of the outer pier and sat down on the low wall looking out across the blue-green sea towards Gribbin Head. Thinking about the past, she realised how very special this place was.

The tide was slowly inching its way in. She watched as the frothy waves sucked at the shingle, each successive wave covering a tiny bit more of the beach. She looked across to what had once been her and her friends special place. It was probably too small to be called a cave, it was more of a large crevice in the cliffs. Now she could see signs of significant cliff fall. Big boulders had fallen by the entrance but other than that it looked pretty much the same as when she, Joe, CJ, Kat, Marco, and Tom had met there to plan their adventures. She couldn't put a number on how many times the six of them had sat in there. It had been their very own private place, which even in high tide, had remained dry. She felt a stab of almost pain. It was so beautiful; she swallowed hard, being here was making her emotional.

The sound of a mother calling her small boy who was racing along the quay, brought her out of her daydreaming. She looked at her watch, it was almost time to meet Kat. Her friend said she had a surprise for her and to meet her in the new coffee shop, the one that used to be Bonnetti's, once owned and ran by Kat's family. Apparently, it was now under new ownership.

Walking down Harbour Road towards the coffee shop, she felt quite nervous. Surprises weren't her thing anymore. She and Kat had been so close; proper best friends, right from the time her own father had re-located his solicitor's practice down to Cornwall from London all those years ago. Even though they hadn't seen each other for a few years, she and Kat had stayed in touch, but even Kat didn't know much about her life after she had split with Joe. Kat had taken a teaching post at the local school and had married their other close friend CJ, who was doing very well for himself by all accounts, his building firm now a major player in the south-west.

As soon as she entered the coffee shop, she wanted to run straight back out again. There behind the counter was Joe's younger brother Tom. There was no mistaking his ginger hair and freckled face. Now looking lean and muscly, Tom's puppy fat was a thing of the past. Pulling her sunglasses from the top of her head, she quickly slipped them over her eyes. Then with her head down, she found an empty table and sat with her back to the counter, in the hope that Tom wouldn't recognise her.

'Ally!' Kat sat down and gave her a big hug. 'Oh my goodness, it's so good to see you again. How are you?'

Although shocked at Ally's appearance, Kat did her best not to show it.

Ally knew her old friend well enough to know that she had not been prepared for how awful she looked and wondered what questions would follow. Kat however, looked well. She had her dark curly hair cut into a short bob which suited her. Marriage to CJ must be agreeing with her.

Thinking back to the last time they had seen each other, she realised it must have been quite a long time ago. She remembered that she and Kat had met in Truro for lunch. Since then, she had been too ashamed and too embarrassed to talk about her abusive relationship with Nick and she had made excuses every time Kat had suggested they meet up.

'Coffees are on me, I've ordered.' Kat grinned and nodded in the direction of the counter. 'Look who is over there? Did you recognise him? It's Tom.'

She nodded, thankful that Tom was too busy talking to one of the waitresses to notice them. 'I must admit it took me back Kat. He looks so different. Just look how tall and slim he is now. What's he doing here? I thought when your mum and dad sold up, that the place would be run by new people.'

'That's the surprise Al. It's now Tom's place. He's just bought it. He only opened a couple of weeks ago. CJ lent him some money for the deposit.'

She looked all around her. The walls had been painted a soft white and there were framed sketches of tall ships hung on the walls. Bonnetti's old American diner style tables with their wipe-clean cloths had been replaced by trendy light oak tables and white chairs with pale blue seat pads. 'Wow, I'm impressed. He seems to have done a lot. The place has certainly changed. It looks lovely; trendy but with a nod to village life.' She glanced at the menu, 'and quite upmarket too judging by the prices.' She turned back to Kat. 'Gosh our cheeky little Tom, now all grown up.' Her face broke into a smile. 'I always knew Tom liked his food,' she joked, 'but never in a million years did I think he'd end up owning a coffee shop, especially this one!'

Kat laughed. 'I think we were all amazed at how well he's done Al. He worked hard, did lots of training with award winning chefs and is a qualified chef himself now. Once the place gets going, he plans to do evening meals and turn this place into a restaurant.'

'I'm really pleased for him Kat, but it's a bit sad too, there being no more Bonnetti's. It's an end of an era, we spent half our life in here when we were kids. Where are your mum and dad living now?'

'Well, after they retired and sold up, they bought a little bungalow off Sea Road, overlooking the bay. It's only small but they are quite content, and relieved not have to worry about running this place anymore.'

'That's good, it's nice there. I'm glad they are both well. What about Marco? What's he up to now?'

Kat laughed. 'You know my brother Al, always wanting the finer things in life. He lives in a classy waterfront apartment block in Plymouth. He lives with his equally classy girlfriend, who to be honest, none of us are that keen on. They both work for a multi-national media company. Marco's a graphic designer and earns mega bucks.'

'Wow, looks like your brother's done well for himself.'

Kat nodded, trying to think of something to cover the moment of embarrassed silence when neither of them mentioned the elephant in the room, the last member of their previously tight friendship group – Joe.

'Anyway, enough about us. Come on Al, while we wait for our coffees, tell me, what's been happening with you?'

She felt her stomach knot. Did she really want Kat to know about her wreck of a life? She knew that she couldn't face Kat's sympathy or kindness because it might make her cry. Everything was still very raw. She decided to skirt around the question. 'Kat, an awful lot has happened since I left Joe. It's not something I'm proud of. It's still quite hard for me to talk about. I'll tell you when I feel better, I promise. But I am getting there, I feel I'm starting to get stronger. Coming back to Cornwall is like therapy and will do me good; I'm sure,' she added for good measure.

'I understand. No worries.' Kat leaned across and patted her friend's hand. 'I'm here if you need me Al, you know that.'

Her eyes moistened. She bit on her lip to stop it wobbling. 'Thanks Kat, that means a lot.'

Sensing her friend was on the verge of tears, Kat stepped up. 'So, how's your mum and dad? I've not seen them for ages,' she asked brightly.

She smiled, relieved Kat had noticed her distress and was trying to make her feel better. 'They're good. My dad has still got his solicitor's practice in Truro and although his staff run the office, he pops in once or twice a week to keep his hand in. Mum has retired from teaching, although she still does a bit of drama supply if they need her. I'm popping over to see them on my way home. To be honest Kat, I'm only just finding my feet. An awful lot has happened which has knocked the stuffing out of me.'

Kat nodded. She didn't want to ask what Ally meant. She knew her dear friend would tell her what had happened in her own time.

There was a moment of silence; only broken by the waitress bringing their coffees. Never had Ally felt more relieved that she hadn't had to come face to face with Tom.

CHAPTER 4

It was the end of the day, and she felt not physically, but mentally tired. Meeting up with Kat had emotionally drained her. It shouldn't have, Kat was her oldest and dearest friend and they had shared so much when they were younger. She knew that she had become so adept at hiding her feelings and at convincing everyone that everything was just fine, that it was now hard to let anyone in and for her to learn to trust again. Would she ever start to feel better and get back to the confident woman that she'd been ten years ago? Had her toxic relationship with Nick destroyed that part of her forever?

Switching on the table lamps, she was looking forward to having an evening curled up on the sofa relaxing in front of the tv. Picking up her phone, she absently scrolled through her social media. She hadn't posted anything for ages but still liked to see what everyone else was doing with their lives. She stopped in her tracks when a time-hop photo popped up on her newsfeed, bringing back memories she had been trying to suppress. She stared at the photo, it was taken at the beginning of her relationship with Nick, not long after she had left Joe. She and Nick looked so happy, that was when she had been so obsessed with him. She pursed her lips and shook her head slightly as a wave of anger and repulsion swept over her. What the photo didn't show, was that shortly after it had been taken, Nick had flown into a tantrum and had broken her wrist. She had ended up at A&E, where she had used her best acting skills to convince everyone that she had tripped over. She had been so infatuated with Nick, that she hadn't been able to tell the truth.

For a while after she had broken her wrist, Nick had been full of remorse, and couldn't do enough for her, doing his best to win her over. Naively, thinking it was a one-off, she had forgiven him. It was when he had returned from one of his jaunts that things started to get worse. She thought back to how she would always make excuses for his abusive behaviour and how she had truly believed that everything was all her fault. It had taken her a long time to start to see Nick's true colours.

Seeing the time-hop post had unsettled her. Feeling slightly shaky, she sank down into the sofa and thought back to the first time she had met Nick. He had come on to her and she had stupidly fallen for his glamorous lifestyle and how good-looking he was. How shallow and stupid she had been. It was at a production party that she had first set eyes on him. He had been so charismatic that she had fallen for him there and then.

Nick had been on the Board of Directors of the production company, one of many directorships that he held, which meant he could turn up at the studio whenever he fancied. When he did, he always sought her out. Blinded by his charisma and charm, their relationship blossomed until he had asked her to move in with him, by that time she was besotted. They often said love was blind, and in her case, it was very true, she thought bitterly.

At the beginning though, she and Nick had lived a good life, for Nick liked money, both earning it and spending it. They had lived a lavish, exciting lifestyle. That was in the early days though, after a while the excitement began to wear off and Nick started to get more and more distant. It had taken her a while to realise something was going on. What with her busy filming schedule and Nick's so-called work commitments, she hadn't been unduly worried when she didn't see him for days. Nick continued to come and go as he wished, and she learnt never to ask where he was going for fear that he would get nasty. If things were going his way, he would be creepily kind but if crossed, or something displeased him, he would turn in an instant. She never knew who Nick was with or where he'd been, he was very secretive. He would fly off in his private plane to goodness knows where, vanishing for days on end, often switching off his phone.

Towards the end of their relationship, she had dreaded him coming home, because after he'd been away, he would often be even more controlling and violent. Nick never accepted responsibility for any mistakes, and she could never predict what mood he would be in. He would pick a fight, then turn it back on her to deflect his own bad behaviour. His favourite saying was that it was all in her imagination and what a snowflake she was turning into. Nick had a way of making her think everything was all her fault. There had been lots of lies told too, over the silliest things, often just to save himself. The stupid thing was, she didn't think Nick ever caught on that she knew he was lying. She had always let it go, fearing the outcome if she challenged him about it. Standing up to him would always provoke him even more, something she had found out to her cost quite early in their relationship. That was Nick, and in the end, she'd had enough. Her health, both physically and mentally had suffered, and her reputation was starting to nose-dive because of her drinking and the prescription pills, which she'd been taking to help blot out her feelings.

Picking up the cushion next to her, she held it against her chest and hugged it for comfort as she reflected on the past few months. She fully accepted that much of what had happened she had brought on herself. She had been blinded by her pursuit of fame and had lost sight of who she really was.

Eventually, realising that she had reached the end of her tether, and wanting to protect her health and sanity, she had quit when her studio contract had come up for renewal. Soon after that, at the earliest opportunity, and while Nick was away, she had packed her things and left. It was something she hadn't regretted. She had gone to great lengths to keep her plans secret so that none of her London friends or those at the production company knew where she was. She hoped she had been successful in hiding her whereabouts, because the one thing she feared more than anything, was Nick's reprisals. The thought of his cold, cruel revenge was something that frightened the life out of her. She had left because she wanted her life back, it had been a risk she knew she had to take.

She glanced over at the pile of self-help books that she had ordered to help her ditch the alcohol and pills and, so far, they seemed to be helping. There was no alcohol here in the cottage to tempt her and her two remaining pills were locked away in a drawer.

Her thoughts turned to Joe. Why had she cheated on him? She had no reasonable excuse, except that around the time she had met Nick, she and Joe had been going through a bit of a rough patch. Although Joe had rarely complained, she had known that living in their pokey little flat was starting to get him down. Joe hadn't settled in his new job either. He had given up his position with the Cornish police and moved to London just so he could be with her. He missed his friends, his family, and his colleagues back home. She had been fully aware of all this, but she had been so hellbent on furthering her career, she had just ruthlessly ploughed ahead in her single-minded search for fame. A feeling of shame swept through her. Why had she been so self-centred? Why hadn't she been more understanding of Joe's feelings? He was kind and caring and had only ever wanted to make her happy. Her quest for fame had made her cold and un-caring; and look where it had got her. She had lost a good, kind man because of her selfishness and her blinkered lust for fame. Not only had she hurt Joe badly, but she had also ridden roughshod over the sacrifices he had made for her. If only she could turn back the clock, for Joe was ten times the man Nick would ever be. What an idiot she'd been. She told herself that she mustn't keep dwelling on the past. Joe could only be a memory and she had to move on. She got up to switch on the television then went to make herself a cup of tea.

Over the sound of the television, she could hear the forecasted heavy rain beating against the cottage windows. Feeling chilly, she slipped her arms into the sleeves of her cardigan. At least she was snug and dry here in her little cottage.

Feet up on the sofa, she settled down to watch a raucous Saturday night quiz show. It took her a little while to realise that there was a strange noise in the room. Turning the television down, she strained to listen, it seemed to be coming from the direction of the fireplace and sounded like flapping wings. Could there be a bird stuck? She walked over to the fireplace and peered up the chimney.

There was no doubt about it, the flapping noise she could hear was coming from high up inside the fireplace. Grabbing her phone, she switched on the torch, and with a sweeping movement shone it all around the inside of the chimney cavity, but as hard as she tried, she still couldn't see anything but black sootiness. Puzzled, she sat back down on the sofa and watched, maybe whatever it was would fly out. After about ten minutes, the sound stopped. The bird must have escaped.

With a sigh of relief, she went into the kitchen to make herself a hot drink. On returning to the room with her mug of hot chocolate she did a double take, for on the flagstone floor, starting from the fireplace, was a single line of wet bird tracks. The bird footprints, about four inches long, had three toes facing forward and one toe facing backwards, resembling an arrow. As she stood there wondering how the wet marks had got there, the bird tracks started to disappear, quickly fading to nothing. In disbelief, she put her drink down and glanced anxiously around the room for any sign of the elusive bird. Still not satisfied, she hurried over to the window and threw the curtains open as wide as they would go. There was nothing there either. Feeling very confused, she started to wonder if she had been imagining things and spent the rest of the evening listening out for more strange noises.

The next morning, as soon as she awoke, she remembered her restless night. It had taken her ages to go to sleep and then she had woken up about 3am after having a nightmare about giant birds.

Eventually she had dozed off again, but now felt awful through lack of sleep. Checking her phone, she realised it was later than she wanted it to be and although feeling sluggish, she needed to get up. A strong coffee would hopefully do the trick.

Taking her breakfast into the garden, she sat on the bench. Last night's rain had cleared, and the garden looked and smelt fresh.

Kraa, Kraa. A big black bird, who she was now certain was a crow, swooped down in front of her. It was looking uncannily like it was eyeing up the slice of toast she was eating. She swept the crumbs onto the grass and the bird began pecking away at them. A thought suddenly occurred to her. She looked down at the crow's black feet and with a start realised that they looked around the same size as the tracks that she'd seen on the flagstones. Was this big bird in her living room last night? And if so, how did it get out?

After her shower, she was scrolling down her phone for any new messages when she noticed there were more missed calls. She looked up the number; it was the same as the previous missed calls. She did a reverse call check to see if she could find out who it was. The number came up unknown. Puzzled, she decided it wasn't worth worrying about and instead decided she would tackle the garden. She would first buy some garden tools from the village hardware shop to help her cut her way through the overgrown jungle the other side of the hedge.

The bell jangled as Ally entered Harries Hardware, which seemed to be a throwback from the 1950's. An elderly man with white hair and rheumy eyes stood behind the old-fashioned counter. 'Hello miss. Wondered when we'd see you in here. You be from London they be saying.'

'Er, yes, I'm staying at Rose Briar Cottage for a while, and I thought I would tackle the garden. I need to buy some gardening tools.'

'Ay, all the garden tools be over there,' he said, pointing. 'By the way, did you know that your cottage used to be the village shop back in the day, that be during the second world war. My family used to run it, lived above the shop too they did. The place was teeming with American airmen back then. My mother used to tell me how they used to bring her chocolates and stockings. Apparently, our Alice, that be my mother's name,' he added as an afterthought, 'was a bit of a looker in them days, not that you would know it now, she not knowing anything and being bedridden an all.'

'Oh, I'm sorry to hear that,' said Ally, taking her receipt.

The man shrugged. 'She just be old that's all. In her 90's she be now, and I be no spring chicken either,' he added with a wry smile.

She smiled sympathetically. 'How come the cottage is no longer a shop?'

'It became too small. Things changed after the war. They started bringing in all that self-service malarky and the owner sold it off. Them that bought it turned it into a dwelling, and it still be like that today. Don't know who owns the place now, never see 'em. Probably some rich Londoner bought it as an investment. It's bigger than it used to be though; had bits built on to it over the years. Did you say you be doin' the garden me dear? You might also need a pair of these.' He took a pair of heavy-duty gardening gloves down from the display.

'Ah, yes, just what I need. There are quite a few brambles to cut through and I'm sure a pair of these will come in very handy,' said Ally, paying for the gloves.

'You take care now young miss. We don't want anything 'appening to you.'

'Thank you,' she said with a smile. 'I'd better get going.' She held up the things that she'd just bought. 'Lots of work to do.'

'As I said, you take care young miss. By the way, my name is Oscar, Oscar Harries.'

As she walked back to the cottage, she wondered why the locals kept telling her to take care. Did they know something she didn't?

Cutting the tags off her newly acquired garden tools, she left them outside on the bench and ran up the stairs to put some old clothes on, instantly forgetting about the strange warnings.

Wearing an old pair of jeans and a faded sweatshirt, she felt suitably dressed for the task ahead. Glancing at her pale face in the bedroom mirror, she knew she looked permanently tired. Fresh air and exercise were good for you. Maybe she would sleep like a baby tonight after chopping through all that undergrowth. Dark eye circles were not a good look.

Pulling open the kitchen door, she was surprised to see the crow pecking at her new gloves. It didn't fly off when it saw her approaching. Instead, looking intently at her it started to *kraa kraa* at her. She shivered. The thing seemed to be talking to her. She had never known any other bird do this.

'Shoo, shoo.' Feeling brave, she raised her arms to make the bird fly away, then slipping on her gardening gloves, headed down the garden with her tools.

It was proving to be hard work. She wiped the sweat away from her brow with the back of her glove and looked up, aware that all the time she had been working that she was being watched by the crow, who was perched on the roof of the brick hut.

It was a few hours later, and feeling utterly exhausted, that she had finally finished chopping her way through the brambles and weeds and had managed to clear the narrow and overgrown path which circled the hut. Deciding to have a look at the now almost weed-free area, she followed the path, stopping in front of a small window. Standing on her tiptoes, she tried to look in through the moss-lined glass but it being curtained in cobwebs on the inside, she couldn't see a thing. It was obvious that no person had been here for many a year. Feeling hot and thirsty, she decided she had done enough for one day.

'Well, that's me done,' she said, looking up at the crow. Then she shook her head. For goodness sakes, had she lost it? What on earth was she doing talking to a bird? She chuckled to herself, she was obviously spending too much time on her own and needed to get out more. She would arrange to meet Kat again. Already she was feeling less stressed, less buttoned up. All this gardening must be doing her good after all.

It was only when she was getting ready for bed that night that she realised that she hadn't thought about taking even half a pill. That night she slept like a top.

CHAPTER 5

There was someone knocking on her front door. Putting down the book she was reading, she went to see who it was. She was curious because she had only been here a week and hadn't really got to know anyone.

She tried not to stare at the elderly, ruddy cheeked and haphazardly dressed person who was standing on her doorstep. Wearing non-matching slippers, rainbow-coloured socks, and an ankle length pinafore over a neon pink dress, which appeared to be covered in animal hair, the woman was a sight to behold.

'Hello,' can I help you?' She asked politely. For a moment there was no reply. Taking in the woman's frizzy shoulder length white hair, she guessed her visitor had to be her neighbour from next door.

'Just come to introduce meself. I'm Edna, I live in the next cottage. I run the local animal sanctuary, take in any lost and strays I do,' she added importantly, her chest puffing out slightly.

Noticing Edna was leaning heavily on a walking stick, she smiled and offered her hand. 'Hello Edna, so pleased to meet you. Would you like to come in?'

Edna didn't smile. 'No, I be alright. It wouldn't be neighbourly of me not to invite you to our knitting circle. Can you knit?' she asked brusquely. 'We are making blankets for the animal sanctuary.'

'Um,' Ally was slow to answer as she wondered what to say. Edna was not coming across as the friendliest person on the planet, her pursed mouth giving her the appearance of sucking on lemons. 'I'm afraid I'm not very skilled in the knitting department Edna, so will have to decline your kind offer.'

'Suit yesself then. I've heard about you London types; think you are better than us locals. I be keeping an eye on you to make sure you don't get up to any funny business. There had better be no wild parties going on, at my age I need me sleep.'

Despite being extremely annoyed by Edna's unfounded assumptions, she answered calmly. 'I quite understand Edna. I can assure you though that there will be no parties. But just to let you know, I was brought up a few miles from here, so I am not really an incomer.' She spoke politely but firmly, not wanting to let the elderly and extremely cantankerous woman get away with anything.

Edna nodded and looked thoughtful as she digested what Ally had just told her. 'I be seeing you then,' she declared, with slightly less antagonism in her voice. 'Knock next door if you need anything,' she said abruptly, before turning to shuffle back down the path.

'Phew,' she leaned back on the door after she'd closed it. What a character. It looked like Edna was going to be a force to be reckoned with, and so far, had been the only villager she had spoken to who had not been friendly.

It was a particularly gloomy Saturday and it had been raining heavily through the night and all morning. She hadn't seen or heard anything more from Edna, which had been a blessing. Through the window she could see it was still raining heavily. A day outside now looked very much off the cards. She was glad that she had made a start on the garden and had been able to clear a path to the shed before it had started to rain. When it brightened up, she would go out there again to see if she could somehow get into the hut.

By the afternoon the weather still hadn't improved. Beads of rain trickled down the windowpane. It was certainly not a day for going out, she would get soaked just walking into the village. She picked up her phone to see what was going on in the world. Someone had tagged her in a post on a celebrity gossip site. Clicking on the post, she felt her stomach turn when she saw a publicity photo of herself. Underneath the photo, someone had written - *'Looks like this one's career is well and truly over. Everyone is asking where this drunken, pill-popping, washed-up actress is now. Apparently, she's gone to ground now she's been sacked from the production. Keep an eye out for her folks and report on here if you see her.'*

Distraught, she let her phone slip through her fingers. It fell to the floor with a clatter. Who had done this? What malicious person knew enough about her life? It wasn't entirely true either; she hadn't been sacked. Her contract had been up for renewal, but she hadn't wanted to renew it. The production team had been supportive and had tried hard to get her to stay, but she had refused, so badly did she want to get away and sort her life out. Who was behind these lies? She wanted to reply and set the record straight but realised that if she defended herself the perpetrator would know she had seen the post and it would probably make things worse.

Resisting the urge to numb it all with one of her two remaining pills, she lay down on the bed and started to sob. It was as if a dam had suddenly burst. As much as she tried to stop herself crying, she couldn't. She stayed there until she was all cried out.

Later, lifting her head off the damp pillow, she reached for a handful of tissues to dry her red, blotchy face and to give her nose a good blow. Why she had taken it so badly she didn't know, but she had. Then she realised that the cruel post must have tipped her over the brink. Up until now she had been determined to be strong, but obviously the strain of it all had built up inside her, and now, a stupid chink in her armour had caught her unawares and rendered her a soggy mess. She told herself that she was being ridiculous. After gathering her thoughts, she vowed to remain strong. Maybe a good cry had done her good, released some of her pent-up emotion.

Getting up off the bed, she headed back down the stairs to retrieve her phone. Checking it for damage, she realised she had been lucky. The screen was still intact. Thank goodness for the sturdy leather phone case that she'd bought before she had left London. Right now, the last thing she needed was the bother of getting a replacement.

Wishing she had someone to talk to, she scrolled through her contacts until she found Kat's number. She tapped out a message. 'Kat, I'm sorry to trouble you but are you free for a chat? I could do with talking to someone right now. Obviously if you are busy and can't, I completely understand.'

Instantly Kat replied. 'Of course. What's wrong Al? CJ's gone to his business club. He'll be gone for hours yet. They all spend ages in the bar putting the world to rights and supposedly doing deals. Shall I come over to yours? It will make a change from sitting here marking homework.'

'Thank you so much Kat. I must warn you though, I'm not in a good state. I'm a soggy wreck and look hideous. Things haven't been good with me for a while and something else has just happened which has really upset me.' She could feel herself welling up.

Worried, Kat bit her lip, she could tell Ally was crying. What on earth had happened to make her friend like this? She grabbed her car keys, and trying not to speed, drove the six miles along the coast to where Ally was living.

Kat lifted the black iron door knocker and gave it a good, firm rat-a-tat-tat. She wasn't prepared for what she was about to see. Ally's tear-filled eyes were like puffy slits. With swollen lips and a red nose, her friend hadn't been exaggerating when she said that she looked a soggy wreck.

'Come i-in Kat,' croaked Ally, her voice thick from crying.

'Oh Al.' Kat threw her arms around Ally. 'Come on, sit down, I'll make us a cup of tea and you can tell me what's wrong.' Her eyes darted around the room. 'Where's the kitchen in this place?'

Ally nodded at the door off the living room.

Kat set the two mugs of tea she'd made down on the small side table. 'Right, come on. Tell me what's wrong.'

Clicking on the malicious post without looking at it, she gave the phone to Kat.

Neither said a word as Kat scrolled down through what was now a long stream of posts added to the original one.

'The person who started this off is plain evil, but Al, just look at how many people have commented. There is a whole stream of supportive comments saying how much they are going to miss you on the show and what a great actress you are. They are all saying they want you to come back on the show because it won't be the same without you.'

'Really? I've not seen them, been too scared to look.' As she began reading through all the positive messages her eyes filled again.

'How did they know all this stuff? Is it true Al? Were you sacked?'

'No,' she sniffed, 'I left of my own accord. They tried to make me stay but I was so stressed, I just had to get away from Nick.'

'Don't let the creep that wrote this get you down. I bet this filthy slur was written by someone you worked with. It's very spiteful and there's no way of knowing who it was either as they've obviously given a false name. Do you think Nick wrote it and that he is trying to find you?' Kat asked, noticing Ally was twisting a soggy paper tissue around and around her finger.

'Maybe. I did wonder about that. He can be extremely nasty and it's the sort of thing he would do.'

'Do you feel ready to tell me everything that's been going on Al,' Kat asked softly.

'Gosh, how long have you got?' Ally joked.

'As long as it takes Al.'

'Kat, I-I think I'm starting to lose it. That post shouldn't have upset me like it did, but I think Nick's constant belittling of me, his violent temper and spiteful behaviour may have finally got to me. I've spent years putting on a brave face and having to tread on eggshells because the slightest thing would set him off. I've put up with his terrible rages and his cruel taunts. I've tried hard to remain strong, but that post was the last straw, it touched a nerve, it broke me. Kat, I'm so sorry to land this on you. I've kept everything bottled up until now, I've told no one else, not even my parents.'

Kat was devastated. This was worse than she had ever thought. Not interrupting, she let her friend continue to speak while reaching over to pull a bunch of tissues from the box on the table.

'Thanks Kat,' she said, gratefully taking the tissues. After dabbing her eyes and blowing her nose, she looked at her friend through tear filled eyes. 'You know, he didn't like me meeting people. Every time I met up with the girls from work, he would be stony-faced and sulky when I got home, even though he thought it acceptable to disappear himself for days on end. Sometimes he was missing for a couple of weeks. It got worse as time went on, goodness knows who he was with and what he was up to, I was too frightened to ask. If I challenged him in any way, he would get very nasty and make me suffer. I always had a bruise or two, which I did my best to disguise. He broke my wrist once,' she croaked, absently pulling to pieces her scrunched up tissue.

'Did you report him?'

She shook her head. 'One time, after we had got home from an awards ceremony, he smashed one of my newly acquired tv awards against the wall in a violent rage because he was jealous. There have been lots of other instances too. He never had a good word to say about me. I'm afraid I stupidly turned to drink and prescription pills; it was my way of numbing it all, something that I now regret and feel ashamed about.'

'Oh Al.' All these years and she'd never had an inkling of what her old friend had been going through.

'It's okay, I'm off the pills now and I've not had a drink since leaving London and I'm determined to keep it that way.'

'Well, that's something positive. Why didn't you walk away from him before things started to escalate?'

'That's the question I often asked myself. The fact is, I was too weak. Nick is a big cheese at the production company, he's also on the Board of Directors there and everyone thinks he is so wonderful. Because I was in the public eye, I didn't want everyone to know what was happening. It would have been too embarrassing, especially if the newspapers had got wind of it. No one wants to admit that their relationship is a failure. Besides, I had my dream job and I wanted to keep it.'

Kat nodded as if she understood.

Ally wiped away another tear. 'On the outside Nick was the perfect partner and liked by all. I didn't think anyone would believe me if I said anything bad about him. Even if someone had believed me, I was quite certain they wouldn't back me over Nick. Nick was the powerful one, he called the shots and could make or break careers. For nearly ten years, my life with Nick was controlling and toxic. Over the years I had told him that I wanted to leave, but he threatened to ruin my career if I did.' She looked up at Kat. 'I made a huge mistake in leaving Joe. It's something I will regret for the rest of my life.'

'None of us are perfect Al, we all make mistakes,' Kat said softly.

'I wish that I had never set eyes on Nick. I thought I loved him until he started to show his true colours, then I saw the real cruel, vindictive man behind the charming facade, but by then I was in too deep. It was only when I started to take pills and drink more than was good for me to numb the pain, that I realised I needed to drastically change my life and escape from his clutches. That's why I left the show and came back here to Cornwall, where I desperately hope he won't find me.'

'Ally, you are going to have to report this to the police to cover yourself just in case something else happens.'

'Yes, I know. I'll do it later, I promise,' she replied, her voice still thick from crying.

'Do it now. There's an on-line crime reporting form. I'll look it up for you.'

Kat sat next to Ally as she filled in the form and pressed send.

'That's that then,' Ally said quietly. 'Let's hope whoever is behind it won't do anything else. I can't think why anyone would want to do this. I can't remember upsetting anyone enough for them to post this nasty stuff.'

'It's probably just a one-off, someone who got out the wrong side of bed this morning. Reporting it to the police is just a bit of insurance that's all, to be on the safe side in case it happens again. I bet it won't though,' Kat quickly added, seeing the look of alarm flicker across her friend's face. 'I don't like leaving you like this Al. Will you be alright?'

'Yes, I'll be fine. Thank you so much for coming over and for your support Kat. I feel so much better now that I've had someone to share things with. Sorry to burden you,' she added, managing a watery smile.

'Ally, please tell your mum and dad what's been happening. I'm sure they'll be supportive.'

She nodded. She knew Kat was right. She just needed to find the right time.

'Listen Ally, you know where I am. Please message me if you are unsure of anything. I won't have my phone on while teaching but I'll get back to you as soon as I can. You don't have to deal with this on your own.' Kat gave her friend a big hug. 'Don't leave it too long this time, we're besties remember, we are here for each other.'

Standing on the doorstep, she waved goodbye to her oldest friend as she drove away. She had meant what she had said to Kat, she did feel heaps better after talking it over with her.

Her head still aching from crying and feeling slightly nauseous, she carried the dirty mugs through to the kitchen. Although not hungry, she realised that the nauseousness was probably due to her not having had anything to eat. Leaning forward, she stood on her tiptoes so that she could take down one of the cans of soup that she'd stacked on the top of the tall cupboard that she had been using as a larder.

'Oh no!' She felt the thin gold chain that she always wore, slither from her neck. She must have snagged it on one of the cupboard's protruding handles. In dismay, she looked down by her feet but there was no sign of the necklace. This was the last straw and not what she needed right now. She started to panic. Where had it gone? Her nan had bought her the necklace for her 18th birthday and since then it had hardly left her neck. It must have slipped through one of the gaps in the boarded floor, there was nowhere else it could have gone. There was no other choice, she would have to move the cupboard to enable her to see better. Using all the strength she had, she pushed the cupboard back a few inches so that it was flat against the wall. Wiping away a thick layer of dust with her finger, she still couldn't see any sign of her necklace. She looked at the dust in distaste, the cupboard had obviously not been moved for many a year. She would have to get the broom to sweep up and then clean the floor. Her thinking that a can of soup would be a quick and easy meal, had turned into a bit of a mare.

Could her day get any worse? She got down on her hands and knees to take a closer look at the old timber floor. Through the floorboards, she saw a glint of gold; it was her necklace, it had slipped through a small gap. She knew that even though she could see her necklace, there was no way she could reach it. There was only one option, the floorboard would have to come up.

After pushing the heavy cupboard to one side, she stood in the middle of the kitchen and wondered what she could use to prise up the floorboard. Her first thought was the bread knife, but as soon as she took it out of the drawer, she knew that it wouldn't be strong enough. An idea suddenly came to her. Flinging open the door to the garden, she ran outside and grabbed hold of her garden shears that were still propped up on the bench. Clutching the shears, she ran back into the kitchen, knowing that there was only one thing to do and that was to just get on with it.

Getting down on her knees, she slid the closed shears into the narrow gap between the floorboards. Trying hard not to splinter the wood, she worked carefully until the thick rusty nails holding the board in place started to work loose, allowing her to pull it free. Setting the floorboard aside, she hesitantly slipped her hand inside the filthy cavity, which was caked in goodness knows how many years of dust and dirt, to retrieve her necklace. As she did so, she noticed that there was something else in there too. Dipping her hand in again, she pulled out an old key. After brushing off the dust, she held the dirty key in the palm of her hand and wondered how it had got there, and more importantly, what it was for.

Depositing her necklace and the key safely on the worktop, she knew she had to replace the floorboard. It would be easy enough to pop it back in position, but it would have to stay loose, because she had nothing to nail it down with. Satisfied that the floorboard had been slotted back in correctly, she grabbed a nearby broom to sweep the floor, then pushed the cupboard back in place. Covered in dust and breathless after her efforts, she laughed to herself at the absurdity of it all - all this faffing about had started with her desire for a tin of soup, but on the positive side, it had taken her mind off the vile post.

After a quick shower and change of clothes, she checked her necklace. The chain was still intact, but the fastener had been bent. She would take it along to the jewellers in Truro and get it repaired. Picking up the key, she held it up to the light. She didn't know much about keys, but this one looked quite old. After washing off years of accumulated grime, and not knowing what else to do with it, she absently placed the key on the windowsill. Her stomach was telling her that she still hadn't eaten. After all the hassle there was no way she wanted soup now, she would make herself a sandwich instead.

CHAPTER 6

'Good morning world,' she murmured, looking out of the bedroom window. Despite everything, she had slept reasonably well. Her long pent-up tears had needed to be shed and she was now feeling quite upbeat about the day ahead. Padding barefoot into the kitchen to make her first coffee of the day, she noticed that the broom she had used yesterday was still propped up against the tall cupboard. She would take it into the garden with her later. It might come in handy to brush away the cobwebs and any spiders lurking around the old hut.

Several cups of coffee and slices of hot buttered toast later, she felt ready to start the day. Dressed in her old jeans and shirt, carrying her tools and the broom, she made her way down to the wild overgrown plot that she now thought of as her little secret garden. She was thinking about how she was going to tackle the enormous job that she'd given herself when she heard a loud flapping of wings. She didn't have to look up to know it was the crow. 'Come on crow, how do we get inside this place?' Once again, she couldn't believe she was talking to a bird. The crow flew up onto the roof of the hut and hopped across to the far side. *Kraa Kraa.* It was like the crow was telling her something. Walking around the hut, she stopped right by where the bird was looking down at her from his high perch. With his head cocked knowingly, the crow's beady eyes continued to watch her every move. *Kraa Kraa.* She looked up at the crow. What was wrong with it, why was it making so much noise? She wondered if it was hungry and looking for food, maybe she would buy some wild bird seed later.

She surveyed the wall of dense dark green ivy. The thick, woody shoots had completely covered the side of the hut and were reaching up towards the roof. Looking closer, she noticed that the ivy was clinging to the wall using tiny rootlets. Seeing the ivy brought back memories of her father moaning to her mother about the ivy, which always seemed to be growing up the side of their house. She could still picture her mother holding on to the ladder to stop it wobbling precariously while her father was on the top rung pulling the ivy away from the wall.

Kraa Kraa. The crow was at it again. She looked up at it and wagged her finger. 'You, my noisy little birdie buddy, are such a hard taskmaster.' Ignoring the crow, using her shears, she started snipping at the ivy, and was pleased when after just a few minutes, she had managed to clear away a reasonably large patch. Taking a step back to admire her efforts, she was surprised to see that she had exposed what looked to be the door to the hut. Spurred on by curiosity, she continued, not stopping until the door was laid bare. She stared at weathered timber door which was still bearing flakes of dark green paint. It appeared quite solid and was showing no sign of rot. Hidden away under the thick ivy, it was no wonder she hadn't noticed the door. She reached in and tried the blackened handle. It moved slightly but the door itself would not budge. Bending down to look closer, she saw there was a keyhole directly beneath the handle. Disappointed, she realised that despite all her hard work, there was no way she would be able to open the door without a key. A thought suddenly occurred to her. It was a bit of a long shot, but what about the old key she had found beneath the floorboards. It had to be worth a try. Quickly running back to the kitchen, she grabbed the key from the windowsill, then sprinted back to the hut.

She carefully teased the key into the rusty aperture. 'Here goes,' she muttered, briefly glancing up to the roof of the hut, where the crow was still perched, looking down at her with interest. She was astounded, when after a bit of jiggling, the key slotted in. With her hopes building, she held her breath as she tried to turn the key. They were soon dashed when it didn't move. Disappointed, but not wanting to admit defeat, she tried some more, hoping it was just a case of perseverance. She told herself that over the years it was hardly surprising that the lock had seized up. All she had to do was keep trying. She continued pulling and twisting the door handle whilst jiggling the key inside the lock, and was just about to give up, when to her surprise, she thought she felt the key turn slightly. Did she imagine it, did the key really move? Heartened, and now even more determined, she pressed on. Finally, she heard the lock click – Eureka - she was in!

The door creaked ominously and grated as it dragged along the rough concrete floor of the hut. Leaning against the door, she realised something was preventing the door from opening fully. Using her shoulder for strength, she continued pressing against the door until it had opened wide enough for her to see that there was a toppled ladderback chair right behind the door. Using the broom, she pushed the chair away from the door. Feeling quite nervous about what she was going to find, she cautiously stood on the threshold of the hut for a moment. After deciding it looked safe, she stepped inside and was relieved to see that it wasn't as bad as she had thought. Yes, she could see cobwebs and maybe some sign of infestation, but it was largely dry and didn't smell too bad.

Taking hold of the broom, she held it out horizontally in front of her to brush away the cobwebs and fend off any spiders. She was quite surprised, for this wasn't some old ramshackle hut. It was a solidly built brick building and there didn't appear to be any obvious signs of damp or decay either. Along one wall there was a dark wood desk that had three drawers down one side. Tucked under the desk's recess was a matching chair. Judging by the amount of wadding hanging out and the large number of droppings, the seat of the chair had obviously become home to a family of rodents. On top of the desk, draped in layers of thick cobweb was what looked like an old-fashioned wooden stationery rack.

After righting the toppled chair, she listened for any sound of rodent activity, there was nothing, all she could hear were birds in the nearby trees. Relieved, she attempted to brush off some of the cobwebs to have a look. In the stationery rack were sheets of paper, which had mottled and curled with age. A dried-up inkwell and ink pen with a rusty nib sat alongside and was also draped in cobweb. There were the remains of what must have been a blotting pad too. It had been gnawed by something and was barely recognisable. To the right of the blotting pad was an old oil lamp. She looked around her. The whole place couldn't have been much more than 8ft square, but it was large enough to house a small sofa that had been pushed against the far wall. Shrouded in multiple layers of dust and cobweb, the sofa's pattern was indistinguishable and was also showing signs of rodent attack.

She went over to the desk and tried the drawers. After a firm tug, the first one opened but was empty except for a couple of curled up dead spiders. When she looked inside the middle drawer, she was surprised to see a bundle of papers, that on closer inspection, appeared to be letters. The letters had been tied with a strand of ribbon. Partly disintegrated, the ribbon's original colour had now faded to a dingy brown. Very carefully she picked the letters up and blew off the layer of dust. She would take them back to the cottage and look at them later. On attempting to open the bottom drawer, she realised something was stopping it from opening. There appeared to be something lodged in the back of the drawer. Carefully taking out the drawer above, she saw what it was. Reaching in, she pulled out a wooden photo frame. Discoloured with age, it held a sepia photo of a handsome man in uniform. She looked at it again, she wasn't sure, but didn't think the uniform was that of a soldier. Could the man be an airman? She thought back to Oscar's words about the US airmen here during the war. Her interest was piqued, she was intrigued and would do a bit of research later; it would give her something to do, something to make the long evening pass quickly.

Clutching the bundle of letters and the framed photo, she locked the door of the hut and headed back to the cottage. She felt slightly sad, for the little hut was like a time capsule, and would have been part of someone's life. It reminded her of something she'd seen on the History Channel. She wondered who used to come here, for it had obviously, a long time ago, been someone's private space, their sanctuary. Maybe once she had read the letters she would know more.

That evening she settled down to look at the letters. Moving the table lamp nearer so she could see better, she carefully unpicked the fragile ribbon tied around them. It soon became very clear that what she was reading were love letters from a US Airman by the name of Frank to someone called Alice. Frank frequently mentioned in his letters how he missed them being together in their secret place and spending time on the lumpy little sofa and of the love he had for her. He also wrote how he missed the village, sailing on the river and going down the local pub, and the villagers who had made him feel very welcome. The envelopes were stamped and postmarked by the US postal service.

By the time she had finished reading the letters, she felt very emotional, for this was a real love story. It was obvious from the letters that Alice and Frank had loved each other very much, but it was reading the last two letters in the bundle that had really upset her. A solitary tear rolled down her face. The last letter had been written by Alice to Frank, telling him how much she loved him and that she was expecting his baby. This letter had remained unsent, probably because the previous letter in the bundle had been from Frank, telling Alice that, although he loved her deeply and would always love her until the day he died, he had responsibilities to his sick wife who needed him in Virginia. He wrote that he was heartbroken that he and Alice could no longer be together. He wished with all his heart that he could bring her to his home in the blue mountains, but it was not possible.

She felt at a loss as she wiped away a few stray tears. What was the matter with her, why did she keep crying? The slightest thing seemed to set her off. In the past she would have poured herself a glass of wine, but those days were gone, and she was glad there was nothing alcoholic in the cottage to tempt her. She was proud of herself for doing well and she wasn't going to cave in over some sad letters. What a story though. She wondered what had happened to Alice. Did she have her baby? The name Alice was ringing a bell. Where had she heard that name recently. Then it came to her. Of course, Alice was the mother of Oscar, the man in the hardware shop. Could it be the same person? Oscar said his mother was in her 90's, so it could well be. Didn't he also say that his family used to live in this cottage when it had been a shop, and that the US airmen used to bring his mother stockings and the like. Maybe she should return the letters and photo. She would do some research first. Grabbing a pen, she noted the town on the faded postmark and the name of the airman and began Googling.

Just as she was about to go to bed her mobile rang. It was that unknown number again. Who could it be? Who on earth would ring her at this time of the night? It was gone eleven for heaven's sake. There was no way she was going to answer it. All the people she wanted to hear from were already in her contacts and the number on her screen wasn't one of them.

CHAPTER 7

The next morning Ally decided to take the plunge and drive into Truro. Enough was enough, she'd spent too long hiding away. Not having been there for ages, it would be nice to have a look around the shops and she could also take her broken necklace to the jewellers for repair.

Having sorted her necklace and treated herself to some new clothes, she turned her thoughts to where she was going to have lunch. Still feeling slightly awkward at the thought of eating on her own, she decided on a pub that she and Joe had frequented back in the day. They had upstairs tables with a view of the busy street below. She would try and get a window seat and do some people watching while she ate. That would be much better than being sat at a table set for one in the centre of a room surrounded by loved up couples and groups of laughing friends.

The pub was busy. She waited in the queue to be served.

'Can I help you?' the young girl behind the bar with perfect long blonde curls asked, looking at Ally as if she recognised her from somewhere.

'I'd like an upstairs table please, by the window if you have one available.'

'Let me see now.' The young girl looked at her screen, and after pressing a few keys, looked up at Ally and smiled. 'You got lucky, table number four is free and it's right by the window too.' She pointed to the narrow staircase to the left of the bar. 'Just go up them stairs over there and you will see table four over by the far window. The waitress up there will take your order.'

'Thank you.' As she headed over to the stairs her eyes started to moisten. Maybe this wasn't a good idea after all. Coming to a place where she had spent time with Joe was making her emotional; she told herself to get a grip.

'Table for one is it?' The waitress at the top of the stairs asked.

'Afraid so,' Ally answered a bit too brightly.

'That's okay dear,' the waitress answered sympathetically. 'I'll just get you a menu.' She then directed Ally to a small table set in an alcove that overlooked the busy thoroughfare below.

She sat at the table that was usually laid for two and cast an eye over the laminated menu card. She felt a lump in her throat when she saw Joe's favourite dish was still on the menu. The food on offer, just like the décor, hadn't changed much since she was last here with Joe, which must have been just before they had moved to London. She could feel her eyes pricking again as she thought about him. He had been her rock; the love of her life and she had stupidly thrown it all away. Why had she done it? She knew the answer; she had left him behind because she had wanted to find fame and have a glamourous lifestyle. She knew that she had been totally self-centred back then and had completely disregarded Joe's feelings, leaving him badly hurt. What a selfish, up herself idiot she'd been. She brushed away a stray tear with the back of her hand. It had all happened too long ago, it was water under the bridge, so there was no point feeling sorry for herself now. She had to stop all this self-pity stuff and accept that she had behaved badly and now must live with the consequences. Kat had let slip that Joe had a girlfriend named Maxine, who was a fellow police officer. She hoped that Maxine would treat him better than she had done. All she wanted now was for Joe to be happy.

'You alright love?' The jolly, rosy-cheeked waitress had arrived with her food and was looking at her with motherly concern.

Ally nodded and looked down, desperate to hide the fact that her eyes were filling. The last thing she needed was someone being nice to her.

'There, you be tucking into this miss. The Chef's Special this is, and it be right tasty too.'

She gave the waitress a wan smile. 'It looks delicious, thank you.'

Stuffed full of veggie lasagne, she pushed her plate away and stared out the window, trying to push all thoughts of Joe out of her head. She had a good view of the road below. As usual Truro was heaving with shoppers and visitors. She looked down at the stop-start traffic, as drivers stepped on their brakes to avoid running over the hordes of people spilling over onto the crowded pavements.

Absently looking down on the hustle and bustle, it took her a few seconds for the penny to drop and when it did, she felt slightly sick. Had she imagined it, or had she just seen Nick's car drive past? She took a few deep breaths and told herself that she must be mistaken. Her imagination was obviously getting the better of her, there must be countless dark blue BMW's just like Nick's in this neck of the woods. Then, with a sinking feeling, she remembered that the colour of Nick's car was personal to him, he had paid a small fortune for it. Maybe it was a trick of the light. She took a sip of her coffee to steady her nerves and told herself not to be stupid.

It was later that afternoon that she felt the need to do something to take her out of herself and pass away a couple of hours. She had an idea; she would walk down the hill into the hub of the village. It would be busy with holidaymakers but if she had her hair pulled back in a scrunchie, wore her cap and sunglasses, she hopefully wouldn't be recognised. There were some lovely little shops down there to look at, most of them aimed at the tourists but nevertheless, very nice.

Dodging families holding ice creams and children carrying colourful buckets and crabbing nets on long sticks, she threaded her way along the busy bunting decorated streets. Taking up corner position in the main thoroughfare, the colourful interior of 'Millie's' caught her attention. She stood in front of the window which was loaded with trays of glazed pastries, plump scones and delicious looking cakes and wondered whether to go inside. The woman behind the counter, who appeared to be in her late twenties, smiled at her. Wearing denim dungarees over a yellow shirt, the woman had a mass of curly copper red hair, tied with a red bandana. It was the woman's wide, genuine smile and open friendly face that made her step inside.

'Hello Ally. I've seen you around the village and wondered if I would get to meet you,' the woman said chirpily.

Ally smiled in return, wondering how the heck the woman knew her name.

'Sorry, let me introduce myself, I'm Millie, said owner of this establishment.' Millie bowed dramatically.

'Oh hi. Yes, I'm Ally, how did…'

Millie grinned. 'Everyone knows everyone around here. Word spread around like wildfire that you have rented Rose Briar Cottage. Welcome to our little village.' Millie glanced around. 'There's a table going over there if you fancy a coffee?'

Ally smiled. 'That sounds good, a latte please,' getting out her purse to pay.

'This one's on me. A drink to welcome you. Go and sit down and if I can, I'll come and join you for a little while. I'm due a break.'

Ten minutes later, Millie, balancing two mugs of coffee and two overfilled strawberry tarts came and sat down next to her. 'I made these tarts this morning, they go quickly so I put a couple aside. You've done me a favour by being here, otherwise I'd have scoffed them both.'

Ally bit into the succulent strawberries which were set in creme pâtissiere, encased in a crisp pastry shell and thought she'd gone to heaven. 'Wow, that is amazing. You made these yourself?'

'Yep, all my own work, I'm a trained a chef.' Millie beamed, delighted at Ally's reaction. Her eyes darted over to the door. 'Oh gosh, I'd better go, a crowd of customers have just come in. I'd love to talk longer but I can't. How about we swap phone numbers? I'll ring you and we can arrange something. I know my friend Ashna would love to meet you too. There are not many women of our age in the village, so we must stick together against all the old 'uns,' said Millie with a wink, after taking Ally's number.

From then on, a friendship was born.

She quickly got in the habit of going down to Millie's and helping her clear up after the last customer had gone and the closed sign was on the door. Both women worked while chatting and laughing as Millie baked and prepared food for the next day while Ally swept the floor and wiped down the surfaces.

Although she hadn't told Millie the whole sad story of her relationship with Nick, she decided to tell her newly acquired friend her worry about the possible sighting of him in Truro.

'Well, if it was him, and it probably wasn't, he had better not turn up here. If he does, we'll set Bolshy Betty on him.'

She tried not to laugh. 'Who on earth is Bolshy Betty?'

Millie's eyes crinkled into a smile. Tucking a stray strand of her red curls back behind her ear, she chuckled. 'Once seen never forgotten is our Betty. Before she retired, she was a primary school teacher.' Millie's brow furrowed, 'or she might even have been a headmistress, but I'm not at all sure about that. Betty regards herself as the matriarch of our community and knows everything there is to know about the village and everyone who lives here. She's a sweet old dear but can be very fierce if her feathers are ruffled or if she takes a dislike to you. Once you get her on side though she's got a heart of gold and will do anything for you. She's also the person behind the fund-raising for the new village hall. Everyone thinks she is marvellous for her age. Betty is one of our oldest residents and I'm almost certain that she was born here. She's quite an age, I reckon she must now be in her late eighties. Everyone looks out for her. It's her daughter who sometimes helps me in the kitchen and I always give any unsold food for her to take home to Betty. Betty has a son too; he lives in the cottage next door to her. You might have seen Rob driving his van around as he maintains the gardens for all the holiday rentals and looks after the village floral displays.'

'I think I may have seen him. Does he drive a little green van?'

'Yes, he does. He knows loads about plants too and if you want to know something garden related then he is definitely the person to ask.'

'Maybe I'll have a word with him if I see him. I'm really getting into gardening.' Ally gave a wry laugh, 'I'm calling it my therapy. Your Betty sounds a bit of a character too. Oh, I've just thought of something. Did you say that Betty has lived in the village for a long time?'

'Yes, I don't think she has ever moved away from here,' Millie replied.

'Then I wonder if she could help me with some old love letters and a photo that I found in the hidden hut at the bottom of the garden?'

'Hidden hut, old love letters and a photo, that sounds ve-ry intriguing,' said Millie, her eyes lighting up.

Ally described the contents of the letters. 'I have an idea who they belong to, but just need to know for sure.'

'Gosh, how romantic. I would certainly show Betty, that's right up her street. She's lived here for donkey's years and knows everything that needs to be known about the place. I'll come with you if you want. She's a bit of an eccentric and might not take to you straight away and could send you packing if you go on your own.'

'That would be brilliant. Thanks Millie. That reminds me, talking about eccentric.' She told Millie about her run-in with Edna next door.

'Ah, Edna.' Millie smiled. 'Edna and Betty are arch-enemies. Apparently, many years ago, before Betty married her late husband, the two women both lusted after the same man, the milkman I believe, or was it the butcher? Anyway, it seems that they've never got over it. I think they also fell out when one of them didn't win a prize at the flower show. Can't remember which one said the other one sabotaged their dahlias or something.'

'Oh my word.' Ally couldn't stop laughing. Being with Millie was like a breath of fresh air and just what she needed to cheer herself up.

It was that evening her mother rang and it was half-way through their chat that her mother dropped the bombshell.

'Did I tell you that I had a phone call from your Nick?'

She nearly dropped the phone. 'No Mum you didn't, and he's *not* my Nick. When did he ring?'

'It was the other day.'

'Mum, w-what did he want?' She asked a little too sharply.

'You know Allegra, you have never really explained why you and Nick split up and why you left London. Nick is such a lovely man, very polite. He asked after you, said he missed you. He also wanted to know if you were in Cornwall as he had some leave due and he wanted to come down and see you.'

She felt her stomach tighten on the realisation that she hadn't been imagining things earlier and that it probably was Nick's car she had seen in Truro.

'Mum, what did you tell him? Did you tell him I was here?'

There was a moment's silence before her mother answered. 'Er, yes, I said you had rented a lovely old cottage down here. I didn't say where though, but thinking about it, I did say you had a lovely view over the river. Why, did I do wrong?'

'No, it's alright Mum. I've not told you the whole story. Nick is not as nice as he seems. I really don't want to see him ever again.'

'Oh dear, I'm so sorry, I might have put my foot in it.'

'It's not your fault Mum. I should have warned you. Look, come here tomorrow and I will tell you more. We can have lunch in 'Millie's'. The food is very nice in there, and Millie who owns the place has become quite a good friend.'

'That would be lovely Allegra, I'll look forward to it.'

'Okay Mum, I'll see you tomorrow.' As she finished the call, she felt sick to the core. She would have to tell her mother what had happened now. She wished she had done it before, then her mother would have protected her. Never in a million years did she think Nick would contact her parents. She didn't even know that he had their home details and guessed it must have been the studio who gave it to him, because she had put them down as her next of kin. Feeling her legs weakening, she quickly sat down. Taking deep breaths to try and calm herself, she wondered if she would ever escape from Nick's clutches? Would she ever find peace? Willing herself to remain strong, she got up and marched determinedly into the kitchen. She wasn't the fragile wreck who had left London, she was tough, and there was no way Nick was going to get to her or hurt her ever again.

The next day, as Ally's mother jumped into her car to go to lunch with her daughter, she had no idea she was being watched then followed by a man driving a dark blue BMW. After parking her car in the public car park at the top of the hill, she headed down the steep incline leading to the village.

Halfway down, she caught a glimpse of the blue twinkling river far below. Stopping to get her breath and to admire the view, she didn't notice the tall dark-haired man a good distance behind her, who was just crossing the road from the car park and heading her way.

As the door to Millie's jangled for the umpteenth time, Ally turned to look. This time it was her mother.

'Thanks for coming Mum,' she gave her mother a big hug.

Her mother looked around her. 'You are right, it's very nice in here Allegra, and very colourful too.'

'You wait 'til you taste the food Mum. Millie cooks it all herself, she trained as a chef in London.' Ally took her mother over to a secluded table at the back of the long room and handed her mother the menu.

Just as they had finished eating, Ally looked up and froze. There, looking through the front window was Nick. Ally grabbed the menu card and held it up in front of her face. 'Mum we need to go – NOW.'

'Why? What on earth is the matter?'

'Just get up Mum. Quickly before he sees us. Follow me, we'll go out the back way.'

'Allegra, what's going on? We left without paying too,' her mother gasped, doing her best to keep up with her daughter who seemed to be sprinting along the narrow streets.

After ramming the key into the lock, she pushed open the front door. 'Quick Mum, get inside.' After checking for any sign of Nick, she slammed the door shut, desperately hoping that there was no way that he would know the twisty back streets of the village well enough to find out where she lived. She didn't dare allow herself to think otherwise.

Noticing her mother's face was very red from all the running, she instantly felt guilty. 'I didn't mean to put you through that Mum. Go and sit yourself down, I'll make us a cuppa,' said Ally, disappearing into the kitchen, feeling quite worried about what she'd done to her mother.

'Just a glass of water for me,' her mother panted, still trying to get her breath.

She returned with a glass of water. 'Are you alright Mum? I'm so sorry about what just happened.'

Her mother nodded. 'I'll be alright in a minute. What about all the food and drinks we had? Won't your friend be out of pocket if we don't pay?' she asked, after draining her glass.

'I'm just going to sort it, Millie's a good friend, I'm sure she'll understand.' She reached for her phone and began tapping out a message to Millie explaining what had happened and that she would settle the bill later. 'There, job done. Get your breath back, then I'll tell you everything that I should have told you before now.'

Her mother leaned back into the sofa visibly upset by all that her daughter had just told her. 'Why did you not tell me? Why did you not report him to the police? He was physically abusing you, that's a crime. And you could have been seriously injured too,' she sniffed, pursing her lips in angry disapproval. 'Why did I think he was such a nice man? I'm afraid that I've been completely taken in by him,' she said, shaking her head in disgust.

'That's what everyone thinks Mum. Everyone thinks he's flipping marvellous and because I was well known for being on television, I didn't want to wash my dirty linen in public as the saying goes. I wasn't sure anyone would believe me either. I'm sorry I didn't tell you or dad, I didn't want to worry you. It's all my fault. I've been very stupid, and I thought you would say that I had made my bed and now must lie in it.'

'Come here girl,' she gave her daughter a big cuddle.'

Ally's eyes started to fill as she nestled in her mother's comforting arms.

'I think you should tell someone, report it to the police?'

'It's too late Mum. I don't think anyone would believe me now, although Kat made me log the on-line trolling that I told you about with the police.'

'Well, that's a start I suppose. If something else happens, you must report that too, straight away.'

'Will do Mum, promise.'

'You should never have left Joe.'

'I realise that now Mum; just a bit too late; ten years too late.'

'At least you are still in touch with Kat. You two were as thick as thieves when you were younger.'

'Yes, we were. I've met up with her a couple of times since I've been back. She knows about Nick. Kat's still there for me but I don't want to bother her too much with my problems as she's very busy what with teaching and keeping CJ on the straight and narrow.' Ally chuckled. 'It's hard to believe that CJ is a respectable businessman now.'

Rolling her eyes, her mother laughed. 'I can still remember all the tricks he used to get up to. What a lad he was, the scrapes he got into.'

'It wasn't only CJ though, was it?' Ally said laughing.

'No, it was all of you, including Joe's younger brother, er, I can't remember his name, what was it?' she looked at Ally.

'Tom.'

'Ah yes, I remember now. Did you know Tom now owns Bonnetti's? It's not called that now, it's something beachy.' Her mother wrinkled her brow as she tried to remember the name. 'I think it's called The Beachcomber or something like that. I've not been in there, but apparently the place is gaining quite a good reputation.'

Her phone started to ring. It was Millie. Having just read Ally's message, she sounded concerned. Ally started to tell her about seeing Nick.

Thinking it best to let her daughter continue talking to her friend, her mother got up from her seat. 'I'll be getting off home now,' she mouthed, patting Ally gently on the shoulder before heading towards the door.

'Hang on a minute Millie,' said Ally, putting the phone aside before turning to her mother. 'Mum wait, you don't have to go.'

'No, you carry on talking to your friend, a good chat will do you good. I'll phone you later to make sure you are okay, but please phone if you are worried about anything.' She gave Ally a kiss on the cheek. 'Speak later and tell Millie the lunch was superb.'

That evening Ally kept a listening ear out for any strange noise but felt reasonably sure that Nick wouldn't find out where she lived. Even so, she had a fitful night's sleep.

CHAPTER 8

It was later the next day that she got a call from an anxious sounding Millie.

'I don't want to worry you Ally, but I think you ought to know what I've just overheard.'

Ally felt her mood tumble. 'Oh no, what's happened?'

'I was in Mort's and that young girl who works there, Kirsten, the one with the purple hair and the thick makeup, well, I heard her bragging to someone that she had been speaking to a 'posh' man from London. The man had apparently told her that he might find her a TV job if she gave him some information.'

'Oh no. Millie, do you think the man was Nick? Do you know what kind of information?' She croaked, her mouth suddenly running dry.

'Ally, I'm sorry, but I think there's every chance it was Nick. Trying to be casual, I went over and asked the girl what the guy looked like, and she told me that he was tall with dark hair and that he was asking about you. The guy told her that he worked on the television series you used to be in. I'm afraid that the silly girl told him that you lived in the village.'

Ally suddenly felt very sick. 'What am I going to do Millie? I'm frightened that he's stalking me. We didn't split on good terms, and I know what he is capable of. He can be very nasty and could physically hurt me.'

'I'll come over later and we can drive to the police station and tell them. They probably won't do anything as he's not harmed you in any way, but at least they can put it on their records.'

'Thanks Millie.'

'Hey, no worries, that's what friends are for. I'll be over after I've finished the food prep for tomorrow.'

The next morning, she absently waited by the toaster to catch her two slices of breakfast wholemeal before they shot out the toaster like a rocket and landed on the floor. She hadn't slept well and now her head was full of yesterday's awful visit to the police station. She had gone there on her own after insisting that Millie stay at home and catch up on her paperwork. To say that the officer on the front desk had thought she was a complete neurotic was an understatement. As she buttered her toast, she recalled the whole embarrassing interchange.

'Do you have any evidence that this man is wanting to harm you?' The bespectacled grey-haired duty officer had asked, looking over the top of the glass screen.

As soon as the officer had mentioned the word evidence, she had known she was going to be at a disadvantage. 'No, not really,' she had answered. She wasn't ready yet to divulge everything that had happened while she had been living with Nick, it was far too private and too raw, besides there had been umpteen people milling about. 'I have logged an earlier issue with you though,' she had said helpfully, giving him the crime number. After several clicks on the mouse, it seemed the officer had found her crime report. Her hopes of any sympathetic recognition of her plight were soon dashed, when after a moment or two, he had peered at her over the top of his glasses, shrugged his shoulders and dismissively told her that there was no evidence that it was the same person.

She had tried not to let her irritation show. 'I am fairly sure it is the same person, because whoever wrote it had information about me that only a few people knew about.' Straight away she could see he wasn't buying it. She was wasting her time, for the officer certainly wasn't showing any signs of understanding how she was feeling. In the end she had lost patience and had insisted that he log her visit down on the system. After watching him tapping away at his keyboard, she could only hope that he had done so. With a curt 'thank you,' she had turned tail and driven back to the cottage, where she had gone straight to bed.

She had then spent the night tossing and turning, her thoughts and fears having kept her awake for most of the night. Now here she was, the next morning, feeling sleep-deprived and fearing what the day would bring.

～

JOE -AT POLICE HQ

It was late morning and Joe was back at his desk at the police station. Having just returned from having his break, he powered up his workstation to catch up on any new crime reports that he had been assigned while away from his desk. Quickly, he skimmed through the latest list that had just come in, which ranged from stolen dogs to a house being burgled. One case immediately caught his attention. The incident had been logged by the front desk late yesterday and it seemed some poor woman had been on-line trolled and was now frightened that the same person, an ex-boyfriend, was stalking her. Joe continued to quickly read through the report. It was only when he referred to the victim's details that he immediately recognised the name of the woman. His stomach turned. He checked again to make sure, but knew without doubt, from the information given, that the person reporting the crime was his former girlfriend and love of his life, his very own Ally. It took a while for it to sink in. He thought Ally was still living in London with that smarmy TV executive that she had left him for. Then he remembered that Kat had let slip that she had been in contact with Ally but hadn't said anything more about it.

Joe just sat there, not knowing what to do. He rubbed his chin, maybe he should get a colleague to deal with it. He was torn. His heart was telling him to go straight over to Ally, but his head was telling him no. In the end he knew that he had to pass Ally's crime report onto a colleague. The last thing he wanted was to rake up all the hurt and memories, memories which he had worked so hard to bury. 'Damn it.' Seeing her name had brought it all back to him. He shut down the report and went to get himself a bottle of water from the vending machine. On returning to his desk, he still felt really unsettled. Maybe he needed a break. He had some annual leave owing to him, he would check with the Guv about taking it soon. Needing to put Ally out of his head, he concentrated on the rest of his workload.

The sun filtered through the front window of the cottage. It looked a beautiful day out there with not a cloud in the sky. Ally knew that if she had not been feeling so down, she would have been able to appreciate it more. It had taken her ages to get her act together this morning and it was already gone 11 o'clock. She had a thumping headache, probably caused by being awake for most of the night stressing that Nick would find out where she lived and turn up on her doorstep. Her ex had a terrible temper and wouldn't hold back. He didn't like to be crossed and it was quite likely he would take great pleasure in hurting her.

Heading into the kitchen, she made herself a mug of extra strong coffee, then, sinking down into the soft sofa cushions, she sipped the hot caffeine loaded drink in the hope it would make her feel better. It didn't. Pacing the floor, she knew she had to do something to keep her mind off Nick or she would go crazy. She'd used the last of the coffee, and she needed other groceries too, maybe a trip to the supermarket would help. She wondered if Edna next door needed anything. Should she risk getting her head bitten off by the acid-mouthed pensioner? Deciding she needed to be brave and build a few bridges with Edna, she knocked on her front door.

Waiting patiently for her elderly neighbour to answer the door, she could hear Edna cursing under her breath as she shuffled down the hallway. After more cursing and fiddling with the lock, Edna finally pulled open the door. Leaning heavily on her wooden stick, the old lady's gnarled fingers tightly gripped the stick's curved handle, exposing her veiny, aged hands.

'Yes?' Edna asked abruptly, looking startled to find Ally standing on her doorstep.

'Morning Edna, I was just off to the supermarket to get some groceries and wondered if you needed anything. I've got the car, so can get anything you find difficult to carry,' she said brightly.

'Oh!' Edna looked taken aback.

'No worries if you don't want anything, I only knocked to be helpful,' she added, wondering if she'd done the right thing.

Edna's stance immediately softened. 'That's very good of you dear. I'm not feeling too good today. Let me see. Do they sell cat food in that supermarket of yours?'

Ally smiled. 'I'm sure they do. Which brand do you want?'

'Just a meat one, nothing fancy. I've taken in a few more strays, eating me out of house and home they be. The amount they are getting through is no one's business, they be costing me a fortune. Get what's on offer dear and I'll pay you when you come back.'

'I'll get you what I can Edna, is there anything else?'

'Let me think. Yes, please can you get a small bag of carrots and a leafy cabbage for the rabbits, and a pint of milk for meself would be lovely too. None of that skinny stuff mind. I used the last of me milk on me porridge this morning. Me arthritis is playing me up today and that will save me having to go out. Thank you dear, food for the strays is starting to get a bit much for me to carry.'

Back from her shopping trip with far more than was on her list, she delivered to her grateful neighbour all the shopping she had asked for, plus a small bar of chocolate as a treat for Edna from herself.

Feeling like she had made some progress with the old lady, she went back home feeling pleased that she had been able to help someone else instead of being completely self-absorbed in her own situation. She carried her own heavy bags of shopping into the kitchen and was starting to unpack them when she noticed that the sink tap was turned on. Quickly turning it off, she chided herself for being forgetful. On opening the fridge to put the milk in there, she froze, for there on the bottom shelf was a dead mouse. She drew back in horror, had the mouse been there all along and she hadn't noticed it? How had it got there? She knew there were fields nearby, maybe it had crept in while she had had the kitchen door open and at the first opportunity delved into the fridge looking for food. Flustered, she quickly disinfected the fridge and deposited the bagged dead mouse in the dustbin outside the back door, not noticing that the door had not been locked. Mouse disposed of, she locked the door behind her, washed her hands and continued to put away her shopping.

The rest of the day was already planned. She was going to spend the afternoon gardening. The beds near the kitchen door needed weeding, then after that, if she had time, she would go down to the hidden garden to work. Gardening was proving to be a good stress buster, and hadn't she read somewhere that it was good for the soul. While not convinced about that, she had to admit it did take her mind off things. She ran up the stairs to change into a pair of joggers and matching top that had been relegated for work in the garden.

After an hour or so of digging, she felt she needed something to eat. She was preparing a late lunch when she heard the doorbell ring. Quickly tearing off a piece of kitchen roll, she wiped her hands and headed to the door to see who it was. There was no one there but glancing down she saw someone had left a cardboard box on the step. She bent down to have a look to make sure the delivery was meant for her. There was no mistake, the box had her name on it.

On picking up the quite heavy carton she could hear the clinking of bottles. Carrying it through into the kitchen, she placed the box down on the worktop, then using a knife, sliced through the packaging tape. Someone had sent her six bottles of wine. After pulling out one of the bottles and checking the label, a wave of fear swept over her as the implication sank in. She knew straight away who had sent it. No one else knew about this obscure brand of wine except Nick, who being a bit of a wine buff had ordered it on-line. There was a small white card enclosed *'Thought you might need a top up you drunken sot.'*

The whole room seemed to be spinning around. Letting the card slip through her fingers and flutter to the floor, she gripped the worktop for support. After a few minutes, she made her way to the sofa where she sat cradling her head in her hands. It was obvious that Nick now knew where she lived.

She started to weep. She didn't know what to do, it was all too much. Her nerves were frazzled, and she was sorely tempted to pull out a bottle of wine from the carton and get blotto. Then her inner voice told her that was exactly what Nick had sent them to her for; it was what he had wanted her to do. This spurred her into action. The low life would not win, he would not get the better of her. She was stronger now and she would beat this.

In a spurt of fury, she marched into the kitchen and snatched the corkscrew from the drawer. Completely fired up by anger and determination, she quickly scooped up the box containing the wine bottles and carried it outside into the garden. Frantically popping all the corks, she tipped all six bottles upside down into the newly dug soil. Not waiting to watch them empty out, she ran back inside and slammed the door behind her, feeling triumphant.

She had mixed feelings. While feeling proud of herself for not succumbing to the temptations of the wine, the overriding fear that Nick now knew where she lived seemed to be taking precedence.

Trying to stop her hands shaking, she scrolled down her contacts for Millie's phone number. Maybe talking it through with her would help.

'Millie?'

'Hi Ally, what's up? Are you coming down later?'

'No, not today. Millie, I've just had a bit of a shock and to be honest I feel a bit shaky.'

'Oh no, tell me what's happened.'

Ally told her about the mouse and the wine.

'Well as I see it, the mouse could be a coincidence but not the bottles of wine, that is downright nasty. Well done you for tipping the wine away. The loser was obviously hoping that you were going to drink the lot,' said Millie, now fully aware of Ally's past.

'Yes, I feel quite proud of myself. I must admit I was tempted for a minute or two but thankfully overcame it. I have to say that I did run back inside awfully quick afterwards though to avoid getting a whiff of it,' she added, resisting the urge to giggle at the thought.

Trying to visualise what had happened, Millie gave a little chuckle. 'As you've been so good, how about I phone Betty and arrange to take you to see her? It will take your mind off all this Nick stuff. You can take the letters and the photo to show her. She may even know who this Alice is.'

'That would be lovely, thanks Millie.'

'What are you going to do now; will you be okay?'

'Yes, I'm over it. I'm going to go back into the garden for a bit more digging and then I might pop to the garden centre to buy some plants. I'm hoping that if I physically wear myself out that I'll sleep better tonight.'

'Good. You know where I am, give me a ring if you feel a bit low. I'll message you if I get a reply from Betty. She's a bit hard of hearing these days and doesn't always hear the phone ring. I may have to go round to see her.'

'I'm looking forward to meeting her Millie, thank you for arranging it for me. I'll see you tomorrow.'

Later, after a mammoth weeding session, she leaned back on the garden bench and closed her eyes, letting the late afternoon sun warm her face. Hearing a gentle flutter of wings, she opened her eyes to see the crow perched right next to her on the arm of the bench. The bird cocked his head, one beady eye fixed on her. 'Well, hello my little friend.' With her voice barely above a whisper, she reached into her pocket and pulled out a half-eaten snack pack of unsalted nuts. She could see the crow showing an interest. 'Are you hungry?' Emptying the remains of the packet into her hand, she sprinkled a few nuts on to the arm of the bench and watched as the crow picked them up with his beak before flying off.

The evening was long. She flicked through the television channels for something to watch. She was just settling down to a repeat of a period drama when a message came through from Millie. *I've*

*arranged for us to go and visit Betty tomorrow morning
if you are up for it. I've asked Ashna if she wants to come
along too (I don't know if you have met her). Ash's
family run the village newsagents. She's lovely, you'll
like her. See you by the church gate at 10.30.*

She smiled at Millie's message; her friend
was obviously trying to involve her in village life.
After sending back a reply, she settled down on the
sofa, pleased that she had something planned for
the next day that would take her mind off Nick. She
was looking forward to meeting Ashna too.

CHAPTER 9

The next morning Ally dressed carefully. Knowing that her confidence was at an all-time low, she wanted to make herself feel better. She raked through her wardrobe for something from her previous life, something a bit smarter than her usual attire, something that didn't symbolize her new life of digging and weeding. Her choice was limited, as most of her decent clothes had been packed away and sent for storage. Settling on her one good pair of jeans, she slipped them on. As she pulled up the zipper of the expensive designer jeans, she was glad that they still fitted her. She had already ironed the white silk blouse which she had hardly worn since leaving London. Surveying her hands and nails, she grimaced. She'd spent ages scrubbing them, but traces of garden dirt were still visible beneath her nails; that would teach her not to wear gardening gloves. Hopefully bit of nail varnish might do the trick; that is if she could find where she'd put it, or even if she had brought any with her. She couldn't understand why she was feeling so nervous about meeting Betty and Ashna. Why was she fussing so; she seriously needed to get a grip.

As soon as the hands on the church spire clock hit the top of the hour the bell started to loudly chime. As she approached the church gate, she saw a slightly built and pregnant Asian lady start to walk towards her.

Smiling broadly, the pretty young woman introduced herself. 'Hi, nice to meet you. I'm Ashna but everyone calls me Ash. You must be A…' Ash's last few words were drowned out by the sound of the church bells. Ashna put her hands up to cover her ears. 'Oh my goodness, what a din, still could be worse, it could be 12 o'clock, then we'd get twelve of the blooming things. It's enough to wake baby up,' she chuckled, patting the bulging tummy under her bright turquoise tunic.

Instantly she felt herself relax. Millie was right, Ash was lovely.

'Coo ee.' They both looked up to see Millie running towards them, her copper-coloured bouncy curls blending in with the red Breton top she wore under her usual baggy denim dungarees. 'Whew, sorry I'm a bit late, I was waiting for my catering supplies to be delivered. All the clotted cream needed be put away and I had a delivery of ice cream that had to go in the big freezer too.' Millie wiped her brow. 'Gosh it's already warm, and it's set to get even warmer this afternoon. I bet they'll be a run on the old ice cream later, I hope I ordered enough. Right, that's enough of my moaning.' Millie looked at them both and smiled. 'I see you two have already met. Come on ladies, let's go and see our Betty.'

Chatting away, they walked to a part of the village that she had never seen before. As they pushed open the gate, she looked with interest at Betty's long and very neat garden, which was divided into two by a gravel path, the sides of which were edged in colourful summer bedding. On the left side of the garden a large wooden cabin took up the first part of the lawn, its door propped open by a white painted wheelback chair. Ally stopped to read what had been chalked on the small blackboard placed on the seat of the chair. '*You are welcome to come in and browse. Please leave money for your purchases in the honesty box.*' In front of the blackboard was an old black metal cash box, rectangular in shape with a little handle on top, under which was a narrow slot to insert money.

'How quaint, can I pop in and have a quick look?' Ally poked her head inside the open door. Every wall of the cabin was filled floor to ceiling with shelves of second-hand books. In front of the books were tightly packed clothes rails, labelled '*Vintage*', each one bowing from the weight of pre-loved clothing that had been crammed onto hangers. There was a table in the corner piled high with bric-a-brac. Under the table was a crate containing an assortment of handbags and pairs of shoes neatly banded together.

Millie and Ashna followed Ally inside the cabin. 'This is one of Betty's fund raisers,' said Millie, lightly brushing her hands along the clothes. 'She does quite well out of it. The holiday makers love to buy from here. Especially the books. All proceeds go to the new village hall fund.'

'What a lovely idea. Next time I want a book to read I will come here for one. I'll donate some too, as it's for such a good cause.'

'Betty will be very grateful; it means such a lot to her.'

The three of them continued up the path to Betty's front door. After pressing the doorbell, they waited for someone to answer.

'She must be in there. I bet she's got the television on and can't hear us,' said Millie. 'Wait here a minute, I'll go around the back and let her know that we are here.'

As they waited for Millie, Ally turned to Ashna. 'Do you know Betty well?'

Ashna shook her head. 'No, I've seen her about, but like you, this is the first time I've been here. I've not mixed with the villagers that much, only Millie. I think Millie felt I needed to get out more and decided to take me under her wing to broaden my horizons.'

'I think it's the same for me too,' Ally nodded, breaking into a smile.

They were both laughing at each other's predicament when Betty's front door opened. It was Millie. 'Come in you two. I was right. She loves a bit of morning telly, but she has it on so loud that she can't hear anything else.'

Ally and Ashna passed a knowing smile to each other as they stepped through Betty's front door. The heat hit them as soon as they walked into Betty's small living room. It was easy to see why it was so hot, the culprit was the gas fire, on full blast, despite it being a scorcher outside. The room had wall-to-wall floral carpet and a pair of pottery dogs had been placed either side of the fireplace. In one corner, a mahogany cabinet with curved legs displayed a Royal Albert Country Rose tea set and in the adjacent corner a matching cabinet was full of crystal glassware. Framed photos decked the top of both. It was a room with a past, and one that reflected Betty's age.

Ally was surprised at just how upright Betty seemed as she stood up to greet them. Her blue veined hands pushed down on the arms of her armchair as she carefully eased herself halfway out of her seat, then sat back down again. No way had this elderly lady let herself go, for Betty was smartly dressed. Wearing a heather coloured tweed skirt and a pale pink twinset, she had completed her outfit with a string of pearls around her neck. There was not a single hair out of place on Betty's rigid and heavily lacquered shampoo and set hairdo.

'Betty, please meet Ashna who lives in the village, and Ally who has recently moved into Rose Briar Cottage, both are good friends of mine,' said Millie.

Feeling Betty's scrutiny, Ally was pleased she had chosen decent clothes to wear. A mud-stained sweatshirt and shabby leggings would have gone down like a lead balloon with this grand old lady.

Betty pointed to the sofa. 'Do sit down ladies.' Her eyes darted from Ally to Ashna, settling on Ashna. She spoke to Ashna first. 'I know a little bit about you my dear; your family run the newsagents. Nice shop. Very good service. I get my People's Friend from there.' Betty's eyes travelled down to Ashna's very pregnant stomach. 'Baby on the way then?' Knowing it wasn't so much a question but more a statement Ashna just nodded.

Betty then turned to Ally. 'And what brings you to the village young lady?' Betty asked politely but pointedly.

The old saying *iron hand in a velvet glove* sprang into Ally's mind but there was no way that she was going to be intimidated by someone in her eighties. Sitting up straight, Ally looked Betty directly in the eye. 'My family live a few miles away. I was brought up here in Cornwall but have been in London working until recently. Because I wanted some independence, I decided to rent here in the village instead of returning to my family home.'

'Yes, I heard that you have rented Rose Briar Cottage, news travels fast around here.' Betty's brow puckered, 'It appears that you live next door to that awful woman Edna.'

'That's right, Edna lives in the cottage next to mine.' Fully aware that she was being tested, Ally decided not to ruffle Betty's feathers by further mentioning Edna. She swiftly changed the subject. 'I do see my parents on a regular basis though. My father is now semi-retired, he is a solicitor with his own practice in Truro and my mother and I regularly meet up when she isn't working. Although retired, she still does some supply teaching when they need her. She used to be Deputy Head at St Cuthbert's, do you know it?'

Ally could see Betty thinking hard about what she had just said.

With a slight nod of approval, Betty eventually answered. 'Ah yes. St Cuthbert's, that's the private school isn't it. Very good.' Seeming satisfied with the information Ally had given her, Betty took hold of her stick and levered herself out of the chair. 'Let me go and put the kettle on.'

'Betty, do you want any help?' offered Millie.

'No, I don't need any help. I'm quite capable of making a pot of tea thank you,' Betty instantly bit back.

Feeling slightly deflated at being put in their place, the three women watched as Betty headed into what appeared to be the kitchen. They could hear her walking stick making a tapping noise on the kitchen's tiled floor and the chinking of crockery.

'Phew, that was quite scary,' whispered Ally.

Millie smiled. 'Her bark is worse than her bite, she's a sweetie really - once she gets to know you.'

'Well let's hope Ash and I pass muster,' Ally answered with a grin, which rapidly disappeared when she saw Betty making her way back into the room pushing a brass coloured serving trolley.

Although Betty's slipper clad feet appeared firmly placed as she walked across the room, the upper half of her frail body seemed unsteady, giving them the impression that she might topple over at any minute without the support of the trolley. With her walking stick conveniently parked on the trolley's lower shelf, and her hands firmly gripping the trolley handle, Betty carefully steered the clattering trolley into the living room.

'Oooh, those cakes look yummy Betty,' said Millie chirpily, eying up the plate of French Fancies artfully arranged on a delicately patterned plate. A teapot, sugar bowl, milk jug and four cups and saucers from the same set competed for space on the trolley.

The three women looked on nervously, not daring to intervene as Betty released her grip on the trolley and used both her trembling hands to lift the quite heavy teapot. After pouring, Betty shakily handed each of them a rattling half-filled cup of tea, which by some miracle hadn't slopped over into the saucer.

Relieved that the tea making was over with no mishaps and Betty was now safely settled back in her armchair, Millie, Ashna and Ally felt they could relax slightly. As they sat chatting, Betty listened, appearing satisfied that Ally wasn't some evil troublemaker from London.

As Ally nibbled on her cake, the talk flowed easily between them. She noticed how the old lady's face lit up when she laughed. Betty was so much nicer now she wasn't giving herself and Ashna a grilling. Ally felt in her bag for the bundle of letters and the framed photo, maybe now was the time to ask Betty about them while she was in a jovial mood. She took a deep breath before speaking. 'Betty, Millie tells me that you have lived in the village for a very long time.'

'Yes dear, I was born here.'

Ally pulled out the letters and the photo and handed them to the old lady. 'I wonder if you know who wrote these Betty. I found them while I was clearing out the old brick hut in the garden.'

'Let me see.' Betty's thin bony hand reached out for the letters. 'I'm going to need my reading glasses for these I'm afraid.' She looked at Millie. 'Millie my dear, will you get them for me, they are in the cabinet.'

Equipped with her horn-rimmed glasses, now perched on the bridge of her nose, Betty studied the photo for a moment. After a slight nod of recognition, she then turned her attention to the letters. 'They look quite foxed with age, but I suppose that is to be expected, given how old they are. My eyes aren't as good as they used to be,' she grumbled, angling the sheets of handwriting towards the light coming in from the window. All was quiet as Betty endeavoured to read every letter. 'Goodness me,' she said, after reading the last one. 'These certainly bring back memories.' Laying the letters in her lap, she looked up at them. 'It all happened so long ago. I was only a youngster at the time.' Betty sucked in through what was left of her teeth. 'It was such a scandal that even I knew about it. I can remember my mother saying how Alice had brought shame on her family and to the village, although at my age I wasn't expected to know why. It was a scandal that rocked everyone. It was the worst kept secret ever. They wanted to send her away you know, but Alice wouldn't go in case her American lover changed his mind and came back to her.'

'Betty, who was Alice?'

'Alice and her family lived above what used to be the village shop, which is now Rose Briar Cottage, where you are currently living,' she said, answering Ally. 'It was all such a long time ago, let me think.' Betty rubbed her chin as she delved back into the past. 'Ah, yes I remember...Alice joined the ATS, one had to in those days you know. Those eligible had to help with the war effort. I think she worked on a nearby farm. Yes, looking back, I sort of remember feeling quite envious of her when she told me she had learnt to drive a tractor,' said Betty, softly chuckling. 'Alice also helped her parents in the shop, which was also the post office. Yes, Alice did give birth to the airman's child, a son, born out of wedlock, and he still lives and works in the village. His name is Oscar Harries. You may have seen him because he owns the hardware store. Alice never married nor did she have any more children;

people say she never gave up on the hope that her airman lover would return to her.'

Ally nodded, pleased that her thoughts about Oscar's mother had now been confirmed. 'Yes, I've met Oscar. Are you saying that Oscar is Alice's son by Frank, the airman in these letters?'

Betty nodded. 'I don't know if Oscar knows much about his father as Alice brought him up on her own, with the help of her mother.'

'Oh, what a sad story. I must return the letters and photo to Alice.'

'She won't understand my dear. I'm afraid Alice has dementia. You could give them to Oscar though, he might like to know how much his mother and father loved each other back in the day.'

There was silence as the three women absorbed Alice's story.

Betty looked at the three sad faces. 'It was so many years ago now. One mustn't dwell on the past.' Her voice suddenly changed. 'Let's talk about the present instead.' The old lady fastened her gaze on them. 'I need help,' she said bluntly. 'I want you three to go on the fund-raising committee for the new village hall.'

'My baby is due soon, I don't think I can,' Ashna said apologetically, patting her tummy.

'Mmmm, you are excused young lady, but not you Millie and you Ally. I need some young blood to liven it up, the committee is full of old fogies like me.'

Millie laughed and shook her head. 'Have you forgotten? I'm already on the committee Betty.

I've got an idea though. What about I take Ally around to our crumbling village hall. It might help to persuade her.'

Betty's face lit up. 'Excellent idea. Now where are the blessed keys to the hall?' She picked up her ancient leather handbag and started rifling through it. 'Ah, here they are.' She handed the bunch of keys to Millie. 'Off you go. Pop the keys through my letter box when you're done. I'm going to close my eyes and have a little nap soon.'

Taking that as a signal that it was time to leave, they all stood up.

'Thank you for the tea and cakes Betty,' said Ally. 'It was lovely to meet you and thank you for the information on Alice. I will take the letters to Oscar.'

'As you please m'dear.'

As they walked home, Millie made plans to take them to the village hall. 'I can't do it today, but what about tomorrow. Let's see.' Millie bit on her lip. 'I don't think anyone uses the hall tomorrow afternoon, what about we go there after I've finished work, say around five o'clock?'

'Suits me, I'm not doing much,' replied Ally.

'Are you coming too Ash?'

'Oh why not. I've nothing better to do either. You never know, I might just join the committee after baby is born,' she said, patting her stomach and thinking how good it would be to be free from the constraints of home where her every movement was watched and judged by her husband's family.

'Too right you will Ash,' joked Millie. 'Once Betty's got you in her clutches that's it. She's probably already assigned a chair with your name on it,' she added, grinning.

'This is me,' said Ally as they reached her front gate. 'See you tomorrow you two.'

'Yes, looking forward to it,' Ashna replied. She really meant it too, for the last couple of years had not been easy. Living with her husband's family had put quite a strain on her relationship with her husband Arun, for even the slightest cross word between them was heard and discussed by the rest of the family. The prospect of spending a couple of hours out of the confines of the claustrophobic flat above the shop gave her something to look forward to. She had told her husband that once their baby son was born, they would put their names down for a home of their own, a home which they could decorate to their own liking, cook whatever food they liked and have the freedom to live as they wished.

Ally was still smiling at Ash's comment as she turned the key in the cottage door. She knew she had found two good friends in Ashna, who was finding it very difficult living a very restricted life with her in-laws and Millie, who didn't talk about it much, but had hinted that she had also come to Cornwall to escape. It seemed that both her new friends had not had it easy either.

The long afternoon stretched out in front of her, maybe she should have a good walk. There were lots of places to explore. Maybe she could drive towards Lantivet Bay and park at the National Trust car park. It was so beautiful up on the cliffs there, looking down on the turquoise waters of Palace Cove.

CHAPTER 10

The next morning Ally was hoping she was going to find blue sky and sunshine, but the weather had turned dull and misty. Lacking any incentive to do work in the garden, she headed down the stairs thinking about how she would spend the day. She had a free morning, and after that she had a few hours to kill before she was due to meet Millie and Ashna. Maybe now was a good time to take Alice's letters and the photo to Oscar. She would first run herself a bath, then after breakfast she would go down into the village.

Throwing a thin cardigan over her shoulders, she tucked her ponytail in her cap, then donning her sunglasses, headed down into the village. As she walked down the cobbles of what constituted the main shopping street, she knew it had been a good decision to choose this place to live. The shops were lovely, and even though they were beautifully decorated to catch the eye of the holidaymaker, she found there was still enough here to satisfy her own need for a bit of retail therapy. Knowing that there was no rush to see Oscar, she took her time, stopping to look in the window of one of her favourite shops, the bakery. Homemade Cornish pasties, bulging with all kinds of savoury fillings and plump sausage rolls filled the window's lower shelves. Very rarely did she pass this place without buying something. She felt a pang of hunger as she scanned the bakery's top shelves which were stacked full of fluffy scones of different flavours. The bread here was amazing too, the smell of it cooking was nearly always her undoing. After dithering, she resisted the urge to go inside.

Moving on, she glanced in the window of the clothes shop to see if there was anything new. The mannequins had been dressed in boho style linen smocks and floaty summer dresses. Designer summer footwear had been artfully placed among the faux fishing nets and seashells and other nautical accessories. It was all lovely, but not what she needed right now.

In a world of her own, completely ignoring the hustle and bustle around her, she continued to meander along the narrow thoroughfare that was the heart of the village. The toy shop was busy, it always was, being a favourite of children with holiday spending money. There was a cute wooden pull-along duck in the front of the window, maybe she would buy one for Ashna's baby.

The last shop in the row was Harries Hardware. She pushed open the door. The shop was empty. Spurred on by the fact that she wouldn't have an audience, she stood by the counter and pressed the buzzer. As she waited for Oscar to appear, she hoped it would be him and not his assistant. She was lucky, a moment later Oscar came through a door at the back of the shop.

'Sorry me dear, was just doing a bit of stock-taking. What can I help you with?'

'Hello Oscar, I've got something here for you.' She reached into her bag and pulled out the framed photo and the letters.

'Oh,' said Oscar, now looking slightly anxious.

'It's nothing to worry about, it's just that I found these at Rose Briar Cottage, they were in the little hut in the garden. Somebody mentioned they might be of interest to you or your mother, so I thought you might like them.' She offered the bundle of letters and the framed photo to Oscar.

Oscar looked puzzled but took them both. 'Er, thank you. Do you want me to look at them now? I'm a bit busy.'

She shook her head. 'No, it's alright Oscar, I'll just leave them with you, but do you have a pen and paper handy so that I can write down my mobile number for you? I would love to hear from you when you have had time to look at them.'

Oscar still looked puzzled but bent down under the counter. She heard him scrabbling around. He eventually popped up holding a pen and sheet of paper, which he slid towards her.

She quickly scribbled her number down and handed it to him. 'There we go,' she said, smiling. 'Please feel free to phone me at any time. If these letters belong to you, I would really love to know more about Alice and her Frank.'

'Thank you, I'll give you a ring when I've looked at them.' As he watched Ally disappear out the shop, Oscar couldn't help wondering what it was all about.

Ally felt pleased with herself. Deed done, letters and photo delivered safely. She would wait to hear back from Oscar. It was time to go home and make herself some lunch. As she passed the bakery, she knew the aroma of freshly baked bread was going to be her downfall. Her willpower crumbling, she succumbed to a crusty loaf still warm from the oven.

As soon as she got back to the cottage, she sliced into the loaf's dark crisp outer and slathered on some butter. The loaf was so fresh she didn't want to spoil it by adding anything else. She savoured the crunch of the crust and the softness of the bread, this was heaven. With a full stomach and feeling pleased with herself, she switched on the kettle to make a cup of tea. Now feeling quite bloated and with time on her hands, she knew it would be a good idea if she went out for a walk to get some fresh air and maybe burn off some calories. Walking was one of the things that kept her sane these days. She would take the circular route to Lantic Bay. The earlier mist had disappeared, and the sun was out, the sea blue, all perfect for a long trek along the white sandy beaches, what more could she wish for. She would pass the church and walk back through the woods. It would be demanding but it was what she needed and would hopefully enable her to get a good night's sleep.

It was early evening, and after a quick wash and brush up, she wandered down into the village to meet her friends.

The hall, signposted as the Community Hall was at the other end of the village, past the church. As she took in the hall's aged pebble-dashed walls, peeling painted windows and roof patched with corrugated panels which were streaked with rust, Ally could well understand why the village was trying to raise money to build a new one. The hall must have been built a good few decades ago and looked to be on its last legs.

'Right then ladies, let's do this.' Millie pulled the door open.

Following closely behind Millie and Ashna, the musty smell hit Ally as soon as she entered the entrance lobby of the building. She looked around the small space. The walls had been painted a drab yellow, now scuffed and marked after years of wear and tear. There was a large coir mat on the vinyl floor which had seen better days, which might have added to the smell.

Millie noticed Ally wrinkling her nose. 'It's the damp you can smell. It's a cross between stinky socks and old mushrooms. It's because the roof leaks like a sieve. The place needs pulling down in my view,' she whispered. 'Come on you two, follow me, it's not so bad inside.'

To the left of the entrance was a small kitchen. On the chipped Formica worktop sat a large chrome tea urn. Next to the urn was an assortment of mugs neatly stacked on a metal tray. Straight away Ally noticed the cupboards not shutting properly and the tap dripping noisily into the stainless-steel sink.

Millie shook her head. 'You can see the hall has had its day and why we want a new one. The Scouts and cubs use this place too, so it takes a bit of a battering with all those kids running around. They dry their tents in here too when they come back from camp, which probably doesn't help with the dampness.' Millie led them into the main hall with its pale blue painted walls and pointed to the far end of the hall. 'Each group that uses the hall has its own noticeboard. This place is highly utilised by the local community, and we couldn't do without it.'

'Gosh, does the roof leak that bad?' Ashna pointed to the buckets, strategically placed to catch drips.

Millie pointed to the chink of daylight coming through the ceiling. 'I'm afraid so. They keep patching it up but then another leak breaks through. The windows don't shut properly either. It gets flipping cold in here in the winter, none of us take our coats off even though they have the heaters on. It's a wonder the council don't condemn it. Have you seen enough? There is a committee meeting at the nearby coffee shop in a minute if you want to come. You can meet the rest of the long-suffering committee.'

Ashna and Ally looked at each other, waiting for the first one to speak.

Ally took the plunge. 'Okay, count me in.'

'Me too.' Ashna said, while trying to convince herself that she'd done the right thing.

'Great. I'll lock up then we can go. Thanks guys.'

'Hi everyone.' Millie smiled broadly at the people sitting around the table in the coffee shop, each of them with a notepad and pen. 'Let me introduce you to our newest recruits. Meet Ally and Ashna, hopefully they will bring some fresh ideas to the table. Shuffle up everyone,' said Millie, dragging over three more chairs.

After shaking a few hands and saying hello, Ally and Ashna sat very quiet, listening to the jumble of voices around the table. Suddenly everyone went quiet when a distinguished looking man wearing a blue wool blazer and cream trousers rushed in.

'Hello Clive,' Ally heard someone say.

'Sorry I'm late, got held up at the Sailing Club.' Clive pushed his chair back and stood before them. After a little cough he started to eloquently address the committee. You could hear a pin drop as everyone listened carefully to what he had to say.

Ally wondered who he was. As he stood there speaking, she took in his tanned face which showed off his professionally whitened teeth. With his immaculate clothing and neatly cut silvering hair, Clive had affluence written all over him. As his upper-class voice boomed around the hall, attempting to put his ideas across, it was obvious that the rest of the committee held him in high esteem. Even she had to concede that the guy seemed to know what he was talking about as they discussed the upcoming events, raffles, and the lettings they hoped for after they had sorted the roof and given the place a lick of paint. There was even talk of sponsorship if someone would do the local marathon, which she thought was a bit ambitious considering the age of the Committee.

She didn't have to wait long to find out who Clive was, for as soon as everyone stopped to order more tea and coffee, Clive made a beeline for her.

'Nice to meet you Ally,' he said, offering her his hand.

'Hello,' Ally smiled as she shook hands with the tall, athletically built handsome man who looked to be in his early fifties.

'Among other things, I'm Chairman of the social committee here. We have quite a few functions going on. In fact, we have one coming up soon. Would you like to come along? You could help me. You would be such a great asset because people know and love you from the television show. You would be our celebrity guest.'

'Er.' She felt a sense of panic.

Clive pressed on. 'You don't have to say now, just sleep on it. If you would like, we could have dinner. What about that?'

Was she being asked out on a date? For his age Clive was quite good looking, and she wondered if she should say yes. It had been a long time since anyone had asked her out. She didn't know what to say.

Seeing her hesitation, Clive backed off. He ripped a strip of paper from his pad and jotted down his mobile number. 'Here, take my number and if you fancy going out for something to eat, I know of a wonderful place that has a top-notch chef and where the food is outstanding.'

On the way home Ally told Millie and Ashna about her being asked out by Clive. 'What should I do? Is he married or anything?'

Millie shook her head. 'Not that I know of. He has a nice house overlooking the marina, it's the big white one with the blue windows. He is a businessman, has offices in London but lives locally. Other than that, I don't know much about him except that he likes to do a lot for the village, which he now calls his home.

CHAPTER 11

After saying goodbye to her friends, Ally headed home. Even after mulling it over, she still didn't know what to do about Clive's offer of dinner. He seemed kind, and although much older than her, he was quite good looking, but was she ready to dip her toe into the dating scene again? Part of her wanted to accept, the other part shuddered at the very thought of it.

As she neared the cottage, she noticed that the side gate to the back garden was wide open and swinging in the breeze. She felt her stomach turn, because having checked everything before she had left, she was certain the gate was shut. She started to question herself; was she losing it? Was her prolonged absence from the workplace turning her brain to mush and making her forgetful and neurotic? Her worries soon subsided, for as soon as she reached her front door, she knew why the gate was open, there had been a parcel delivered and the delivery person had left it just inside the gate. Puzzled, she carried the cardboard box inside. It had her name on the top, so it must be for her. The box felt quite light, and as hard as she tried, she couldn't think what could be inside. Maybe she had ordered something and had forgotten.

Placing the box on the little dining table along with her keys, she went into the kitchen to put the kettle on for a coffee. Then, with her curiosity getting the better of her, she decided to open the parcel while waiting for the kettle to boil. For the life of her she still couldn't remember ordering anything but hoped it was something nice. Using her key to score along the parcel tape, she lifted the flaps of the box. Inside was an ivory-coloured silk chemise. Tucked in the folds of the silky garment was a blister pack of her old prescription happy pills. She couldn't stop herself from yelping and leaping back in horror, for it wasn't just the pills that had spooked her but the fact that the chemise had been splattered with a blood red liquid which had seeped deep into the fabric. With her heart banging like a drum, she knew without doubt that the box had to be from Nick. It couldn't be from anyone else. He had used what looked like fake blood too. He must really hate her to do this. Was the fake blood a threat? Was he out to seriously harm her?

A surge of anger shot through her. 'I so hate you Nick Curtis, you are the most despicable man alive,' she screamed. Clenching her fists, she forcefully swept the box clean off the table, where it fell to the floor with a thud. Her eyes filling, she stared in disgust at the box, which had landed upright, with its contents still intact.

Feeling the hysteria building inside her, she took several deep breaths and told herself to keep calm. Her legs had turned to jelly. Leaving the box where it was, she walked unsteadily into the kitchen. With shaking hands, she re-boiled the kettle. Scooping an overfull teaspoon of instant coffee out of the jar, she cursed under her breath when her trembling hands caused the spoon to miss the mug, scattering granules all over the worktop. Doing her utmost to control her shaking hands, she tried again.

Holding the mug of coffee with both hands to keep it steady, she went into the garden. After carefully placing the mug on the arm of the bench, she sat down and began inhaling and exhaling deeply, doing whatever she could to keep her hands and knees still. After a while, the shaking started to ease, and instead of crying, she was able to think rationally about what she should do next. She toyed with the idea of ringing Kat, but somehow it felt like she was admitting to her old friend that her life was a complete train wreck, which at that precise moment, was exactly what it was. Maybe she'd phone Millie. First though, she needed to put her practical hat on and collect evidence.

Returning to the living room, she picked up her phone, then walking around the box, used her phone camera to take photos of the box and its contents from all angles. It was only on further examination, that she realised the chemise was the same colour and brand as the one she already owned, which she had brought with her. This confirmed to her even more that Nick was behind it. This was going to the police. She messaged Millie.

Ten minutes later there was a knock on the door. 'Ally, it's me.'

Cautiously, she opened the door a crack, then after looking both ways down the lane to check for any sign of Nick, she let Millie in, along with her dog Charlie, who she had been out walking.

'The creep must be sick in the head to send this.' Millie stared at the box in dismay.

Ally nodded. 'And, you know what is even sicker, it's the same chemise that I've already got. I ran upstairs to check. My one is still in my drawer. He must have gone and bought another one, it's identical.'

'Where did he get the pills from?'

'I think I must have left some in the flat.'

'I don't know what to say Ally. The situation stinks, it's awful.' Millie could see her friend's eyes filling. 'Look, I think it's best if I stay with you for a bit until you feel better. What an evil thing to do. The guy needs reporting. The sooner, the better too in my book.'

'Yes, I know. I'll do it.' She brushed a tear away. 'I'll just make you a cuppa first. Will Charlie be okay? Does he need a drink of water or something?' She bent down to stroke the lively black cockapoo, who was looking up at her with his tail wagging in anticipation of getting some fuss.

'He's gorgeous Millie. Maybe I should get a dog, but one with big teeth to see off Nick,' she quipped, only half joking.

Millie smiled, relieved that her friend was still able to find some humour in the situation. 'Thanks, just a small bowl of water for him Al. He'll probably have a sleep now he's had his walk. You could always get a little cat. My neighbour's cat, a gorgeous ginger tabby, has just had some kittens. Next time you come for a coffee we'll both go and have a look. Right now though, you need to get your laptop and report what has been going on to the police.' Waiting until her friend had completed her on-line incident report and being satisfied that she was going to be alright, Millie made her move to go. 'Ally, please phone me straight away if anything worries you and I will come back.'

After saying goodbye to Millie, Ally went into the kitchen to look for something to eat, something quick and easy. She was just beating some eggs for an omelette when she heard her phone ringing. Her body immediately tensed. She could feel her heart thumping as the phone continued to ring. Taking a deep breath, she stopped what she was doing and told herself to get a grip. She looked across the room at the ringing phone, too scared to even go near it. The voice of reason within her told her that all she had to do was wait for the phone to stop ringing before checking to see who it was. Pushing the half-beaten egg aside, she waited until the phone was silent before tentatively retrieving it from the sofa. She stared at the screen not knowing what to do. It was a number she didn't recognise. A minute later she received a text. The call had been from Oscar Harries. With a sigh of relief, she rang him back.

Oscar was feeling quite emotional. He had read the letters and studied the photo Ally had given him. He had never met his father, but straight away had seen there was a distinct likeness to himself. All he knew was that his father was an American airman and that he had returned to the United States. His mother and his grandmother had brought him up. Every time he had asked about his father it had ended in a frosty wall of silence or a telling off, so he had given up asking. He was pleased when Ally returned his call.

'Hi Oscar, it's Ally, you left me a message to ring you.'

'Hello Ally, yes. Thank you so much for the letters and photo. They have given me a very much appreciated insight into my father's love for my mother.'

'It was a pleasure. I'm glad you found them interesting.'

'Ally, I was wondering if you would like to come and meet my mother? She's very frail but seeing a new face might do her good. To be honest, I have got a bit of an ulterior motive. I know next to nothing about my father and I'm hoping that if my mother recognises Frank from the photo, that she might start speaking about him.'

Ally put down the phone. She fully understood what Oscar wanted her to do. He wanted her to try and coax information out of his elderly mother so that he could find out more about his father. She would give it a go, whether it would work or not she didn't know, but she would give it her best shot, besides she sorely needed a diversion from her thoughts.

The next morning, still feeling unsettled after the chemise incident, she walked down into the village to Oscar's shop. She knew she was entering unknown territory and didn't know quite what to expect or what was expected of her. Pushing firmly on the shop door, the bell jangled. Oscar looked up.

'Good morning me dear.' Oscar acknowledged her with a smile from behind the counter where he was serving a customer. 'Won't be a jiffy.' As soon as the customer exited the shop, Oscar reached over to a small cabinet behind him for Alice's letters and the photo. 'Here you are. I must admit these really got to me. I didn't think I was a softie but reading the letters brought a tear to my eye.'

'I know what you mean, they got to me too Oscar.'

'I'll just put the closed sign up, then I'll take you upstairs to see my mother. You do understand that her mind is not what it should be, don't you?'

he said, trying to forewarn her as he locked the shop door and turned the sign over.

Ally nodded. She didn't know why, but she was feeling a bit anxious as she followed Oscar up the carpeted staircase leading to a narrow passageway, which was mostly taken up with a zimmer frame and a commode. Squeezing past them, Oscar knocked on a door and called out 'Ma, it's me, Oscar. I'm coming in.'

'Some days are better than others. I don't know if she'll even know who I am today,' Oscar said quietly, before entering Alice's bedroom.

As Ally entered the room, she was pleasantly surprised. Oscar had obviously done his best to make the room as comfortable for his mother as possible. The room was bright and colourful. The pink floral curtains and bedspread matched and toned with the carpet and there were framed photographs hung on the walls, including one of a large group of men in uniform. The television in the corner was blaring out a morning television show on full volume. There was a shelf with books and jigsaw puzzles next to the bedside cabinet. The other side of the bed, and directly in front of the TV was Alice, who was sitting upright in an orthopaedic chair and clutching a baby doll dressed in pale blue knitted clothing. Beneath a wheeled cantilever table, Alice's raised legs were covered by a crochet blanket, all except for her slipper clad feet, which were sticking out at angles.

Alice's whiskery face lit up when she saw Ally. 'Maud, I can't find my ration book, can I have one of your coupons so I can get 4 oz of sherbert lemons, or if they've not got any, some barley sugar twists; me mouth be as dry as the bottom of a parrot's cage.'

Ally looked at Oscar, then quickly realised that Alice had confused her with someone else. She made a mental note to buy Alice some sherbert lemons.

'Ma, this isn't Maud, it's Ally. She has something to show you.' Oscar turned to Ally and whispered. 'I believe Maud must have been one of her friends as she often mentions her.'

She nodded slightly to let Oscar know she understood, before looking over to Alice. 'I love sherbert lemons too Alice. I'll get you some from the shop,' she added brightly, hoping she wasn't overdoing it.

Alice beamed and clapped her hands together like she had won the first prize in a raffle. 'Thank you, Maud.'

'Ma, look what Ally's got.' He indicated to Ally to hand the letters to his mother. 'Hold back on showing her the photo though,' he whispered from behind his hand.

'What's these? Do I know these?' Alice's thin veined hands pulled the letters from the envelopes.

'Here Ma,' Oscar handed Alice her reading glasses.'

Alice shakily put them on and stared down at the handwriting. It was a few minutes before she looked up. She had tears in her eyes. 'My Frank, my beloved Frank.' She looked around the room. 'Is he here? Has he got leave? Has he come to take me back with him to his home in Virginia where the mountains are blue?'

Oscar stepped forward. 'Ma he's not here, but look, there's a photo for you.' He took the photo from Ally and gently placed it in his mother's lap.

With shaking hands, Alice picked the photo up and stared at it. 'My Frank.' A big fat tear rolled down her face as she held the frame to her lips and tenderly kissed it.

Ally bent down and patted Alice's hand. 'Your Frank loves you very much Alice.'

'We are going to be wed you know, but he has to go back to America to see his family first. Did you know he made shoes? He promised me a pair of leather boots.' Alice continued to weep. 'He loves me; he really does.' In a distressed state, she started to rock back and forth.

'Alice, we know how much he loves you.' Ally didn't know what else to say. She felt like she had made a huge mistake by re-opening Alice's wounds. Pulling a handful of tissues from the box on the table, she handed them to Alice to dry her tears. 'Shall I look after the letters and the photo for you?' She spoke softly, leaning forward to comfort the old lady who was dabbing her face with the tissues.

'Yes Maud, take them; you are such a good friend to me. Don't forget those sherbert lemons now, my mouth feels like the bottom of a parrot's cage,' she repeated, smacking her lips.

'Of course, I'll go and get you some now,' Ally replied, relieved that Alice had been diverted away from her painful memories.

Oscar smiled at Ally. 'Think me ma may have had enough now.'

She completely understood. 'I'll pop to the shop and get her some sherbert lemons, that's if they have any. Here you are Oscar,' she passed the letters and the photo over to him. 'It's best that you keep them,' she said, reaching for the door handle. 'Don't worry, I'll let myself out while you see to your mother.'

'Thank you for your help,' said Oscar, his voice gruff with emotion, as Ally got up to leave.

CHAPTER 12

Ally looked out at the darkening sky. The weeks had flown by, the days were gradually getting shorter, and it was difficult to tell whether the gloomy light was a result of the night drawing in or of the predicted storm. It wasn't long before she had the answer as heavy spots of rain began hitting the window before turning into a deluge.

Pulling the living room curtains shut, she headed into the kitchen. What a foul night. She had a fancy for something comforting, something sweet, and was just reaching for the biscuit tin when a sheet of lightening illuminated the garden. This was quickly followed by a loud clap of thunder, which made her nearly jump out of her skin. 'For heaven's sake woman,' she muttered under her breath. She never used to be this jumpy. Her nerves being well and truly shot, she took two chocolate hobnobs out of the tin.

She couldn't settle. The six o'clock news went completely over her head. The newsreader could have announced that aliens had taken over Cornwall and it wouldn't have registered. Her mind was in turmoil, chock full of stuff – mostly about Nick, but there were other things nudging in there too.

Restless, her eyes landed on the crumpled paper bag she'd left on the table containing the last remnants of fudge. She was addicted to the stuff. She'd swapped one addiction for another, she thought glumly. There was a tiny bit left, and she wasn't going to waste it. Holding up the bag, she tipped the remaining crumbs into her mouth. Straight away they hit the spot. Savouring the fudge's salty sweetness, she told herself that if she didn't try harder to put her fear of Nick out of her mind, she would probably end up going crazy and, if she kept on eating fudge like this, she would end up being the size of a house too.

With huge determination, she pushed Nick to the back of her mind and instead thought about her earlier visit to Alice. She had taken Oscar's mother a bag of jelly babies and it had heartened her to see how the old lady's face had lit up when she entered the room. While there, it had become obvious to her that Oscar was a good man and had his mother's best interests at heart, because before handing the sweets to his mother, he had tipped them out of their original bag and put them into a more nostalgic plain paper one.

Still restless, she idly flicked through the tv channels for something to occupy her mind. The room was hot and stuffy. The storm had passed but hadn't got rid of the humidity. Needing some fresh air, she got up to open the kitchen door and was surprised to find that it was ajar. Immediately she cursed herself for being careless, especially after everything that had happened. She quickly brushed aside the feeling that she was sure she had locked the door.

Standing on the kitchen doorstep, she let the slightly fresher air cool her skin. Feeling much better, she came back inside but as she went to shut the door behind her, she noticed the door wouldn't close properly. Bending down to see what was wrong, she noticed that there were splinters of wood on the floor. Frowning, she ran her fingers over the jagged door frame. It looked like the door had been jemmied. Who had done this? She hadn't heard the door open, or the sound of the side gate opening or anything else suspicious while she'd been home, and she was now certain she had properly locked up before she had left to go to visit Alice. She could feel the fear creeping up inside of her as the situation started to become clear. Someone must have been inside her home, her sanctuary, without her knowledge while she had been out.

It was one thing after another. She felt like screaming with frustration. Raking her hands through her hair, she asked herself if this nightmare would ever stop. Turning to get the dustpan and brush to clear up the mess, she did a double take. Why she hadn't noticed it before she didn't know, but there sitting on the kitchen windowsill was a shoe sized box. The box's black plastic wrapping had been clumsily sealed with clear sticky tape. How long had the box been there? More importantly, who had put it there? The package looked a bit odd, like it had been amateurly packed. She felt a sharp stab of anxiety as she remembered the last parcel she had opened. There was every chance that the person who had left the parcel was the same person who had tampered with the lock on the kitchen door.

As the implications sank in, she just stood there staring at the parcel. This had to be Nick's doing. He was playing his spiteful games again. She didn't think she could take any more; living in fear of Nick was destroying her. Suddenly it was all too much. She couldn't halt the flood of tears that were now streaming down her face. Running into the living room, she flung herself down onto the sofa and sat with her knees tucked under her chin. With her arms tightly clasped around her legs, she gently rocked back and forth while weeping.

Hearing the church clock strike eight, she knew she couldn't hide for ever. She had to face her demons, the demons being whatever was in that blasted box. Maybe she was over-reacting, maybe she had got it wrong and what was in the box was completely innocent and unthreatening. Telling herself to get over it, she rubbed her cheeks to liven herself up, then picking up her phone, she returned to the kitchen. Still too scared to touch the box, she stood in front of it trying to summon up the courage to open it. Calm down and think logically was her mantra as she took several deep breaths and used her phone to take photographs of the unopened box, desperately hoping they wouldn't be needed, and that she was being ridiculous.

The time had come for her to bite the bullet and open the box. She knew she couldn't face her fears if she didn't. She didn't think anything else could sicken her, but what was revealed when she carefully opened the box, both sickened and shocked her to the core. A nurse Barbie, with its arm pulled off, lay on a bed of black tissue paper which had been sprinkled with tombstone confetti. The doll's uniform and the snapped off arm were smeared with fake blood. A feeling of nausea swept over her when she noticed a thin rope, also smeared in fake blood, had been looped around the doll's neck. Knowing she was going to be sick, she rushed up the stairs and held her head over the toilet bowl.

She lay on the bed trembling. Grabbing hold of her pillow, she buried her head into its deep softness to stifle the sound of her racking sobs, which didn't stop until she had no more tears left to cry.

The bedroom was in darkness. She slowly lifted her head from the damp pillow. She had a pounding headache and had no idea of the time. It could be the middle of the night for all she knew. Leaning over, she saw 22.59 on her phone screen, her usual bedtime. There was no way she would be able to sleep now. Everything was racing through her mind like a runaway train. She was certain it had been Nick who had left the parcel, although she had no proof. She asked herself how the heck did he get into the garden? The gate attached to the side of the cottage had a bolt on it, didn't it? She had to check. Despite feeling unwell, she forced her feet into her slippers, grabbed her phone, then holding on to the stair rail, made her way down the stairs.

Switching on her phone's torch, she cautiously opened the kitchen door. Putting her head out, she listened for anything unusual. The night was dark and silent as she stepped out into the blackness of the garden. Being careful not to trip up, she aimed the torch at the path, then slowly made her way down the side of the cottage. On reaching the gate, her heart missed a beat. The gate was wide open. On closer inspection, she could see that whoever had done this had used force, for the bolt had been sprung and was now hanging by only one screw. She had her answer. That's how *he* had got in. First thing tomorrow she would buy a bigger bolt and a strong padlock. In a spurt of anger, she tried to tell herself that she wouldn't let Nick frighten her anymore. It was just brave talk though, because there was no denying the fact that she was absolutely petrified.

Back inside the safety of the cottage, she sat on the sofa thinking about what to do. She knew her first job in the morning would be to contact the police, but first she needed to capture more evidence; she needed to photograph the contents of the box. Where was her phone? She had it a minute ago. With swollen eyes, and still with a headache, she couldn't think straight or see clearly. She ran her hands across the sofa, then looked underneath it. Her panic building, she dragged all the cushions off the sofa. There it was. It had slipped down and had somehow managed to wedge itself between the gap in the seats. With a sigh of relief, she retrieved it. With shaking hands and jangling nerves, she attempted to focus on the phone's small screen to access its camera but found she couldn't see properly. Keeping hold of her phone, she ran into the kitchen to splash her swollen eyes with some cold water.

CHAPTER 13

Ally was woken by the morning light filtering through the bedroom window. She closed her eyes tight, attempting to shut it out. It had taken her forever to fall asleep last night, or should she say the early hours of the morning. She knew that she should try and get out of bed, but couldn't face what might happen next, it was like she was living in a nightmare, a nightmare that was getting increasingly sinister. Trying to ignore her developing headache, she re-arranged her pillows, and rolling on her side, closed her eyes again.

Ring, ring… It was her phone, which was next to her bed. With some trepidation, she reached over to see who it was and was relieved to see Millie's name on the screen.

'Afternoon Ally,' Millie chirped cheerfully.

'Gosh, what time is it?'

'It's just after 12. I have some exciting news; Ash has just had her baby. A healthy little boy.'

'Oh, that's wonderful. I bet she and Arun are over the moon.'

'Yes. He's a good weight too, 8lb something. Both mum and baby are doing well.'

'Fantastic, I'm really pleased for them.' She did her best to sound animated, even though her head felt like it was being hit by a thousand hammers.

'Listen Al, there's a committee meeting later to discuss the Autumn Fayre. Are you coming? There's so much still to be done. I've got someone to cover for me at the coffee shop and I will be taking some cake and scones from the café so everyone will be fed.'

'Um, er.'

'Are you alright Al? You sound a bit groggy.'

'I had a bad night. I've only just woken up. I'll grab a quick shower and I'll be there. I promise. I needed something to cheer me up and the news about Ash has done the trick.'

'Are you sure Al?' Millie asked, concerned. Her friend didn't sound right.

'Yes, I'll see you there. I need something to take my mind off things, besides I love your cakes,' she added, with false brightness. 'See you later.'

She flung back the duvet, then clutching the stair rail, she took the stairs slowly, one by one. Her head was banging. She headed for the kitchen cupboard for the pack of paracetamol she had stashed away and popped two out, which she took with a glass of water. Realising that the headache was being made worse through dehydration and hunger, she drained the glass and made herself a slice of toast. After a shower she felt better. The headache had not quite gone but was nowhere near as bad, for which she was very grateful, as she firstly contacted the police and then the local carpenter to come and fix the door. She would stop at Oscar's to buy a new bolt and padlock on the way down to the village hall.

At the village hall she found herself seated between Clive and Millie.

'What's happened Al? I was worried about you earlier.' Millie could tell her friend wasn't her usual self, in fact she looked awful.

Ally first looked at Clive, then back at Millie, who was waiting for an answer. Oh heck. She could see Clive was all ears and showing a keen interest. She didn't know how much to divulge. Throwing caution to the wind, she told herself that it didn't matter if Clive knew her business; at this stage she was past caring. She started to tell Millie about the nurse Barbie with Clive listening in.

'That's horrendous. Did you report it to the police?'

'Yes, an officer is coming to see me later.'

'No wonder you sounded a bit out of it earlier.'

'Tap, Tap, Tap.' The leader of the Autumn Fayre committee rapped on the table with a big spoon. 'Right ladies and gentlemen, let's get this meeting started.'

Ally was never more relieved for the diversion away from her own troubles.

The meeting was progressing well. She had been going to run the tombola stall with Ashna, but obviously not now. A cheer went up in the room when Millie announced Ash's new arrival and plans were made for a whip-round for a baby present. It wasn't long before the hissing from the urn and the chink of china was heard coming from the small kitchen.

'Come and get it,' one of the fellow members yelled through the serving hatch. In an instant there was the scraping of chairs and a queue for hot drinks and some of Millie's cakes and scones.

Clive taking his chance, sidled up to Ally. 'I was listening to what you were telling Millie. I had no idea you had been under so much stress my dear.'

She smiled weakly. 'Yes, it's not been easy.'

'If I can help in any way, please let me know Ally.'

'That's very kind of you Clive. I've reported it to the police and that's all I can do for now. Thank you for your support though.' She felt a surge of fondness sweep over her. Clive appeared to be a nice man. She noticed his expensive blazer; he was quite well-dressed too. Clive obviously liked her, but what came next took her by surprise.

Clive cleared his throat and puffed his chest out. 'Ally, would you do me the honour of coming out with me?' He paused. 'I think I'd like to get to know you better.'

She didn't know what to say. She really liked Clive, but only as a friend. She really did need a shoulder to lean on, but it was too soon and there was no flicker of chemistry on her part either. She felt flattered but quite sad. She was a complete wreck, and it was a massive confidence boost to have someone find her attractive in her present state, but she knew Clive was not for her. She wished he was though, because at times, she had felt quite lonely.

She needed to stop dithering and let him down gently. 'Clive, I'm so sorry, I can't,' she said softly. 'I like you, I really do, but as a friend. I'm afraid I'm not in a good place right now. I'm not good company and I don't feel ready to start seeing someone. Sadly, I think it will be a long time before I will be in that frame of mind.'

Clive looked taken back, as if he thought his offer was the best thing since sliced bread. His face darkened; all pretence of being kind and considerate had completely vanished. 'Oh, never mind. Plenty more fish in the sea m'dear.' With that he took off, marching out the door, still holding his cup of tea.

She watched Clive storm off. She hadn't expected that reaction. Clive obviously wasn't as nice as he appeared.

Seeing her standing on her own, Millie came over. 'Where's Clive gone? It looks as though he left in a bit of a hurry.'

Red-faced, she explained what had happened.

'Oh dear,' Millie was trying very hard not to laugh at Ally's predicament. She shook her head. 'He's acting like a spoilt child Al. Take no notice. You are better off without him anyway. I've been doing a bit of digging on your behalf, and according to village gossip, our Clive's a bit of a womaniser.'

'Oh really, shame you didn't tell me that before,' Ally joked.

'I didn't know. It was only when another member of the committee noticed him chatting you up just now that she mentioned that she didn't like him, and I asked her why.'

'I'm glad I said to him what I did now.'

'Yep, lucky escape. He's a pompous prat. Come on, the meeting's starting up again. Another hour then we can all go home. What time are the police paying you a visit?'

'Around five o'clock, I think. I need to get a bit of shopping on the way home too, so I can't hang around.

CHAPTER 14

After her visit from the police, Ally was feeling a bit more confident. She had got the impression they were, at long last, taking her complaint seriously, which was a great comfort, but she did wonder if there was something they were not telling her. The two officers had stayed for quite a while, and she had been asked to report any further incidents and to take any evidence along to the police station at the earliest opportunity.

Once they had gone, she ran herself a relaxing bath, made herself a mug of hot chocolate then headed, with a book under her arm, upstairs to bed. After a few chapters her eyes became heavy. Finding it hard to stay awake, she switched off the bedside lamp and was soon asleep.

Deep in the night and after much tossing and turning, she awoke with a start. Was that the letterbox on the front door being pushed open? Was someone peering through it? Snuggled down under the duvet, she stayed still and silent, barely daring to breathe, listening out for anything unusual. After a while, not hearing anything, she pulled the duvet up under her chin, shut her eyes and tried to sleep. But it was not to be, for try as she might, sleep would not come. She opened her eyes and stared into the darkness. It was no good, she would have to go downstairs and check that everything was alright.

Using her phone torch, she crept down the stairs and into the living room. Slightly pulling the curtain back, she cautiously peered through the window. There was no sign of anyone being outside. She then checked the front door. It appeared securely locked. She was probably imagining things or maybe it was just a bad dream, both understandable given everything that had happened. It could even have been the wind rattling the cottage's old wooden windows. The TV weather bulletin had warned that there could be another storm brewing. As if in answer to her thoughts, a gust of wind whistled down the chimney. With her mind now at ease, she went back to bed, falling asleep to the sound of the wind blasting against the windows.

Next morning, she looked out the front window. She could see that the weather forecast had been well and truly accurate, for there had indeed been a storm in the night. The garden was littered with fallen branches and leaves. There was a huge puddle by the stone wall where the garden sloped. She stared at the dismal state of the garden and wondered the best way to tackle it. Her thoughts were interrupted by a loud *kraa, kraa*. Straight away she knew it was the crow, who she hadn't seen for a few days. Leaning into the window, she watched the crow swoop down onto the grass then strut around the garden as if it owned the place. Her lips twisted into a slight smile as she suddenly saw the funny side. What had happened to her? How had she gone from being a well-known television actress to being a lonely neurotic bird nerd. She continued to watch the crow's antics through the window. It had probably been hanging around this place for years, so there was every chance that it had, indeed, claimed the garden as its own. She noticed that the crow had hopped across to the path and was now pecking at and tossing something metal around with its beak.

More out of curiosity than anything else, she unlocked the front door and stood on the doorstep watching as the bird attacked the small coin shaped object. 'What have you got there Mr Crow?' She asked softly, realising that she must be crazy talking to a crow like it was her best friend. Immediately, the crow took the piece of metal into its beak and hopped over to her, promptly dropping it right by her feet. Bending down to pick it up, she saw it was a silver button. She held the button in the palm of her hand. It seemed familiar, where had she seen it before? Then she remembered Clive's blazer, it had buttons like this. Still holding the button, she turned to go back inside, only then did she notice the bunch of shrivelled black roses propped against the wall right next to the door. A small white envelope had been placed among the thorny stems. She opened the envelope and pulled out the card inside. The word '*Bitch*' had been written in capital letters on the card. A red mist came up. Not something that happened to her very often.

'Dead black roses. How dare he!' Tipped over the edge like someone demented, she furiously rammed her feet into her wellies. Not even considering getting dressed or brushing her hair, she yanked her old gardening coat off the hook. Seething with rage, she slammed the door behind her. Holding tightly onto the button, she marched through the village towards the marina, angrily determined to find Clive's house, rehearsing in her head exactly what she was going to say to him.

Remembering what Millie had said about Clive's house being white with blue windows, Ally's welly clad feet stomped down the small, but exclusive cul-de-sac of expensive houses that overlooked the marina, not stopping until she came to a house with white rendered walls and blue windows. Still seething, she didn't even stop to think if it was the right house. Standing on the doorstep of the impressive home, she began furiously pressing the doorbell over and over.

The door opened. Clive, who was still in his dressing gown, looked both indignant and annoyed at the person who had been repeatedly ringing his doorbell. When he realised who it was, he looked startled. 'It's a little early my dear,' he said sarcastically, taking in Ally's dishevelled appearance.

Ally completely lost it. 'Don't you dare "my dear" me. What a despicable thing to do, just because I turned you down.' Ally shoved the button under Clive's nose. 'This is yours, isn't it? You lost this button when you left those disgusting dead roses by my door last night, didn't you? I know you have a blazer with buttons just like this one. Explain yourself, you creep.'

Clive took a step back to protect himself from the mad woman in her pyjamas and wellies who was berating him on his doorstep. He let her continue ranting until she eventually ran out of steam and insults. Then, closing the door on her, he disappeared inside, to appear moments later holding his blazer. 'Here, see this. *This* is my blazer.' He thrust the garment at her. 'Even a fruit loop like you can see the buttons on this are different,' he raged, his face now an unattractive shade of pink. 'AND look, surely you can see that they are all firmly attached,' he snorted in derision. 'Now just you take your nasty accusations somewhere else. If you don't leave now, I'm calling the police. I know nothing about dead roses. I realise you have been under a lot of stress my dear, but I'm afraid you are barking up the wrong tree. Looking at the state you're in, I'm jolly glad I didn't take up with you now. Maybe you should seek help.' he added nastily.

'Oh.' On realising her mistake, red faced and with her anger deflating like a punctured balloon, Ally wished the ground would swallow her up.

Gulping, she attempted to stutter out an apology. 'Clive, I'm so t-terribly s-sor-ry, I...'

Clive obviously wasn't in a forgiving mood.

Making his feelings very clear, he slammed the door shut just inches away from her face.

Blinking away the tears, she stared at the closed door.

She couldn't blame Clive, she deserved all she had got. She turned away. As she walked back down Clive's neatly manicured garden path, she knew that she had reached a new low. She had had a complete meltdown. Maybe Clive was right, maybe she did need help.

With her head bowed, she pulled up the hood of her coat and made her way home. She knew that she had behaved very badly and was deeply ashamed of herself. With a feeling of numb despair, she let herself back into the cottage, and without stopping to take her coat and wellies off, sank down into the sofa. She wanted to cry but no tears came. Suddenly, with little warning, her hands started to tremble, then her legs. Pretty soon her whole body was shaking as her held back emotions were finally released.

Not able to shake off her thumping headache, she rinsed her face with cold water. She had never cried so much in her life as she had lately and knew that she couldn't go on like this. She made herself a comforting mug of instant soup. Hugging it with both hands, she returned to the solace of the sofa and tried to make sense of everything. There could only be one culprit, Nick.

This was just the sort of thing he would do. Why on earth hadn't she stopped to think before making an utter idiot of herself by going ballistic at Clive. She had acted like a raging bull and had gone hammer and tongs at Clive based on a button and his ill-tempered reaction to her turning him down. Sighing, she shook her head, she was seriously losing it.

Picking up the button, she looked at it carefully. It had to be Nick who had left the dead roses, there was no one else it could be. Was it him she had heard in the night? Had he been peering through her letterbox? Although feeling woolly-headed and finding it hard to think properly, an image flashed into her mind. It was of a function she had gone to with Nick. It had been at his flying club. He had just got his PPL, his private pilot's licence, and was bragging about his blazer resembling a pilot's uniform. She was almost certain that Nick's blazer had buttons like this. If the button belonged to whoever had left the dead roses, then it had to be Nick's.

Nick was obviously still somewhere in the area. The thought of it sent a chill through her. She would take her evidence, including the button and the withered roses to the police tomorrow. Needing distraction, she looked towards the crates of tombola prizes for tomorrow's Autumn Fayre which she'd stacked by the door. She'd forgotten that the numbers still needed sticking on. Reaching for the book of raffle tickets and the roll of sticky tape, she was thankful for something to do.

The next morning she was up early. She had been to the police station first thing. They had bagged all the evidence and had taken details and told her they would be in touch. Her heart had leapt when she thought she saw Joe walking down a corridor but dismissed it as wishful thinking. She sat clutching her now cold mug of coffee. How she yearned to turn back the clock but what was done was done as the saying goes. Her life was one big mess and she had to live with it.

Deciding that there was no point sitting here wallowing in self-pity, she checked the time on her phone and decided it was time to get a move on. She was needed back at the village hall to help at the Autumn Fayre and was running late.

Arriving at the village hall, her timing couldn't have been any worse even if she'd tried, for there right in front of her, was Clive enjoying his cup of tea. There was no way of skirting around him either as he was standing right in the centre of the doorway, blocking the way through to the main hall. Awkward, embarrassed, remorseful were among the words that sprung to mind to appropriately describe how she felt when finding herself face to face with the man whom she had, quite shamefully, wrongly accused. After taking a deep breath, she decided she had no choice, no matter how painful, but to take the opportunity to reach out to him.

Feeling anything but brave, she walked up to Clive and tentatively extended her hand to lightly touch his shirt-sleeved arm. Seeing the look of utter distaste flicker across his face her heart sank. It was obvious that Clive was not going to be easily won over. She knew she had no choice but to persevere; she had to try and clear the air. 'Clive, I got it wrong. I-I'm truly sorry for what I did and what I accused you of.'

Visibly flinching, he backed away from her. 'Apology accepted,' he said gruffly, before scurrying off like a frightened rabbit to hide in the kitchen. After that, he avoided her like the plague, which was difficult, and at times quite comical in the confines of the small hall. Ally didn't blame him. He was, quite rightly, absolutely appalled by her behaviour. Maybe what he said was true, and she did indeed need to book an appointment with a therapist.

The hall was buzzing with activity. Betty was in control. Armed with a clipboard and pen, she sat in a chair by the door ticking each helper's name off her list as they came in, before directing them to their stalls. This was much to Edna's annoyance, who thought she was being too bossy.

After claiming the stall earmarked for the tombola, she went out to her car to fetch the crates of prizes she had prepared. She was pleased she had lots to do because she didn't want to risk being anywhere near Clive more than was necessary. Laying everything out on the wooden trestle table so it looked reasonably attractive, would certainly keep her occupied until the Fayre opened its doors to the public.

At 13.59 on the dot, Betty's gnarled hands gripped the wooden handle of the heavy old-fashioned school bell as she vigorously rang it several times. 'Right, everyone, it's time. Stand by your beds, let the Autumn Fayre begin. Go over and open the doors Clive.' Everyone immediately stopped talking and shuffled into place. Each stallholder looking on expectantly as Clive sauntered over to admit the people who had been patiently queuing outside.

The Fayre had gone well, and the last few stragglers had gone home, after which all the stallholders had counted their takings. The word had gone around that a sizeable amount of money had been raised and every person seemed pleased with their achievement. As she packed the last of her stall away, she smiled as she remembered what one of the other stallholder's had told her and Millie about one of the more comical moments of the day, the interchange between Betty and Edna. It had brought a smile to both their faces when they had found out what had happened.

Betty had been serving on the homemade jam and chutney stall, which was right next to Edna's hand-knitted goods stall. Every time Edna sold something, Betty had tried to outdo Edna, and vice versa. Both ladies had ended up getting louder and louder as they sought to attract customers and compete with one another. In the end someone had rudely told them both to 'pipe down and put a sock in it.' This hadn't gone down too well with either Betty or Edna and had resulted in both ladies going off in a huff, marching into the tea tent, where they had shared a pot of tea together, commiserating with each other for the first time after many years of hostility. It had been a good outcome as far as she and Millie were concerned.

As she drove home, she knew she had quite enjoyed the afternoon, that was apart from the awkward moment with Clive, which was still a source of embarrassment. As she pushed the key into the lock to let herself into the cottage, she knew that although she had had a nice time, she was still very glad to be home. Closing the door behind her, she took great pleasure in sliding the bolt across. She had found the day emotionally and physically draining, and her feet ached, having been on them all day. Throwing off her coat and shoes, she padded over to the sofa in her socks and wearily sat down. Leaning back into the soft cushions, she closed her eyes. She'd been running on adrenalin all day but now she was home, the feeling of tiredness was starting to overwhelm her. Willing herself to stay awake, not wanting to ruin her chance of a good night's sleep, she got up to make herself a hot drink. She hadn't slept well the previous night and was determined to do better tonight.

CHAPTER 15

It was early evening, and ominous black clouds were gathering, making it look prematurely dark. As she switched on the lights, she heard a boom of thunder, followed by a flash of lightening, and knew without doubt, that they were in for another storm. Minutes later the heavens opened. She peered through the window, she couldn't see much, the glass being mostly obscured by the lashing rain. Was that something moving around outside? She strained to listen above the noise of the rain and thought she heard the hollow thud of something treading on one of the loose paving slabs. She leaned in closer to get a better look but whatever it was, there was no sign of it now. It was probably just a fox out there or some other wild animal that Edna next door had taken to feeding, probably running for shelter in the driving rain. She knew she was far too easily spooked these days and walked away from the window telling herself to stop being foolish. Just as she was about to sit down, the lights briefly flickered. Seconds later, the room was in near darkness. The power had gone down.

She sat on the sofa feeling vulnerable and quite jittery. Her nerves were obviously getting the better of her. Storms didn't usually bother her, and she couldn't understand why she was feeling so anxious about this one. Knowing that she couldn't even make a hot drink until the power came back on, she decided to make the best of it. Using her phone torch for light, she reached for her book. She would read a few chapters and hope that the storm would quickly pass.

Later that evening the phone rang. It was Millie calling for help. The storm had been a bad one and some of the homes in the lower part of the village had been flooded. After ending the call, she ran up the stairs to change into some warm clothes. Pulling on her wellies and wearing her raincoat, she headed down into the village to help in any way she could. She felt so sorry for the villagers flooded out of their homes, a lot of them were elderly too. She hoped Betty and Oscar hadn't been affected and counted herself lucky that Edna's cottage, like her own, had been built high on a hill.

Next morning, after a long night spent handing out refreshments to flood victims at the village hall, she sat on the bench outside her back door. Warmly wrapped in a thick cardigan, she sprinkled some crumbs on the bench next to her for the crow. Sipping her coffee, she thought about how the season had changed. There had been lots more rain, and the nights were starting to draw in. The holidaymakers had mostly gone home. There was quite a lot of flood damage in the village from last night's storm and she had promised to go down there again later to help.

Wrapping her fingers around her hot drink to warm them, she noticed that a chilly brisk wind had sprung up, with every gust bringing down more leaves. She watched a robin pecking at the ground then suddenly fly away. Straight away she saw the culprit, it was Edna's tabby cat Baxter, a born hunter if there ever was one. The robin had had a lucky escape. Glancing around, she noticed the bright berries decorating the hedge and the defiant single rose on the bush by the door. Autumn seemed to have arrived early this year.

Reflecting on how long she'd been living here, she wondered if it was time to move on. The last incident with the dead roses had nearly tipped her over. The way she had raged at Clive, who had been quite innocent, had given her a wake-up call. She had done her level best to get her life back on track. She had not had a drop of alcohol since returning to Cornwall, nor had she taken a pill, instead she had been immersing herself in self-help books and podcasts. She had been doing lots of walking and felt she had climbed over almost every stile on this stretch of the southwest coast path. All she needed now was to keep a firm hold on her sanity.

There had been a call from the police. They had lost track of Nick, which was very worrying, but they had also given her some positive news. After an extensive search of Nick's London premises and after looking into his finances, they had found the bottle of fake blood, on-line receipts for the nurse Barbie and for the chemise and roses. They had also found a dated order for the bottles of wine. The police had told her that they were continuing with their enquiries and would keep her informed. She had put the phone down relieved that she hadn't been losing her mind but felt slightly mystified. She had got the impression that the police were keeping something back about Nick. Why had they been going through his finances? More importantly, where was he? Was he watching her? She felt a shiver run through her.

Her phone rang. It was Kat, who having heard about the flooding, was ringing to check on her. 'I've not been flooded Kat, but I've got a lot to tell you. Can we meet for coffee?'

Sitting in the coffee shop, Kat sat there shocked as she tried to take in everything that Ally had just told her. Ally had not held back, and she had listened, quite horrified as her friend spoke about the trauma of the recent events in shocking detail.

'The guy sounds utterly despicable and dangerous. He should be behind bars. I don't know how you have stayed sane Al.'

She shook her head. 'I'm not sure that I have stayed sane Kat. And even worse is that Nick could be anywhere watching me. The police told me he's gone AWOL. For my own sanity I need to get away from it all.'

'I really feel for you Al, what you have been through is horrendous, nobody should have to put up with that, but where will you go?' Kat looked at her childhood friend, who looked a shadow of her former self.

'I'm not sure. I've been giving it a lot of thought and think I might fly to New York for a few days shopping and seeing the sights. After that, and I know it sounds a bit crazy, I would like to go to Virginia to try and track down Oscar's family.'

'What!'

Smiling at Kat's reaction, she continued. 'The one thing I am certain about though, is that I must get away from here for a bit.'

Recovering from her friend's bombshell, Kat shook her head. 'Are you sure Al? I can understand why you want to get away from the Nick situation and I get the New York thing, but Virginia is a long way to go, especially on a whim. Why not come and stay with me instead? I'm sure CJ will be pleased to see you again.'

Ally looked at her friend's concerned expression. 'I can't bring my troubles to you Kat, it wouldn't be fair. Besides, there's more. I'm afraid that I've made a bit of a fool of myself. I'm sure what I did is already common knowledge in the village and people are gossiping.' She started to tell

Kat about her accusing Clive. 'I need some time away from here, either that or I need to see a shrink. I can't go on as I am. What Nick has done to me will take me a long time to get over. The sooner I can get away, the better. I've got money saved, enough for a nice break.'

Kat nodded sympathetically. 'I understand why you want to get away but please take some time to think it over Al, please don't rush in and do something reckless.'

She smiled. Kat was always the sensible one. 'I promise I won't. I think I'm going to take a drive up to Roche Rock tomorrow. A day away from the cottage will do me good, then I'll pop in and see my parents on the way home.'

'Roche Rock, is that the ancient chapel built on top of a pile of rock?'

'Yes, that's the one.'

Kat shuddered. 'It's not my favourite place, it gives me the creeps. Isn't it supposed to be haunted by hermits or something?'

'Yes, that's what they say. There are so many legends about the place, some also say a medieval landowner hid himself away there because he had caught leprosy and didn't want his family to catch it. Others say it was a hermitage. Who knows what is true. Either way it's a very special place, even if a little spooky. Not many people go there either, I suppose that's why I'm fascinated by it.'

'Talking of spooky, do you remember that abandoned holiday park from when we were kids?'

'Now that *was* creepy,' said Ally, laughing.

Kat glanced at the clock on the wall. 'Hey, Al, look at the time, we've been so busy chatting the time has flown by. I had better get going, I've still got loads of marking to do.' She got up to leave. 'Please message me to let me know your plans when you know for sure. Oh, and please don't go climbing up any high rocks, no matter how special they are,' she added jokily, but still meaning it.

'I won't. See you later Kat, and thanks for the coffee and chat, it has made me feel a lot better.'

Kat couldn't get everything that Ally had told her out of her head. All the way home in the car she thought about it. When she got home, she mentioned it to CJ, who straight away told her to tell Joe, adding that if she didn't, then he would. Kat could see by the look on his face that he had taken it badly too. She scrolled down her phone for Joe's mobile number and began repeatedly ringing it. He wasn't picking up. After several attempts at trying to contact him and leaving him voice messages, she had an idea, she would phone Tom to see if he had his brother's home telephone number.

'Hi Tom, I'm trying to get in touch with Joe, he's not answering his mobile. Do you have his home number?'

'Hiya Kat, good to hear from you. How's things with you and CJ?'

'We're doing well Tom, but I am worried about Ally and want Joe to know what's been going on with her.' Kat gave Tom a brief outline of everything.

'Good grief, that sounds awful Kat. I know Joe was thinking of taking off somewhere for a week or two. He's not been happy at home. Y'know, thinking about it, I don't think he ever got over Ally leaving him. We were all gutted when that happened. Hang on a minute, I'll get his landline number for you.'

'Thanks Tom. Let's all have a catch up soon. I think it's well overdue, don't you?'

'Definitely. How about you all come and eat at my place, I've just started a new menu and need customers to try it out on.'

Kat laughed. 'Okay, we'll come and be your guinea pigs and test it out for you, as long as you don't give us a dose of food poisoning or anything,' she joked.

'As if I would – but make sure you've got some life insurance before you come! Seriously though, I would love to see everyone again.'

'We'll make a date. Let me sort this Ally thing out first though. Thanks Tom.'

Kat put the phone down and immediately rang Joe's home number.

'Hello, is Joe there?'

'Who is this?' the curt voice on the other end of the phone demanded.

Kat gulped. This was not going to be easy. 'It's Kat, married to CJ, do you remember, we all went to that Barn restaurant over Bodmin way last year. Is that Maxine?'

'Yes, it is Maxine. Joe is away.'

'Oh, how long will he be away for?'

'Not sure, a couple of weeks maybe. I've not heard from him. He's probably up a mountain somewhere in Wales with no signal.'

Kat didn't know what to say. Maxine's attitude was quite frosty, verging on rudeness. 'No worries, I'll catch up with him another time. Thanks Maxine, please say hi to him when he gets back, bye for now.'

Kat put the phone down. Joe's girlfriend was hard work.

That night as she lay in bed, Ally started to make plans. She would go and see Oscar tomorrow and talk to him about finding his father's family.

The next morning, she headed down into the village to see Oscar. He was serving a customer and gave her a wave as she walked in. She waited until the shop was empty of customers before approaching him. 'Good morning. Oscar, I wonder if I can run something by you. I've had an idea.' She explained to Oscar what she wanted to do.

'You would do that for my mother and I?' He looked surprised.

'Oscar, it's not just for you and Alice. I'm doing it for myself too. I need a break. Things have been getting on top of me lately. I have some money saved, it will be a lovely and well overdue holiday for me and may also help you to find out more about your American family.'

'Hmmm. Hang on a minute young lady.' Oscar disappeared out the back of the shop. After a couple of minutes, he returned clutching Alice and Frank's letters and the framed photo of Frank. He handed them to Ally. 'Here, have these. Take them with you, it might help to substantiate your story if you ever get to speak to Frank's family.'

'Are you sure?'

Oscar nodded. 'Best you have them now in case I forget to give them to you. Keep 'em safe until you go.'

'That's wonderful, thank you, Oscar. I'll guard them with my life, and you shall have them back as soon as I return.'

Oscar smiled. 'I hope it won't be too long until you come back to us Ally. I know some people have been gossiping, but most of the village are with you and will stand by you. Some of us folk think that Bossy Clive is a bit up himself; not mentioning any names though,' he added with a wink.

Ally gave Oscar a hug. 'You don't know how much that means to me Oscar. Thank you.'

As soon as she left Oscar's, she messaged Millie. 'Millie, have you got a minute, I've got something to tell you.' Then she messaged her mother. 'Mum, can I pop over later?' She had set the wheels in motion.

Walking down the hill towards Millie's, she thought about what she had got planned for the day. She needed to stay occupied, realising that any distraction from her thoughts would help her to keep her anxiety in check. She was looking forward to seeing Roche Rock again.

As soon as she entered Millie's, she could see it was busy and that most of the tables were full. Millie was working behind the counter and looked up when Ally came through the door.

'I'll be two minutes,' Millie mouthed, pointing to the only empty table, before continuing what she was doing.

A short while later Millie hurried over and sat down next to Ally, pushing a plate with two cherry scones towards her. 'Just come out of the oven they have, tuck in.'

'They look yummy Millie, don't mind if I do, she said, helping herself to one.

'Right, come on, I've got zilch time to spend slacking off, so spit it out. What have you got to tell me?' asked Millie eagerly.

'I'm off to America, I want to find out about Oscar's American family.'

Millie's mouth dropped open like a gaping fish. 'Crikey, I was not expecting that Al. Tell me more.'

Ally explained how she needed to get away, especially after the Clive incident.

'I really do get how you feel Al, but as far as the Clive issue goes, from what I gather, the villagers here don't care much for him, so they wouldn't hold it against you in any way.'

Ally smiled. 'That's good to know, but I think my mind is made up. It's not just what happened with Clive, I also need to get away from here for my own sanity.' Her voice started to break up. 'I'm in constant fear of Nick and what he might do to me,' she whispered hoarsely, biting on her lip as her eyes started to fill. 'Who knows where the vile bully is. He could be anywhere, could be near here for all I know,' she said, nervously looking around her.

'Hey Al, come on,' Millie reached out and patted her friend's hand. 'No tears now, be strong. I get where you are coming from and, I honestly think it's the right thing to do. It will probably work wonders for you, being a change of scenery and all that.'

'Thanks Millie. Please can you let Ashna know about my plans when you next see her, I don't want to bother her, she's got enough on her plate with the new baby. After a quick drive to Roche, I'm off to tell my parents what I'm going to do. Their reaction will be much like yours I imagine, only far worse!'

'You know I will, and I am sure Ash will be pleased for you too. Good luck with your mum and dad. Keep me updated about your plans.' Millie glanced over at the counter. 'Oh my word, just look at the queue. I'd better go Al. Speak soon, stay in touch.'

She watched her friend hurry back to work before walking back to the cottage to collect her car for the drive up to Roche Rock.

Her journey to Roche had been painstakingly slow. She had been stuck behind one farm vehicle after another, but eventually had been able to make a break for it in a gap in the oncoming traffic. While relieved she had made it, she did feel slightly sorry for the people still stuck behind her.

Turning into the village, one couldn't fail to miss the 15th century chapel. A few miles inland, and well away from the tourist trail, the chapel, built from local granite, rose to a magnificent 20 metres high. She stared in awe at the stark two storey tower, which was looking hauntingly beautiful against the cloudless sky. Emerging from its rocky outcrop, and resembling something from a film set, the chapel was so atmospheric and steeped in history, that it got to her every time she came here. Her first visit to the chapel had been while on a school trip when she was about fourteen. Then it had felt magical, and she had let her imagination run riot, believing the place to be haunted by ghosts from the past. She smiled to herself, these days she was much more level-headed, but had to admit, she was still fascinated by the place.

After parking her car, she threaded her way through the shrubby terrain until she came to the two iron ladders which, although not for the faint hearted, gave access to the chapel. Although a bit scary to climb, there was no way she was going to miss out on going up to the chapel again. She put her foot on the first rung of the rust-coloured ladder to carefully test it, then deciding it was safe, continued to climb until she had reached the top.

There was not a soul about. With the wind blowing in her hair, she was in her happy place. She leaned over the chapel's ancient wall to look at the amazing view. Soaking up the atmosphere, she thought back to the stories from her school days. Over the years there had been so many tales told. According to folklore, this place had it all. Lepers, hermits, monks, lords, giants, and even the odd evil spirit; many myths and legends had been passed down through the centuries. Not for the first time she wished the walls could talk and tell their story. The tale she liked the best though, was the one about the two medieval lovers, Tristan and Isolde, who allegedly hid here from the King, and whose story was supposedly to have been the inspiration for Guinevere and Lancelot.

It was so peaceful, there was not a sound except for birds chattering in the bushes below. With the sun warming her face, she closed her eyes and let her imagination about the people who had supposedly lived here over the centuries run riot again.

Her daydreaming was interrupted by the sound of a car pulling up in the road below. She moved to the far side of the chapel which overlooked the road, and glancing down, did a double take when she saw that a blue saloon had parked up right behind her car. The car's distinctive blue colour instantly revealed the name of its owner. The car was a BMW, and it was Nick's. Panic stricken she watched the car door swing open. Without a second glance, and with no time to waste, she knew that she had to get away from here. Nick had obviously followed her and must have been caught up in the traffic that had built up behind the slow-moving farm vehicles.

Climbing back down the rickety ladder as fast as she could, she decided to take the lesser known but longer route back to her car. Figuring that as Nick wasn't a local man, he wouldn't know about it, nor would he be able to see her, as she would be hidden in amongst the rocks and shrubbery.

On reaching the road, she ran to her car. Nick's BMW was still parked next to hers – she had had a lucky escape. He must have remembered her speaking about the chapel when they were together. Never had she been more thankful for slow-moving farm vehicles; if it hadn't been for them, she would have come face to face with Nick. She dreaded to think what might have happened to her if he'd cornered her up there in the tiny chapel with its treacherous 20 metre drop. Breathless and extremely agitated, she attempted to unlock her car, but her hands were shaking so badly she dropped her keys. Cursing her own stupidity, she scooped them up and tried again. This time she was successful, and not wasting a second, she started the car and sped down the road. Ignoring the flashing speeding sign, she headed towards the safety of her childhood home.

'Hi Mum, Dad.' Putting on a brave front, she was determined to hide her inner turmoil, knowing it would worry her parents even more if they knew what had just happened.

After too many cups of tea and slices of cake, she climbed into her car to drive home. Her visit hadn't exactly gone to plan. Like she had foreseen, it hadn't been easy telling her parents about her trip to America. Explaining what she was going to do had not gone down well. Her parents had thought she was heading off on a wild goose chase and had pleaded with her not to go, that was until she had explained how she needed to get away for safety reasons, and to save her sanity. In the end they had visibly softened and agreed that she needed to get away from Nick. As she waved goodbye to her parents, she noticed the worried look on their faces and was glad she had stood by her decision not to mention the scare at the chapel.

As she turned the key to let herself into her cottage, she knew her first job would be to contact the police to let them know that she had seen Nick's car in Roche and that she believed he had followed her there.

CHAPTER 16

The next couple of weeks whizzed by in a bit of a blur. There had been no more nasty packages delivered, nor had there been any further sightings of Nick. When she had contacted the police, they had told her they were doing their utmost to look for him. They had also given her a direct line phone number to use if she felt she was in any danger. Two days after that, she had received a call from them to say they had found Nick's car parked near an airfield and that it was highly likely that he had flown the country and could possibly be somewhere in Europe. On hearing this news, she had felt relieved, for if Nick was out the country, then he couldn't be anywhere near her.

Instead of fretting about Nick, she concentrated on her forthcoming trip to America. She spent ages on-line researching the Blue Ridge mountains area of southwest Virginia where she believed Frank's family had lived. It was a bit of a long shot, as the only information she had was from Frank's letters and the snippet from Alice that Frank had once made shoes. The earliest flight and accommodation that she could book were for the end of November. If nothing came of her search for Frank's family, at least she would get herself a decent holiday.

It was a cold, drab late November day when Ally looked around Rose Briar Cottage one more time before shutting the door behind her. She would miss her little sanctuary; because that was exactly what the cottage had been. She knocked on Edna's door to say goodbye and was quite surprised by the old lady's reaction.

'I heard you were off on a bit of an expedition dear. I will miss you but go and do this for dear Alice and her Oscar.'

Feeling a stab of fondness, she wondered whether to give Edna a hug. Would that be pushing their truce too far. She decided to go for it and leaning forward gave Edna a gentle hug. To her surprise Edna's arms came up and hugged her back. 'Stay safe dear and hurry back.'

Ally could swear she saw Edna's eyes moisten. Maybe all those little treats she'd bought the old lady and the errands she had run for her had paid off. When she got back from America, she would have a word with Millie and maybe they could try to get Betty and Edna together again, after all they had been good friends once.

As she started her long drive to the airport, she felt good for the first time in months.

∾

JOE

Joe looked through the windscreen for a parking sign. He had been wild camping for a few days now and had driven into the nearest town to buy a few essentials. While there, he was hoping to get a signal and find somewhere to charge his phone. He had been doing a lot of thinking. Camping in the Welsh wilderness had cleared his head and confirmed what he had always known but had kept buried, that he still loved Ally. It was time to put all the bitterness and anger behind him and start connecting with her again; that is if she felt the same way, something he wouldn't know unless he reached out to her. Maybe they could meet for coffee somewhere, start off slowly and see how it went. The thought of seeing Ally again lifted his spirits and after finding somewhere to park his car, he walked into the small market town with a spring in his step.

Satisfied that his phone now had some charge, Joe switched it back on. In quick succession the missed call notifications and messages started to ping through. He stared at the screen wondering why his phone had suddenly gone manic. There were umpteen messages, quite a few were from Maxine but even more from Kat, which was unusual. After speaking to Maxine, he tried Kat's number. It went straight to voicemail. She must be teaching. He played Kat's messages and was shocked by what she had to say. He had had no idea about the latest threats Ally had received because, thinking it the best thing to do, he had handed the case over to a colleague to deal with.

While working for the police, he had seen some shocking things over the years, but when it was happening to someone he cared about, it cut very deep. After frantically searching his car, he found an old pen in the glove box, then attempted to write on the cover of his newly bought magazine, the important points in Kat's voicemails. He shook his head in disbelief when he read through what he had scribbled down - the vile note sent with the carton of wine, pills, blood-stained chemise, the dismembered Barbie doll with a rope around its neck, the shrivelled black roses. All these things, in addition to what Kat had mentioned about the traumatic life Ally had led in London, amounted to serious harassment and the person responsible needed to be caught asap. As a police officer, he had always tried to be objective, but this time it just wasn't happening, this felt too personal, and he wanted vengeance for whoever was doing this to Ally.

Decision made. He would go back to his tent and pack up his camping gear then head straight home, in the hope that he could catch Ally before she left for the States. He kicked himself for not having had his phone available and for missing Kat's messages.

As soon as he crossed into Cornwall, Joe had only one thing on his mind and that was Ally. He drove as fast as legally possible towards the house where Ally's parents still lived, hoping they would give him her address.

Ally's mother answered the door. She looked surprised to see him. 'Oh, hello Joe, long time, no see. How are you?'

'Hi. Er, sorry to trouble you, but I need to see Ally. Do you have her address?'

'Really sorry, but you are too late Joe, she's not here. Ally is in America.'

'Oh no!' Joe shook his head, not even trying to hide his disappointment.

'Why are you so upset Joe? What's wrong? Is there something we should know?'

'Kat told me about what's been going on with Ally. I've only just found out, I've been away camping, no phone. I really wanted to see her.'

'Yes, she's really been through a lot, but she's bound to phone us soon, and when she does, I'll certainly let her know you have called. I'm sure she'll be pleased. I don't think she ever quite got over you Joe. Do you want her mobile number?'

Joe hesitated, thinking carefully before answering. 'No, it's alright. I need to see Ally face to face. Please don't tell her that I've been in touch when she rings. An awful lot went on between us which can't be put right in a phone call. I'll wait until she comes home. Please can you let me know as soon as she gets back? Here's my work card, you can reach me at the police station, there's a mobile number on there too.'

She took the card. 'Of course. I'll keep this safe Joe and let you know when I hear anything.'

'That's great, I really appreciate it, thank you. I'll be off now. I need to get into work to check something. It was good to see you again though.'

'Same here. Goodbye Joe, look after yourself.' She watched him drive away. He was a good lad. Both she and her husband had been devastated when her daughter had left him all those years ago.

Back at the police station, at the first opportunity, Joe sat at his workstation and pulled up Ally's incident reports. After reading them, he raked his fingers through his hair in despair.

CHAPTER 17

It had been a long, tedious drive but eventually she had arrived at the airport without any mishaps. Although her body felt slightly stiff and weary from the journey, Ally felt a tingle of excitement as soon as she entered the airport terminal. The place was busy, the coffee shops and eateries all having long queues and full capacity. Her suitcase being large and cumbersome and far too heavy to lug around, she headed to the baggage check-in point. Knowing that she still had a couple of hours to kill until her flight boarded, she decided to hit the duty-free shops. Six months ago, she would have tried all the perfumes and probably would have purchased one or two bottles, along with some expensive accessories. This time though, her heart wasn't in it and after looking in several shops, she realised that she had lost her taste for luxury goods. Giving up on the shopping idea, she decided to join one of the long queues for something to eat.

After finding a seat, she had time to think. As she ate her salad filled baguette and sipped her much needed coffee, she thought about her parents. She had deliberately not told them the full details of everything that had happened, because what they didn't know, they couldn't worry about. She would give them a quick call though before she boarded, just to let them know that she had safely arrived at the airport.

Had Kat been right? Was she bonkers travelling over 3,000 miles across the Atlantic on a whim? Millie and Ashna had appeared fully supportive of her plans though, both saying they were quite envious. Although that didn't quite ring true with Ashna, who was fully loved-up and completely immersed in being a new mother. They had both told her that they were looking forward to all the gossip when she got back. She hoped she would have something positive to tell them.

Finishing her coffee, she thought back to the long chat she'd had with Millie a couple of days ago. Her friend had divulged a bit more about her past and told her that she had once co-owned a small restaurant with her then boyfriend. The boyfriend had managed the financial side of the business and Millie had looked after the catering side. The boyfriend had turned out to be a complete rat, because unbeknown to Millie, he had been squandering the profits while cheating on her with one of the waitresses. All the money had disappeared by the time Millie had realised what had been happening, leaving large amounts of debt, forcing the sale of the restaurant. Millie had told her that she had struggled after that, not only financially but mentally too, and it had taken her a long time to get her head together. It was only after her grandmother bequeathed her some money, enough to re-locate to Cornwall and start over, that she had found herself solvent again. Millie had said that it had been tough when she had first moved to Cornwall. After buying the coffee shop there had been lots of sacrifices and hard work. All her hard work had paid off though, and now the coffee shop was doing well and rapidly gaining a good reputation. Millie had said she felt much stronger and was determined that she would never be stupidly caught out again, no matter how cute or charming the guy was.

As she sat there thinking about Millie's story, she knew there were similarities, the main one being that they had both been mentally scarred by their ex-partners. She had felt inspired by Millie's guts and determination. If her friend could successfully start over, then so could she. She promised herself that when she got back from America she would answer one of the many messages she'd had from her agent offering her work. Hearing her flight being called, she finished her coffee and headed to the check in gate.

Climbing the steps to board her American Airlines direct flight to JFK, she felt a surge of happiness, something she had not felt in a long, long time. She had flown before, quite a few times, she had even been to New York before, but this time felt special, and she was going to make the most of it. Tucked under her arm was the novel she'd just bought from WH Smith. She'd been swayed entirely by the book's attractive cover and it being a New York Times best seller. She hoped it would turn out to be a good read.

Settled in her seat, she thought about her plan, which was to spend a few days shopping and seeing the sights in New York, then she would fly to the town in southwest Virginia where she believed Frank was from. If she was unable to find any information on Frank or his family, then she would enjoy a jolly good holiday in the Blue Ridge mountains, either way it was a win-win scenario.

Through the small window, she watched the plane take off and the UK coastline fade into the distance. As she lay her head back in her seat, she glanced sideways at the book the grey-haired lady next to her was reading. The lady, sensing Ally's interest, lay her book down in her lap and smiled.

'Are you interested in the psychic dear?'

Ally could feel herself reddening. 'Sorry, I didn't mean to be nosy.'

'It's alright dear. Let me introduce myself, my name is Anne and the reason for this book is that I'm a practicing Psychic Medium.' Anne pointed to the book in her lap. 'I'm having a bit of a read-up. I've got a Psychic reading engagement at a small venue in New York. To tell you the truth, I'm a bit nervous about it, that's why I'm doing a bit of revising. Are you travelling to New York for a holiday?'

Warming to her flight companion, who had kind eyes and a nice genuine feel about her, she offered her hand. Smiling, she introduced herself. 'Hello Anne. I'm Allegra, but most people call me Ally. I'm having a few days seeing the sights, then I'm off to Virginia.' She didn't know why, but she told Anne about Frank and Alice's letters.

'Oh my goodness, what an adventure.'

'Yes, it is. I know the whole thing sounds a bit mad and impulsive, but I just needed to get away from everything. I'm afraid that I've had a bit of a rocky time lately,' she confided, her voice breaking slightly.

After digesting what Ally had just said, Anne turned to face her.

Being completely unnerved by Anne's scrutiny, she could feel herself starting to blush again. Why on earth had she divulged her personal life to a stranger? Why hadn't she kept her mouth shut, for it now seemed that Anne was looking deep into her soul, and it felt uncomfortable. What could she see?

'I can sense that you have been through the mill and that there has been unhappiness in your life Ally,' Anne said gently, her eyes still on Ally's face. She paused slightly before adding, 'but after a bumpy ride my dear, I am certain that you will eventually find true happiness.'

'Oh. I-I'm not sure I believe in all that stuff.'

'Ally, everything will be alright. Be true to yourself my dear. You will be rewarded,' she said, reaching over to gently pat Ally on the arm.

Not quite knowing what to say, Ally knew that somehow, she had found Anne's words comforting.

Settling down in her seat, Anne picked up her book and began leafing through its pages. 'Now where was I, ah yes, Chapter 7. Time for some more homework,' she said, softly chuckling to herself.

Ally opened her book. After a few chapters she could hardly keep her eyes open.

It wasn't long before both women had fallen asleep, their books discarded.

PART TWO

NEW YORK

After landing at JFK, Ally saw no more of Anne. She summoned a yellow taxi to take her into the city and to her hotel, which was a small boutique hotel in midtown Manhattan. Although feeling slightly jet-lagged, she knew she had to make the most of her short time here. In a matter of minutes, she had already unpacked her case and was ready to get out and start exploring the fabulous iconic city.

Stepping outside, she checked her map. Fifth Avenue was a short stroll away, she would go there. She wanted to stock up on a few bits of casual clothing more suitable to her new Cornish lifestyle, then if she had time, maybe go to Saks for a bit of upmarket browsing. Her mother had an important birthday coming up and she wanted to buy her something special. First though, she needed to eat and knew just where to go. She'd read about Katz's Deli, and had always wanted to go there, because it was said they had the best pastrami sandwiches in town. It was a bit of a trek, but the walk would do her good after the long flight.

Later, with her feet aching like mad and holding several carrier bags, she stopped at the Starbucks near Times Square for coffee. It wasn't long before she realised two women were looking over at her and whispering behind their hands. Seeing Ally had noticed them, they got up out their seats and walked over to her.

'Er, excuse us, sorry to disturb you.'

Putting down her cup, Ally looked up at the two women. Puzzled and sensing they weren't going to give up, she smiled fleetingly at them, wondering what was going on.

'You are Nurse Sally from the tv show, aren't you?' the younger of the two gabbled enthusiastically.

Ally nodded. 'I hadn't realised it was on over here.'

'Sure is, we watch it every week. We love it, don't we Sis? Please can we have your autograph?' asked other woman, who resembled her sister and looked to be in her forties. The woman scrambled about in her handbag and fished out a pen. While her sister went over to the counter and grabbed a couple of paper napkins. 'Here you are, one for each of us would be fan-tastic.' They placed the pen and napkins on the table in front of Ally.

'I'm glad you are enjoying the show, Ally said warmly, taking in their satisfied expressions after writing on the napkins. She had always had time for fans, they meant a lot to her, and she was pleased, that even over here in America, that she was able to carry the flag for the show that she had been proud to be part of. 'Here you are then.' She handed back the pen and the two signed napkins.

'Thank you ma-am, that's real good of you,' both women said in unison, smiling broadly at Ally.

'Have a nice day both of you.' She watched the two women exit through the double doors and out into the busy street. The encounter had lifted her spirits and had also brought back memories of a different life.

Deciding she'd had enough retail therapy for one day, she decided that after dropping off her shopping bags back at her hotel, she would pay a quick visit to the Guggenheim Museum, which had been on her bucket list for many years. If she hurried, she would get there before closing time, and after that, she would go and find somewhere to get some dinner. On her wish list was Ellen's Stardust Diner but she was beginning to have second thoughts about that. Was she in the mood for watching the lively diner staff bursting out in song and dancing on the table-tops while she was here on her own? She would decide later. First stop was to see the museum, she was going to soak up the art and become a bit of a culture vulture.

It had been a full-on day and evening. Dog-tired, she had fallen asleep as soon as her head hit her hotel pillow. What seemed like halfway through the night, she woke with a start. She sat up in her bed and listened. What was that sound? Was that the door handle rattling? Was someone trying to get into her room? She felt the all too familiar stab of fear strike her. Her heart thumping, she leapt out of bed and cautiously approached the door. To her relief, she realised that the sound she had heard was a breakfast trolley being wheeled along the corridor. She checked her phone; it was gone eight o'clock. Someone was obviously getting room service. She laughed at her own stupidity.

CHAPTER 18

The next day was a full one. The shops were in full Christmas mode, and the Rockefeller skating rink was already full of skaters in colourful clothes whizzing around the ice. The famous Rockefeller Christmas tree was in situ but not yet lit.

As soon as she stepped outside the hotel, Ally realised, that despite the cloudless sky being a beautiful blue, it had turned very cold. As she walked along, her fingers were starting to feel like blocks of ice. She pulled up the collar of her coat and decided to head for the H&M by Times Square, they were bound to have some warm gloves and a hat she could buy that wouldn't cost the earth. She was already feeling slightly guilty about her mini splurge in Saks, where she had bought her mother some very expensive earrings for her birthday.

Wearing her new gloves and matching bobble hat, she decided to visit Macy's to stock up on her favourite makeup, which was cheaper than back home. She was hovering around the cosmetic counter when the sales assistant offered to give her a makeover. Her first thought was to say no, but after a moment's hesitation, decided she had nothing to lose. 15 minutes later, she hardly recognised herself when the sales assistant showed her the mirror. Armed with a small fortune in cosmetics, and her credit card having taken a big hit, she knew that when she got home it would be even more beneficial to her bank balance to make contact again with her agent.

Walking down 3rd Avenue, heading towards the ferry, she decided to take a walk around the East Village. This time she resisted buying one of the giant salty pretzels on offer from a street seller that she'd had the last time she'd visited. Instead, she went into Russ & Daughters to buy a smoked salmon and cream cheese bagel. It was so delicious that she was sure she'd still be dreaming about it about long after she was home.

Quickening pace, she found the queue for the ferry. She was so looking forward to seeing the Statue of Liberty and the view of the towering blocks of Manhattan from the river again. She'd seen it all before, but it was still a wonderful experience. Clutching her ticket, she boarded the ferry. Feeling confident in her new makeup, she leaned over the ferry railings and let the breeze blow against her face. She didn't even mind being chatted up by a fellow passenger as the ferry cut through the steely blue-grey water.

As she looked back at Manhattan's impressive skyline, the view was amazing, as was the weather, which was crisp and bright and not at all bad for the time of year. The sky was a beautiful blue but even standing in the sun it felt cold and she was very grateful for the gloves and hat she'd just bought.

Back in Manhattan, everywhere was so busy. Traffic was almost at a standstill with tour buses, cars, and yellow cabs bumper to bumper along the main avenues.

She looked for somewhere to have dinner. She decided to walk back to the bright lights of Times Square, where there were lots of places to eat. Maybe Bubba Gump's or Hard Rock Café, she'd been to both before. As she approached, she could see both were busy. She could see groups of people queuing outside waiting for tables and knew she needed to find somewhere quieter. Walking along Broadway, she wondered if she should try and get a last-minute theatre ticket. Undecided, she walked on some more, coming across a small bistro which didn't seem too busy. The bistro looked quite nice inside and wasn't packed to the hilt like the eateries in Times Square. Pushing open the door, she stepped inside. Before she even had a chance to pick up a menu, she heard someone call her name. A few feet away from her sat Anne, her psychic plane buddy.

'Anne, so good to see you.' She was genuinely pleased to see a familiar face. It had felt strange being in New York on her own.

'Come and sit down my dear. Are you eating?'

'Yes, I think I am. All the other restaurants seem so busy. This little place looks ideal.'

'Yes, they do nice food too. I always come in here when I'm in New York. I've just finished my Psychic engagement. I think it went well, but one does always have a few doubts,' she said, a with a brief flicker of concern. Then as if pushing the thought away, her face brightened. 'Now then, tell me Ally, what have you been up to? Are you having a good time?'

'Yes, I have been quite busy.' She told Anne the places she'd been to. 'It's not the same being here on your own though. I feel sort of vulnerable and a bit lost to be honest.'

'Well, my dear, I've a suggestion. How about we join forces and do a bit of sight-seeing together. I'm free now for a few days, then I fly home to the UK. We could take in a Broadway show or maybe get a carriage ride around Central Park.' Anne clapped her hands together and chuckled. 'I've not done the carriage ride thing for many, many years. Oh my, it would be such fun,' she chortled, her eyes shining. 'You know Ally, there are still lots of places I've not been to in this wonderful city, and to tell the truth, I would also appreciate a bit of company.

I've always wanted to see the architecture in the SoHo district. I think it's something you might like too, because it's become quite arty and trendy now and has some nice shops. Things haven't been the same since I lost my poor husband,' Anne said softly, her eyes sad. 'We were married for over forty years you know, and it was such a loss when he died, and I still miss him.'

'Oh, I'm sorry.'

'It's alright dear, it's not recent. My Harvey died a good few years ago. I'm learning to live with it, but I still miss the grumpy old beggar. He was a New Yorker, brought up across the bridge in Brooklyn. I suppose that's why I like it here and keep coming back. We used to get a pizza from Roberta's and eat it under the shadow of the bridge on the tiny bit of beach there,' she said wistfully. 'Never mind, one mustn't dwell on the past.' Anne looked thoughtful.' You said you went to the Guggenheim, how about we visit some of the other museums? There is one in Brooklyn worth a visit, and I can show you where my Harvey used to live.'

Ally smiled. 'Count me in. I would absolutely love that. Thanks Anne. You are such a godsend. I'm so glad that we bumped into each other.'

'So am I Ally. It will be wonderful fun showing you around. Shall we order?' Anne lifted the menu from the stand and studied it. 'They do wonderful blueberry pancakes in here, so save some room.'

The next couple of days passed in a blur. One of the highlights was the lighting of the Rockefeller Christmas tree.

As usual Anne was very knowledgeable and very good company. The two of them stood shoulder to shoulder with the crowd of people who were, like themselves, watching the live performances prior to the big switch on. It was so cold they could see their breath.

Struggling to be heard over the loud music, Anne started to tell Ally about the history of the magnificent tree in front of them. 'Let me tell you about this tree Ally. In 1931 the Rockefeller workers pooled their money to buy the first tree, it was said they did it because they were grateful to have jobs in the Great Depression. The tree was 20ft high, and they decorated it with handmade garlands. After that, it was decided to make the tree an annual event. Then in 1936 there was a skating pageant here on the Plaza, on the new ice rink. In 1999 they had the largest tree ever here. I believe it was something like 100ft tall.' Lowering her voice slightly, Anne continued. 'You have obviously heard of 9/11 when the twin towers were attacked. It was such a terrible time for the city, lots of lives lost and families devastated. That Christmas, 2001, the tree was lit up in patriotic red, white and blue and people from all around the world came to see it.' Anne smiled, so my dear, you can see this tree is important to the people of New York and a big part of the city's Christmas festivities, a bit like the Christmas tree in London's Trafalgar Square.'

'Gosh, you know so much Anne. Thank you. You have made my time here so much nicer.' She genuinely meant it and knew she had found a good friend in Anne.

'Aw, thank you dear. I must confess I did a bit of reading up on the tree before we came out, so I'm not that good,' she said, with a wink. 'We must stay in touch Ally. We'll swap numbers later. Oh, here listen, they are announcing something, maybe they are starting the countdown. It will be absolutely stunning; apparently there are 50,000 lights on the tree.' Anne looked up to the sky. 'Was that a couple snowflakes I just saw come down?'

CHAPTER 19

It was as she was waiting for her internal flight to Virginia that she saw a call coming through on her mobile. Straight away she recognised the number. It was the police station back home in Cornwall.

'Hello, it's the C.I.D office, just a quick call to update you on your case and to reassure you that our investigation is still on-going. Unfortunately, up until now, our enquiries have drawn a blank. I'm sorry to say that Nick Curtis' whereabouts are still unknown. We've been informed that the hunt for him has been widened. It has now gone nationwide. The word is that the search for Curtis is also going international.'

'I don't understand. What has he done?' She asked, feeling a bit confused.

'I'm afraid I don't have the full picture. The case is being investigated at a high level, but the indications are that Curtis may have got himself mixed up in international organised crime.'

'What does that mean?'

'We don't have any details. I'm sorry, I can't tell you anymore. The powers that be are keeping it under wraps. Sorry the news isn't more positive. The direct line phone number we gave you still stands though, and you must call it if you feel you are in any danger from Curtis.'

'Yes, I will, thank you. I had no idea that Nick was involved in anything like that.' Shocked to the core, she struggled to take in everything that the police officer was telling her.

The officer went on to say that Nick was a person of interest to the London police and that the case had virtually been taken over by them, but that the Cornish police would still be in contact with her to pass on any information, if relevant to her case.

'Thank you for calling. I'm in America for a couple of weeks. I'll be in touch with you again as soon as I get home.'

As she closed her phone, she was finding it difficult to absorb everything the police officer had told her. What the heck did it all mean? Had Nick been living two lives? One as a respectable businessman and one as a kind of international criminal? What had Nick been up to, apart from terrorising her? She knew he had a dark, nasty side, because she'd frequently been on the receiving end of it. She tried to recall if Nick had given her any indication of his criminal activity but could think of nothing that had made her suspicious, apart from his absences. All she knew was that he had often looked worse for wear, quite ill even, after he had returned from one of his increasingly longer and more frequent jaunts. Towards the end of their relationship, she had hardly seen him, so he could have been up to anything. She had never questioned him, knowing that she would probably come off worse if she did. Where was he? Nick had not been seen at his London flat or at any of his business addresses and the police had already told her that his car had been found by an airfield, so the chances are, that he had left the country.

It was all too much. She was finding the whole thing hard to believe and very disturbing. She tried to convince herself that it was pointless worrying about it while she was here. She would only be in America for a couple of weeks, and she needed to put Nick out of her mind for her own sanity.

Her vow to forget Nick was proving easier said than done. The whole way through her flight to Virginia, she hadn't been able to think of anything else. The call from the police had re-awakened her awareness that the problem had not gone away, and that she would have to face it again as soon as she got back home. She was sick of constantly looking over her shoulder. Her stomach felt queasy remembering the feeling of panic every time she had heard a strange noise at the cottage; be it someone treading on the loose paving slab in the garden, or the back gate opening. Feeling herself getting hot, she fanned herself with the magazine that she'd bought before boarding. She had been foolish to think the problem would be sorted by the time she returned to the UK and now the news that her ex was a wanted criminal and on the loose somewhere made her even more worried. She felt stupid for being so naïve about Nick. Oh how she hated him.

"WELCOME TO VIRGINIA." She felt more than a pang of apprehension after reading the sign on the roadside. Had her parents been right? Was on a wild goose chase? All her previous bravado had disappeared. She was somewhere she had never been before, seeking information on a person long deceased. Fully aware that she had no real connection with Frank, she wondered if she was indeed on a fool's errand. All she had was a bunch of faded letters and an old sepia photograph, which thank goodness, Oscar had given her permission to bring, otherwise she'd have nothing to show as evidence.

Ally sat in the back of the taxi which was taking her to her hotel. The brilliant blue sky looked stunning against the backdrop of crimson, burnt orange, and golden hued leaves, which lined the two-lane highway. It was beautiful, and with the smoky blue mountains peeking over the horizon, it was scenery that any photographer would die for.

After checking in at the hotel and unpacking her case, the reality of the situation suddenly hit her. With her confidence hovering around zero, she didn't think she had the slightest chance of finding Frank's family. She sat down on the bed to think things through. She told herself that she was doing this for Oscar, and there was no way she could wimp out at the first opportunity. She had to remain positive. Before she had left the UK, she had done some internet research on the town but knew she needed to dig further. Maybe now she was here, the hotel could give her some local information, or at least tell her where to look. She would also try and find the town library, that's if they had one.

Having got over her wobble, she looked around her room. The hotel she had chosen was mid-priced and in the centre of town. Her room was not grand but was clean and well-appointed and she could tell that her stay here would be comfortable. The fully tiled bathroom had a decent sized bath and a shower cubicle. There was a complementary tray of toiletries, along with a selection of white fluffy towels which had been left on the countertop. The bedroom was plenty big enough and had a large flat screen TV fixed to the wall. There were also multiple electric and charging points, more than enough for her needs.

Finishing the big bag of potato puffs and the bottle of water she'd bought at the airport she sat on the edge of the bed thinking what to do next. Picking up the freebie notepad and pen from her bedside cabinet, she started to plan her next move. Her first stop had to be the public library. She picked up her phone and started to search the internet. It wasn't long before her eyes became heavy as a wave of tiredness swept over her; the long journey was taking its toll. Time to call it a day. Snapping her phone shut, she decided she needed to make a fresh start tomorrow, she would be far more productive after a good night's sleep. She ran herself a warm bath, then slipped into her pj's and climbed into bed, where despite the hum of traffic outside, she was soon asleep.

The next morning, dressed for the weather, she felt good as she stepped outside. The day was cold, but bright and sunny, perfect for a bit of exploration. Her internet search had found the town's library. According to the map on her phone, it would take her ten minutes to walk there from the hotel. First though, she would look around the town, which from her first impression, looked interesting. Armed with her complementary paper map, she headed towards what appeared to be the hub of the town. Taking pride of place in the town square was a colourful and bustling market. People were queuing to buy fruit and other fresh produce from the attractively laid out stalls. She looked around her; this place seemed to have it all. There were quite a few trendy tourist shops too, all decked out to entice the Christmas visitors, and all within walking distance of her hotel. She looked at her map. There was obviously a theatre here too, but she'd leave that for another day. Today her main objective was to find the library. After rummaging around in her bag for her phone, she tapped on Google maps, then keeping a close eye on where it was taking her, carried on walking until she found the library.

Pulling open the library's heavy swing doors, Ally quickly glanced around, taking in the quiet, studious atmosphere. The place was huge and filled with row upon row of tall bookcases. On the far side of the room there was an elderly man sitting at a long table reading a newspaper. To the left of her was the check-in desk. There was nobody there. Maybe if she went and stood over by it someone would see her and come over. Feeling a bit conspicuous, she waited patiently, rehearsing what to say in her head. Out of the corner of her eye she saw a middle-aged lady with bobbed auburn hair hurrying towards her.

'Can I help you?'

Ally summoned up her widest smile, she didn't know why she was feeling nervous, but she was. She hoped that after explaining why she was here, that the woman wouldn't think she was barking mad.

The woman looked at her expectantly.

'Oh yes please. This is a bit of a long shot, but I wondered if you would be able to help me with something?' She pulled Alice's letters and the photo of Frank out of her bag then went on to explain what information she was looking for.

After listening to all Ally had to say, the librarian looked at her long and hard. 'I'm trying to place your voice. I'm sure I've heard it before. You are a Brit aren't you.' It was not so much a question but a statement.

Ally wondered if being a Brit was perceived to be a good or bad thing in this neck of the woods.

'Have I seen you before?' The woman's tone was direct and not overly friendly.

'Erm yes, I'm English, and no, I don't think we have ever met. This is my first time in this town.'

The librarian looked puzzled. 'I'm sure I know you from somewhere.'

Suddenly the penny dropped. 'Maybe you have seen me on the television. I'm an actress. I played a nurse in a UK television drama,' she offered by way of explanation, hoping that it might make the woman less hostile towards her. 'I understand that the show is currently running here in the US.'

'Yes! Nurse Sally! It's you!' In an instant, the librarian's attitude completely changed. Suddenly she was all smiles and treating Ally like an old friend. 'I knew I had seen you somewhere before,' she gushed, flushed with excitement. Giving a little chuckle, she turned to Ally. 'What a story, there was I thinking it was going to be yet another tedious day and then you turn up.' She thought for a moment. Then, as if having a light bulb moment, her face lit up. 'I have a great idea!'

'You do?' Ally replied, smiling.

'Well, this library publishes a weekly newsletter. I'm the editor of it actually,' she added importantly. 'The newsletter goes out online too, that's where most of the local people read it. It's due out first thing tomorrow. Before it runs, how about I put a piece in the newsletter about your story? I'll insert some pictures of the letters and the photograph of Frank too. It will bring your quest into the public domain, and maybe one of Frank's family will come forward. We can put the library down as a contact number and then we can pass any information we get straight to you, so you won't get any cranks or time wasters.'

Ally couldn't believe her luck. She wanted to give the woman a big hug. 'Gosh, that will be fantastic. Thank you so much. I'll give you all the information that I have about Alice and Frank and the hotel where I'm staying.' She scribbled the information on the sheet of paper the librarian gave her. 'I've written my mobile number down too, so please contact me if you hear anything.'

'Of course, by the way my name is Catherine and I'm the head librarian here.'

'Catherine, I'm very pleased to meet you. I feel I've been very fortunate today, as I really didn't know how my search for information about Frank's family would go.'

'It's a pleasure Nurse Sally,' Catherine winked. 'I hope it all works out for you. I'll just take some photos of the letters and the framed photograph before you go. Er, would you mind me also taking one of us both together? My friends will be so jealous, it's not every day one meets Nurse Sally,' she giggled girlishly.

Ally laughed, thankful that her career was bringing some rewards instead of just grief.

A few days later, to her surprise, she had a call from the hotel's reception to tell her that there were media camped out in the hotel foyer. The local television station had somehow found out about her search and wanted to interview her.

It was a good job she was accustomed to being in front of the camera, because the interview had taken place in the busy hotel foyer. As well as the cameraman, there were also curious hotel staff and what seemed like half the population of the town looking on. Two easy chairs had been set out adjacent to each other, one for her and one for the interviewer. The questions about Frank and Alice she had found easy, but the interviewer had obviously picked up on her Nurse Sally role, which when questioned about, had made her feel uncomfortable. The crew had taken photos of Alice and Frank's letters and the photograph of Frank.

After the crew had packed away, Ally didn't know what to do with herself. She ordered a coffee and sat in the hotel lounge reading through the local 'What to do Guide' that had been left on the coffee table.

'Can I recommend somewhere ma-am?' asked the young waitress, scooping up Ally's empty coffee cup and placing it on her tray.

Ally looked up from the guide and smiled. 'That would be great. I have a few hours spare.'

The young girl took the guide from Ally and started to leaf through the pages. 'Here you are. How about this. The river gorge and the mountains are not too far. It's a fantastic place to listen to the roar of the water, and you can walk among the rocks down by the river. You'll have to be careful though as it can be a bit slippery, I've nearly fallen in a couple of times. I just love it there, because it's a place where you can lose yourself in your thoughts, it's very relaxing. Hopefully it won't be too busy either. People go there to do fishing too, but I don't suppose you'll bother with that. Wear some sturdy shoes though, it might be a bit muddy.'

'It sounds ideal,' said Ally. 'How do I get there?'

'By cab, I can call you one if you like. There are lovely views and it's well worth a visit.'

She looked at the girl's name badge. 'That's very kind of you Amy. Please can you book a cab for me in, er, say fifteen minutes? I want to pop up to my room and change into some warm clothes and boots, something more suitable for walking in.'

'Sure ma-am. Have lovely time won't ya.'

'I will, thank you Amy.'

After the taxi dropped her off, Ally followed the signposts for the river trail. It was only a short hike down to the riverbed but a lot of steps going back, and she was glad she'd worn her walking boots. The trek was well worth the effort though. Just like Amy had said, just being alongside the river, hearing the roar of the tumbling water and walking among the stones was therapeutic. As she stood there listening to the water lapping against the rocks, it felt magical. Feeling brave, she had also ventured out onto the extremely high bridge looking over the river but, having no head for heights, had not stayed there long.

Feeling quite exhausted and with her feet aching after trailing around all afternoon, she decided that she would retire to her hotel room and would run herself a hot bath. Easing her sore feet out of her boots, she padded into the bathroom and turned on the taps which fed the large white bath. After emptying an entire mini bottle of pine essence into the water, she watched the bubbles form. The smell was amazing and just what she needed. After a good soak, she ordered some food and mentally prepared herself for the task of wading through the long list of people that had contacted her through the library. She was very grateful to Catherine. The librarian had done her proud and had typed up all the details in the order of what she thought would be the most likely to be useful.

The little red digital clock on the bottom of the TV was showing that it had gone eleven o'clock. She yawned, it was, without doubt, time to turn in. It had been a long evening, but she had eventually whittled all the messages down and had made a short list of those who she thought may have a connection to Frank. That would have to be a job for tomorrow though. She climbed into bed, plumped up her pillows and fell into a dreamless sleep.

CHAPTER 20

She spent the next morning in her hotel room making calls and leaving messages, in the hope that someone from her short-list would make her visit worthwhile. Also, a tiny bit of her was wanting to prove to her parents that she had been right to come here, and that she wasn't on some stupid wild goose chase. It wasn't looking promising though, she thought bleakly, as she looked down at the list of people she had already crossed out. It seemed that most of the people she had rang had not proved to be at all sincere. A couple of them wanted to know if there was a reward and one man seemed to be thinking it all a huge joke and just wanted to get himself seen on tv.

Feeling despondent, she picked up the guidebook. There was no point in coming all this way and not having a holiday and doing the tourist thing. Flicking through the pages, she noticed that one of the places on her wish list was within walking distance. A walk would do her good. The photographs in the book showed there was some stunning scenery, including a small waterfall and wonderful mountain views, everything she wanted to see. In a more positive mood, she put on her boots and warm coat, and with her map at the ready, set out to explore and hopefully find, the nearby area of natural beauty seen in the book. Although the fall was a little past its peak, Amy had assured her that some of the trees were still showing magnificent colours and would still be beautiful.

Kicking through the crisp dry leaves, Ally explored the woodland, which smelt of soft leaf mould. It was stunning and picture perfect. The cloudless blue sky being a perfect foil for the fiery red, yellow, and orange hues of the foliage. Stopping for a moment to get her breath, she was sure that she would feel like she had done a workout by the time she had finished her walk.

Looking around her, she knew she had picked a good day to come out. The low afternoon sun, filtering through the branches, enhanced the amazing colours and was certainly lifting her spirits. The only words she could think of to describe what she was seeing, were nature's fireworks, because that's exactly what they were.

The sun was starting to go down, and it was getting chilly. Now was the time to head back to her hotel. She looked around for a familiar landmark or building to guide her, but for the life of her, she just could not recognise anything. She hadn't a clue where she was and realised that she must have wandered off track, and to make matters worse, she had lost her paper map. There was no Google map to follow either as her phone had just run out of battery, probably flattened by all the photos she had taken.

For at least an hour she walked aimlessly, trying to re-trace her footsteps. Her anxiety level was now sky-high knowing that she was in an undesirable, non-tourist part of town. She told herself to remain calm and to look for someone trustworthy who could help, but apart from a rough sleeper in a shop doorway, there wasn't a soul to be seen. She glanced around her; this was not the kind of place that a solo woman tourist should be, especially when the daylight was rapidly fading. Trying to ignore the blister she could feel forming on her heel, she walked on, and couldn't believe her luck, when even in the semi-darkness, she recognised the side wall of a tall brick building. The wall had been spray-painted with colourful street art, and instantly she knew that she had passed it by earlier. She looked around her and could have wept with relief when she saw the road which would lead her back to her hotel.

Although she had felt extremely anxious when she had lost her way, she was still glad that she had made the effort. Exhausted by her afternoon trek, she wearily sat down on the` freshly made bed. Her head was starting to ache quite badly, maybe it was all the walking and the stress of getting lost that had bought it on. Placing her fingers on each temple, she gently massaged them to try and ease the pain. She reached in her bag for her bottle of water, thinking that she could also be dehydrated. Feeling no better after drinking the whole bottle, she knew that she would have to go out and find the pharmacy downtown to buy a pack of paracetamol. She needed more plasters too, having just used her last one to cover the nasty heel blister that had now popped and was throbbing like mad. Grabbing her bag and coat she reluctantly closed the door behind her, the last thing she had wanted to do was to go out again.

Acknowledging the duty receptionist's wave with a quick smile, she headed out into the cold, dark evening, which was threatening rain. Looking both ways, she tried to remember where she'd seen the pharmacy. After walking to the end of the street, she saw that the road forked four ways. She hesitated, unsure which way to go, for the daytime colour and hustle and bustle of the streets had disappeared and now everything looked so different. It was hard to get her bearings. There was hardly anyone about either, probably worsened by the forecast of imminent bad weather.

Taking a chance, she turned down a narrow street to the left of her, keeping a look out for a pharmacy sign. She had only been walking a few minutes, when she thought she heard soft footsteps behind her. After looking over her shoulder, she was relieved when she saw that there wasn't anyone there. The street looked deserted and unless the person had slipped into one of the tight gaps between the buildings, which was highly unlikely, she knew the footsteps had been a product of her over-active imagination. Instantly, she told herself she was being stupid for letting her nerves get the better of her. It must have been the rustling leaves which were swirling around on the ground that she had heard. Feeling a drop of rain fall on her face, she looked up at the sky. Another drop fell. Quickening pace, she continued down the shadowy thoroughfare.

Where was the blasted pharmacy? She could have sworn it was down here somewhere. She wished there were more or brighter streetlights, the lack of proper light was making her feel vulnerable. She couldn't get over how empty the streets were. The high buildings looked formidable and for some reason made her feel hemmed in. Suddenly the heavens opened. The promised bad weather had arrived with a vengeance. Now the only sound she could hear was the roar of heavy rain, which was bouncing off the ground. The driving rain was slanting towards her, and she was getting soaked. She would probably look like a drowned rat by the time she got back to the hotel. The wind was getting up too. She pulled up the collar of her coat as another gust hit her. Hopefully the pharmacy, when she eventually found it, would sell umbrellas like some of them did back home. As she wiped a raindrop off the end of her nose, she knew that coming out had been a crazy idea and, headache or not, she now wished she hadn't bothered.

Passing a long hedge, she heard a car fast approaching. A rain puddle, the size of a mini lake, had formed in the road next to her. Knowing she was likely to be heavily splashed by the surge of water as the car drove through, she turned slightly, moving closer to the hedge. Just as the car sped through the puddle, she thought she heard a rustle. It sounded like someone was behind the hedge. She instantly discarded the thought. It was probably just the sound of the water hitting the speeding car, or possibly the wind catching the trees. It was only when she looked back and caught sight of a shadowy figure ducking into a dark alleyway, that she became worried that someone, was indeed, following her. Head down, her pulse racing, she carried on walking.

Trying to remain calm, she continued at a fast pace. Feeling increasingly spooked, she decided to cross over to the other side of the road where the streetlights were more frequent. Standing on the edge of the sidewalk, with one foot already in the road, she noticed a scruffy man leaning against a streetlamp opposite. Wearing a bulky dark coloured padded coat, the man appeared to be looking over at her. His face was partially obscured by his hood and the sunglasses he was wearing, which she felt was a bit odd considering the time of year and it being dark.

Feeling extremely vulnerable at the sight of the man, she decided against crossing the road.

Stepping back on to the sidewalk, she continued walking. A short distance on, it was with great relief that she finally saw a red neon pharmacy sign.

Never was she more pleased to see the store, which seemed to sell everything under the sun, including windproof umbrellas. After purchasing her goods, she knew she had to face the walk back to her hotel. Looking both ways before she left the pharmacy, she was relieved that there was no sign of the man.

Striding purposely, it didn't take her long to reach the hotel. As soon as she walked in through the hotel's swing doors, she felt safe and welcomed by its warmth and protection. She saw Amy talking to the receptionist.

Amy beckoned her over. 'Oh my, you're soaked through. How come you went out in this?'

Ally held up her pharmacy bag. 'Needs must. I had a banging headache and went to buy some paracetamol and a pack of Band Aid.' She took her chance. 'Er, Amy, I saw a scruffy man in a padded coat. I think he might have been following me.'

Amy smiled. 'It's probably old Stan. He won't hurt you. He's often seen around town, especially around here. He's a bit of a lost soul, likes wandering the streets and ever since his wife died, he seems to be doing it more and more. Our chef always saves him a plate of food at the end of the day, he was probably hanging around waiting for that.'

'Does he wear sunglasses?' asked Ally, still not sure.

She laughed. 'Our Stan wears anything that takes his fancy but he's completely harmless.'

'Ah, okay, that's put my mind at rest. Thanks Amy.'

Back in her hotel room, she checked her phone, which she had left on charge. She had been so busy taking photos, that she hadn't checked her messages since early that morning. When she did so, she felt a tingle of excitement…there was a missed call from a lady called Gertie Kelly.

CHAPTER 21

Straight away Ally called the number. 'Can I speak to Gertie Kelly please?'

'Can I ask who is speaking?' asked the thin, shaky voice on the other end of the phone.

'Hello, my name is Ally, you contacted me. It's about Frank.'

'Ah yes, thank you for calling back. Are you the young lady from the UK that was on our local news?'

'Yes I am.' The voice sounded like it belonged to a wizened old lady, and she hoped this was a genuine call and not some pranker pretending to be an elderly person.

'Good. One moment, let me get comfortable, I have a lot to tell you.'

After a lot of shuffling and clattering Gertie picked up the phone again.

'There, I'm all sat down. Are you still there, young lady?'

'Yes, I'm here Gertie and ready to listen.'

Gertie began to speak, explaining that she was Frank's younger sister and the only one of his three siblings still alive. 'Frank and I had two older brothers named Gerald and Henry, both now sadly deceased. Both Gerald and Henry have offspring who are now involved in running the family business. Frank though, was a different story, he died poor. Everything he had was spent on medical fees and residential care for his mentally ill wife. The family supported Frank until he died. Frank had twin daughters by his wife, but they died very young, long before the war, struck down with Diphtheria. It was a terrible time, a real tragedy. We all think it was the grief of losing the twins that finally turned her mind. She got progressively worse after that and was never the same again, neither was Frank. Their marriage had never been strong. I'm afraid Frank's wife was a heavy drinker, which got worse after the loss of the twins. It was also rumoured that she had other men. I'm not surprised my Frank found love overseas. His wife wasn't a very nice woman and I think he was glad to get away from it all.' Gertie gave a little cough before speaking again. 'Our family originated from Ireland you know. Anyway, I digress. I had always suspected Frank had secrets and that something had gone on while he was overseas. He became very quiet after he came back, not his usual self. It was like he had given up. He never said what was wrong, and instead put everything into looking after his wife, who by the end, didn't even know who he was.'

'That is quite a sad story. Thank you so much for getting in touch with me Gertie.'

'It's a pleasure young lady. Would you like to come to see me and then we can talk face to face? I don't like doing this kind of thing on the telephone.'

'That would be lovely, thank you. Are you far away?'

'The other side of town. I'll send my driver over to pick you up tomorrow, say around two o'clock. He will report to your hotel reception.'

'Thank you, that's very kind of you.'

'I'll see you tomorrow then young lady; will look forward to it.' With that the phone went dead. Gertie had ended the call.

The next day, at two o'clock, she was ready and waiting for Gertie's car. When it arrived, she was a bit taken back, for the car was a shiny black limousine. She watched as the uniformed driver approached the reception desk.

'Car for Miss Ally.'

She stepped forward.

'Right then ma-am, let's take you to Ms Gertrude. She is sure looking forward to meeting you.' He ushered Ally out through the double doors onto the sidewalk and opened the rear door of the limousine for her to climb in.

The car sped smoothly past big houses with neat lawns until it swerved off the main road and headed down a long gated driveway, where it stopped in front of a sprawling red brick mansion. She gulped at the sight of the grand house, the size of a stately home. Never in a million years was she expecting Frank's family to be so affluent.

She was shown into a large, crystal chandeliered drawing room. As she looked all around her, she became slightly unnerved by the opulence of it all. One of the first things she noticed were the tall arched windows, each one festooned with floor length richly embroidered swags. Large plump sofas in matching fabric had been placed facing each other either side of the big stone fireplace. Through French doors leading out into the garden, there was a beautiful, manicured lawn with wide steps leading down to a large, paved terrace. In the centre of the terrace was a grand marble fountain, which had water cascading down from three levels, each one graduating in size with the biggest bowl at the bottom.

The sun was beating through the windows, the room was stifling. As she waited for Gertie to appear, she could feel herself starting to perspire. A sweaty face was not a good look, and she was in the process of mopping her brow when the door opened. A dark-haired lady in a plain navy dress came into the room, followed by an immaculately groomed elderly woman, leaning heavily on a walking stick. The dark-haired lady helped the elderly woman ease herself down into one of the many armchairs.

'Ally, so nice to meet you,' said the elderly woman. 'I'm Gertie, Frank's younger sister. Do sit down my dear.' Gertie indicated to a chair opposite. 'Maisie dear,' Gertie smiled at the dark-haired lady, 'please bring us some refreshments. Tea or coffee Ally, which do you prefer?'

'Tea, please with a dash of milk, thank you.'

With a discreet nod, Maisie left the room, only to return ten minutes later with a full-blown afternoon tea.

'Would you pour Ally?' Gertie nodded towards the teapot.

'Yes, of course.' Ally carefully poured the tea into the delicate teacups, placing one on the table next to the elderly lady. 'What a beautiful home you have Gertie.'

Gertie nodded. 'This is my nephew's house. He and his wife have taken me under their wing. I was once the youngest sibling. My three brothers always treated me as the baby of the family, but sadly I'm now the matriarch of it, because I'm the only one left now that Gerald, Frank and Henry have kicked the bucket.' Gertie smiled at her own fate. 'Now then Ally, enough about me, tell me everything.'

'Of course.' She began explaining how she had found Alice and Frank's letters and the photo in the cottage she was renting and had given them to Oscar, who was Alice and Frank's son. She told

Gertie about meeting Alice and how Alice in her muddled mind was still waiting for Frank to return.

Reaching into her bag, she pulled out the letters and photo of Frank. 'This is what I found,' she handed them to Gertie.

Gertie's face lit up as soon as she saw the photo. 'It's the same photo that I have, Frank sent it to us during the war.' Her eyes moistening, Gertie looked down fondly at the photo. 'My Frank was such a handsome man.' Putting the photo down, she turned her attention to the pile of letters. After opening the first one, Gertie instantly recognised her brother's distinctive handwriting. 'That's my Frank alright. I'd recognise his scrawly, spidery scribble anywhere. We were very close growing up you know.' Working her way through the pile of letters, Gertie quietly took her time to carefully read each one.

Having read them all, Gertie placed the letters on the table next to her. 'I loved my brothers, but especially Frank. He was the one that I was most fond of. Frank was a gentle and honourable soul, and I don't think he would have let Alice down if it hadn't been for his commitments back here. I'm so pleased that he managed to find someone who loved him, even though it was overseas. I wish it had turned out better for Alice and Frank. Frank had no interest in the family business; it wasn't his thing. He made leather goods and shoes instead. Frank always liked working with his hands. He wasn't cut out for business.'

Ally smiled. 'Alice, even in her muddled mind, remembered that Frank had promised her a pair of boots.'

Gertie laughed. 'He did make some fine boots. Made me a pair too, I've still got them, even though my feet won't fit into them anymore.'

Gertie looked Ally straight in the eye. 'So, Ally it appears that you do not have any real connection to Alice and Oscar, so what made you come all this way?'

'Yes, I realise that it does seem a bit extreme. Even my own parents thought I was crazy. I can't go into it all now, but I had been very stressed out by things happening, things I had to report to the police. Needing to get away from it all, I decided to book a holiday. I hadn't visited the US for many years and had always wanted to come back. I spent a few days in New York doing the tourist thing before coming here.'

Gertie leaned forward in the chair. 'So, tell me Ally, why you decided to come here to Virginia.'

'It was Alice and Frank's letters. Reading their story resonated with me. Alice and Frank must have loved each other very much. Oscar had invited me to see his mother, who is suffering from dementia and is very fragile. While I was visiting her, Alice appeared very confused, but the one thing that came across loud and clear, was that she was still pining for her Frank and was still waiting for him to come back to her and take her to his home in Virginia's Blue Mountains. This really impacted on me. Also, Oscar, who is a lovely man, didn't know anything about his father and I wanted to help him find out more. After reading Frank's letters and listening to Alice's ramblings about the Blue Mountains, I had a rough idea of the area where Frank was from. I thought it would be a good idea to combine my search for Frank with a much-needed break. Also, after the hustle and bustle of New York City, I wanted to go somewhere completely different, somewhere scenic with beautiful autumnal colours. I thought that if I had no joy in finding Oscar's family, I would still be able to enjoy a nice holiday here in Virginia. I know it all sounds a bit far-fetched, and I can understand why you asked,' she added lamely.

'My dear, you took a big chance on finding us,' Gertie said softly.

'Yes, I know, but when Oscar gave me his blessing and permission to bring the letters and photo to help with the search for his American family, I knew I had to try. It was with Oscar's full agreement that I came here. I had no idea how things would work out. It is only because the television station here picked up on it that you found me.'

'Yes indeed, that's how we heard about you from the TV coverage.' Gertie softly chuckled. 'I even made Maisie find the show you were in this morning and we both watched you in your role as Nurse Sally. You were very good.'

'That's kind of you. Thank you, Gertie.'

Gertie reached for the small wooden box which was sitting on the table next to her. Lifting the lid, she took out an envelope. 'This is the letter my Frank wrote to me shortly before he died. He wrote about his life and the special things that had been important to him, one of them being his love for your Cornish village and how one special woman, who he refers to here as "my dear A", had meant the world to him. He didn't name the woman, but I think it must be your Alice. Although he didn't have any money of his own, he asked that the family donate a sum of money, on his death, to the village in his memory. Obviously, he didn't know Alice was carrying his child.' Gertie gently shook her head. 'Things might have turned out different if he had. I've never told the family about this letter, but now I will. I feel sure they will want to honour Frank's last wishes.'

'I'm sure Oscar will not want anything from your family Gertie. He leads a simple life running the village hardware store.'

'Well, maybe we can get our legal people to investigate, and if it all checks out, maybe we can donate something to the village in Frank's name. Does it have a community hub or something?'

'Yes, there's a village hall. It's seen better days and leaks all over the place.'

'Then we shall look into putting some money in that direction.'

'Gertie, I'm sure Oscar would love that. Thank you.'

The drawing room door flung open. A tall blonde woman walked in. The woman looked Ally up and down disdainfully.

'Ally, meet Georgina, she's my eldest brother Gerald's grandchild. The apple of his eye until he passed away.'

There was no warmth in Georgina's eyes as she shook hands with Ally.

'Maybe we can arrange a video call to Oscar?' Gertie suggested. 'Georgina dear, you know about these things, could you set it up for me?'

'Does Oscar have the internet?' Georgina turned to face Ally.

'Er, I'm not sure. He's quite old fashioned in his ways. It's a very close-knit community though and there are plenty in the village that do have the internet who would be happy to help, including myself. We can certainly sort something out.'

'I'll look into it for you Aunt Gertie. Now let me show you out Ally. My aunt looks tired, she has to rest before our Thanksgiving dinner, all the family will be there.'

Gertie looked up. 'Ah yes, Thanksgiving. Would you like to come to our dinner Ally?'

Out of the corner of her eye she could see Georgina looking daggers at her. 'I'm afraid I have plans Gertie but thank you for asking me.'

Taking the hint that her time was up, she followed Georgina out into the large hall and was just about to leave the house when Georgina abruptly swung around to face her. Startled, she was quite unprepared for what was to come.

Georgina obviously wasn't in the mood for holding back her vitriolic anger. Only inches from her face, and so near to her that she could feel the woman's breath, Georgina vented her fury.

Georgina's face twisted into a cruel smirk. 'You may have schmoozed your way into Gertie's good books, but you have not fooled me. I've been digging into your past. You are hardly Snow White, are you?' she sneered. 'There's no money here for you. Frank died broke. All the money is on my side of the family and you, and this, whatshisname, Oscar,' she spat the name out, 'won't get your hands on any.'

How dare this woman accuse her of wanting money. Standing tall, she looked Georgina straight in the eye. 'I can assure you that is not the reason I'm here. I have nothing to gain by this, nothing at all, nor does Oscar. He just wanted to find out about his father.' With that, she ran down the steps to the waiting car.

Shaken by Georgina's insinuations and the malice in her voice, she quietly fumed as Gertie's driver took her back to her hotel in the black limousine.

She was getting ready to go down to dinner when her phone rang. It was Gertie's number. What did she want?

'Hello my dear, Gertie here.'

'Oh, hello Gertie,' she wondered what was coming next.

'Don't sound so worried my dear. I'm calling to reassure you. I understand young Georgina wasn't very pleasant when she showed you out earlier.' Gertie paused, waiting for Ally's reply.

'No, I'm afraid she wasn't Gertie. She accused me, and Oscar, of scheming to get the family money. Please believe me, it's not true. Oscar just wanted to find out about his father, and I said I would help. That's all there is to it, I promise you. How did you find out?'

'The walls here have ears my dear, or rather Maisie has. She overheard what Georgina was saying and passed it straight on to me.'

'Oh.'

'Look, I don't want to air my family's dirty linen in public Ally as I believe some things should remain private, but Georgina has been warned she will be cut out of inheriting any of her father's estate if she doesn't mend her ways. I suspect that is why she acted so hostile towards you. I can only apologise for her bad behaviour.'

'Gertie, thank you. What you have just said means a lot to me and I appreciate you calling.'

'My dear, you are very welcome. Using the information that you have given me, I will start the ball rolling and, if all goes well, I will be able to get in touch with Oscar soon. Hopefully, your visit to Virginia won't have been in vain.'

Feeling appeased, she went down for dinner. She had made a real effort with her hair and had put on her nicest outfit for the hotel's special Thanksgiving evening and was feeling good. She was sleeping better too. There were no longer any dark circles under her eyes, and her skin seemed to be brighter. It wasn't only her sleep and skin which had improved, her hair was starting to get its shine back and was looking better than it had in a long while. Whether it was her giving up the booze and ditching her pills or her regime of healthy living, self-help podcasts and books that was doing the trick, she didn't know, but something obviously seemed to be working. Tomorrow she would ask Amy for more of the best places to go, but in the meantime, she would enjoy her turkey dinner and everything that went with it.

Taking off her makeup, she thought about the last few days that she had left in Virginia and was determined that she was going to make the most of it. She also wanted to do something very American before she went home, like go to see some Christmas lights and eat brightly coloured sugar cookies and frosted cinnamon buns, just like she'd seen in all the cheesy Hallmark Christmas movies that she watched every year. Maybe she would ask Amy about that too. As she lay her head down on her pillow and sleepily closed her eyes, she felt content and at peace with herself.

CHAPTER 22

'Thank you.' Ally tipped the cab driver who had brought her back to the hotel. As she entered the hotel lobby, she felt slightly sad that her stay in Virginia was now nearly over. Her holiday had flown by. She had had her doubts when she had first arrived but now had no regrets about coming here. She had found Frank's family and had some great memories and photographs to take home with her. Her flight back to the UK was booked but she had no idea how her life would pan out once she was back home. The one thing she did know, was that she was now feeling much stronger and more confident. Hopefully, she would now be in a better place to deal with anything that might happen.

As she headed for the elevator to take her up to her room, she felt fulfilled. The whole day had been completely brilliant and just what she had needed to celebrate her last hours here. She had visited an artisan market where she'd eaten a frosted cinnamon bun, delicious and still warm from the oven, and had treated herself to some gorgeous little wooden tree decorations for her first Christmas in the cottage. She had even found a stall selling the iced Christmas cookies that she'd been craving. Spoilt for choice, she had bought four, two for herself and two for Amy to say thank you. She knew that she wouldn't have been able to visit half of the wonderful places she'd been to if it hadn't been for Amy. Slipping them inside her bag, she was happy in the knowledge that she'd ticked another box on her wish list.

It hadn't ended there either, for as the night started to draw in, she had got a cab to a light festival, where she had wandered around, taking in the amazing light displays which had been strung along the paths and installed high in the trees. She had stood by a large lake and watched the lights from the submerged fountains as they continually morphed into every colour of the rainbow, reflecting magically onto the smooth water. Thanks to Amy's knowledge and guidance, she'd had a fantastic last day,

Pressing the button to summon the elevator, she felt optimistic. She had already been in touch with her agent, who although surprised to hear from her, had been supportive and happy that she was thinking about going back to work. There would be no more hiding away either. As far as she was concerned, Nick, wherever he was, could go and do one. She was determined to get her life back on track, not her old way of life though, that was well and truly over. With a pang of emotion, she thought of Joe and how selfish she'd been. She never wanted to be like that again. She was a different person now; lessons had been learnt. She had paid the price of fame and no longer wanted it. She was going to be positive and look to the future, albeit a different kind of future.

Today had been wonderfully busy. Feeling happy and content with all she had accomplished, she let herself into her hotel room. Flinging her bags onto the bed, she slipped off her coat and padded gilet and turned to hang them on the hook behind the door.

'Hello my darling. You took your time; I've been waiting for you.'

The voice, soft and sinister, was instantly recognisable and sent a chill running through her.

In a state of shock, she froze. She could feel her airways tightening like they were closing in.

She heard him snigger. He was obviously enjoying her reaction.

Summoning her inner strength, she spun around. Seeing the cruel smirk on Nick's face as he leaned nonchalantly against the entrance to her bathroom awoke something in her. A feeling of immense hatred instantly consumed her, turning her shock into anger. She opened her mouth to scream but nothing came out.

He laughed mockingly at her.

It made her blood boil. She went to run but he was too quick for her. Blocking her path, he grabbed hold of her. Clamping his hand firmly over her mouth, he dragged her over to the countertop, where using his free hand, he pulled out a chair and pushed her down into it.

Pulling a gun out of his trouser waistband, he bent down to her level, aiming the gun at her. 'Right, you hoity-toity bitch, make any kind of noise and you'll be in trouble.' As he went to pinch her cheek, she ducked her head. His breath was foul.

Turning to look at him, she asked. 'H-how d-id you g-get in my room?' It came out as a croak, for her mouth had suddenly become very dry. Her all-consuming fear of him finding her had been realised and she knew it was only her anger that was stopping her from passing out.

Looking pleased with himself, Nick pulled the hotel key card from his jacket pocket. He held it out in the palm of his hand for her to see. 'I got lucky. The receptionist was busy dealing with a large group queuing to check in. The other woman behind the desk hadn't a clue what she was doing. All I had to do was show her those flowers,' he pointed to the bunch of flowers that had been tossed into the bin, 'and say how much I wanted to surprise my darling girlfriend. The stupid woman fell for it hook line and sinker and gave me the key.'

She looked at the gloating, unkept man standing before her, and was shocked at how much he had changed. With a good few days of growth stubble, which mostly concealed the lower half of his pale face, her ex's wild eyes and greasy hair made him almost unrecognisable and far from the immaculate man she remembered. She stared at the clothes he was wearing, and it was then that the penny dropped. It had been Nick who had been following her the other night and not, as she had been led to believe, some local lost soul who went by the name of Stan.

She sat there, not daring to move, fully aware that the gun that was pointed straight at her might be loaded. Her worst nightmare had come true. As the implications of her dire situation began to sink in, she knew that she had no choice but to pull herself together. She had to think on her feet. It was sink or swim, there was no time for tears and hysterics. She took a deep breath. Willing herself to remain calm and not show any sign of weakness, she waited.

Nick laughed nastily. 'You are all over the US TV and media my darling, with your quest to find the family of some old guy from that boring Cornish backwater where you were hiding. I couldn't believe my luck when I saw you on the TV. You played right into my hands my sweet.' He gave a little snort. 'Like a lamb to the slaughter,' he added spitefully.

She tensed her body to stop it shaking. With her hands firmly clasped together, she placed them in her lap and continued to stare mutely down at her feet. Nick, however, had plenty to say. As he continued to speak, she vowed she would not allow herself to show any kind of emotion. No way would she give him the satisfaction of seeing how terrified she was.

'In case you were wondering my sweet, I didn't follow you over here. I was already in the States; had some outstanding business to settle. I've been hiding out a few miles from here.' A sardonic smile flitted across his face. 'I got in the country on a fake passport, it was a tad tricky though.' He smirked, showing his unbrushed teeth. 'I had to use a bit of ingenuity.' He looked down at her for some kind of reaction.

If Nick thought she was going to show him any admiration for his efforts, then he was very much mistaken. She didn't answer.

Not put off by her silence, he continued. 'I grew a bit of hair fuzz too so I wouldn't be recognised. By the way, do you like it?' He ran his hand over his chin.

He had a nerve. The man looked disgusting, and she felt sick just looking at him. Keeping her thoughts to herself, hoping he wouldn't pick up on her burning hatred, she looked up at him. 'Who have you been hiding from?'

He hesitated before replying. 'Questions, questions. You're a bit nosy, aren't you? If you must know, there's a price on my head from a rival gang because I shot one of them. 'I'm in heavy, very heavy. Another outfit was trying to muscle in on our business. One of them took a step too far and now, would you believe, the Feds are after me for homicide,' he chortled, obviously finding it funny.

Her stomach somersaulted. 'Are you telling me that you have killed someone?' She couldn't believe she was asking this of someone she had once shared her life with.

'Yes, my sweet. The guy got what he deserved. It was either him or me and I got there first.' He bent down and looked her full in the face. 'Be a good girl for me and you won't meet the same fate,' he said quietly, leering at her.

A wave of fear swept over her as she realised that the gun that he was pointing at her was probably loaded. It was highly likely that if he's already used it to kill someone, there was a real chance that, if riled, he would use it on her. It was patently obvious that Nick was off his head and dangerous. Her legs started to tremble. She pressed her knees firmly together and placed her fists on top to try to anchor them down. She had to be brave, there was no way she was going to show him any sign of fear.

'Nick, why?'

'It's all about the money, my sweet. I'm in deep. Sold my soul for the Bolivian white powder.' Moving in close, he gripped her by the chin. His spittle spraying her face as he spoke. 'Why did you leave me? Nobody dumps Nick Curtis and gets away with it. This is all your fault woman and I'm going to make you pay.'

Although seemingly unhinged, she recognised the pattern of narcissistic abuse that she had been familiar with and that he was still acting true to form by blaming her for everything. Realising that she was in imminent danger, she knew she had to quickly think of something. 'I'm

sorry Nick and very sad that it's come to this.'
Seeing him soften slightly, she took a chance. 'I still
have feelings for you Nick,' she lied, trying to
appease him.

He hesitated then lowered the gun slightly.

She could tell her lies had done the trick. His
ego was bolstered, for the time being at least.

It didn't last. Raising the gun again, he used
his other hand to reach over and tug her coat off the
hook. 'Here, put this on,' he growled, throwing the
coat at her.

She wrapped the coat loosely around her
shoulders like a cloak. With his fingers digging into
the back of her neck, she was then pushed towards
the door. Fully aware that under her coat his other
hand was pressing the gun into her back, she didn't
dare resist.

Glancing both ways to check there was no
one about, he pushed her down the corridor
towards the elevator. 'Call the blasted thing. Press
street level. We are going for a little ride.'

With a trembling hand, she summoned the
elevator. She could feel his sour breath on her
cheeks. The hard metal of the gun was cold and
digging into her back through her thin top. She
listened, hoping for the sound of another hotel
guest in the corridor so that, even though her
mouth was dry with fear, she could somehow
signal for help, but there was no one about. As he
pushed her into the elevator, there was no let up in
the pressure of the gun that he had pressed into her
back.

The elevator pinged. 'Ground floor,' the automated voice announced. Immediately the doors opened. He gave her a little shove. 'Walk and don't make a sound,' he hissed into her ear, before smiling lovingly at her, solely for the benefit of anyone who happened to be nearby. As he led her past the receptionist, who was busy at the check-in desk, it seemed that no one gave a second glance to the man with his arm around his girlfriend, but who was in fact, pressing a gun into her back under her coat. Pushing her through the swing doors, he ushered her around the back of the hotel to a deserted car park.

'Please let me go Nick, please don't hurt me.'

'You'll find out soon enough what I've got in mind,' he tittered. There was only one car in the car park, a battered old Ford. He pushed her towards it.

Unlocking the car door, he gave her a further shove. 'Get in.' When she didn't move, he pushed her forcefully down into the front passenger seat and slammed the car door. Climbing into the driver's side, he waved the gun at her. 'One peep out of you and I'll use this, and keep your feet off that hold-all,' he said, pointing to the canvas bag by her feet. She heard the click of the car doors being locked.

Petrified, she could tell he wasn't bluffing. Her ex seemed crazed as he drove recklessly down the highway, out of town, to goodness knows where. She watched through the window as the car whizzed past buildings, leaving the affluent town centre behind. Nick drove like a demon. The car sped down narrow and badly lit roads, passing boarded up buildings and shabby fronted shops. After a while, she heard a change in the engine. The car slowed down before it swerved into a large space between tall buildings. Looking out of the window, she could see he had pulled into the car park of a small seedy looking motel. The light filtering through the steamy windows of the adjoining diner threw dappled light across the unlit and pot-holed car park. All the windows in the flat-roofed, single storey block were unlit, the rooms seemingly unoccupied.

'Get out the car. Any squawking and I'll use this.' He held the gun close to her face, while his other hand reached for the hold-all.

'Room 5,' he growled, pushing her towards the row of shabby painted doors. Fumbling around, he produced an old-fashioned brass door key from his shirt pocket and inserted it into the lock. After kicking the door open, he roughly pushed her into the motel room. He switched on the light. 'Not quite as nice as our London flat is it, but it will do for my needs.' He made a show of locking the door behind him, slipping the key back into his shirt pocket.

She didn't know what to do. A feeling of despair swept over her on the realisation that she was now locked inside this awful room and held captive by her crazed and gun-toting violent ex.

CHAPTER 23

Terrified and with a strong sense of foreboding, she stood there. Everything was racing through her mind. Would this awful motel room be the last place she ever saw? Would she ever get to see those she loved ever again?

'Welcome to my humble abode, my sweet.' Nick's voice was creepily silky with a menacing undertone.

Humble or not, the room was revolting. Nick was obviously oblivious to the mess. The stench of body odour, stale beer, cigarette smoke and take-out food was overpowering. She could feel her shoes sticking to the tacky surface of the worn carpet. A grey metal framed bed took up most of the room and was facing towards the door. She stared at the unmade bed. A soiled bottom sheet trailed on the carpet, leaving the sagging and stained mattress top exposed. It looked as though the room hadn't been cleaned for a very long time, for the countertop was littered with empty takeaway food containers, whisky bottles, cigarette butts and what she guessed to be drug paraphernalia.

He smirked seeing her reaction. 'Not quite what you are used to is it?'

Ignoring his taunts, she decided to play for time. 'Nick, I need to use the toilet.'

'Go on then. Leave the door open so I can see you. I don't want you escaping until I've done with you.'

His words sent alarm bells ringing in her head as she realised, although quietly said, they had been loaded with innuendo. Pretending to use the toilet, she lifted the lid. The smell coming up from the filthy toilet bowl made her heave. Holding her breath, she quickly put the lid down. Telling herself to calm down and think rationally, she looked around the bathroom for a window to enable her to escape. There was none. With a sinking feeling, she knew that she had no choice but to go back into that disgusting room and face whatever she had coming.

He patted the gun that was tucked into his trouser waistband. 'Just do as you are told, and I won't have to use this.' Bending down, he picked up the hold-all that he'd carried in from the car. After rummaging through it, he pulled out some handcuffs and a bottle of whisky. Turning the hold-all around, he unzipped one of the end pockets and produced a clear plastic bag of white powder. 'Getting the picture now are we, my precious? His voice hardened. 'Get down on the bed, it's payback time, my sweet.'

She stood firm. Hell would have to freeze over before she would get anywhere near that bed.

Realising that she wasn't going to move, his face darkened. He raised his arm as if he was going to hit her. 'Do as I say and get down on the bed, or I'll knock six bells out of you, you sanctimonious has-been.'

Knowing she would rather die than be mauled by him, she was even more determined to stay put.

'You are being a tad stubborn, aren't you my sweet,' he said silkily. In a flash, and catching her unawares, he raised his arms. Using both hands he forcefully pushed her down onto the bed. 'Think you are so smart don't you,' he sneered, as he yanked her arms above her head and shackled her to the bed using the handcuffs. 'There is no point in wasting your energy yelling either, my sweet. There is no one about, only us.' He stopped what he was doing and looked down at her. 'This place is just perfect for what I want it for,' he murmured.

Quietly sobbing, she lay there helpless and unable to move, the tears rolling off her face, soaking into the stained pillow beneath her head. She watched through tear-filled eyes as he opened the whisky, and after downing most of the bottle, began sniffing up the white powder. How had it come to this? She was finding it so hard to take in how low her ex had sunk.

Unsteady on his feet, he unzipped his trousers and approached her.

Just when she thought her fate was sealed, she saw him put his hands up to his stomach. His face, which was pouring with sweat, had turned a deathly white. His body swaying, he stared unseeingly at her. Suddenly, his eyes began to roll. Stumbling, he grabbed hold of the end of the bed. Then placing his hands on the side of the bed for support, he slowly inched his way along the mattress to the other side of the bed, where he collapsed. His whole body appeared to be jerking. It looked like he was having a seizure. After a while the convulsions stopped. Somehow or other he had managed to roll onto his side and was facing away from her. The room was silent.

Unable to see his face, she lay there listening for any sign of life coming from him. What if he died next to her in this stinking and isolated room? Would anyone hear her if she shouted for help? She knew she had to try.

'Help. Help.' She repeatedly shouted at the top of her voice. No one came.

She couldn't hear him breathing and she began to wonder if he was unconscious. She pushed away the thought that there might be a dead body on the bed next to her.

Then, as if in answer to her fear, he coughed and started to move.

She side kicked him to get a response. 'Nick, Nick,' and was rewarded with a grunt. At least he was still alive.

Slowly, he began to come around. After a while he eased himself up off the bed. Lurching towards the bathroom, he looked back at her, and spat, 'later, you stuck up bitch.'

She could hear him being violently sick. Shutting her eyes, she turned her head away, wishing she could cover her ears. Later, not saying a word to her, he walked unsteadily back to the bed. A few minutes later he began snoring like a warthog. Shackled to the bedframe, she lay there wondering how this would end. Was this day going to be her last? She heard him gag and could tell by the smell that he had vomited again, this time into his pillow while asleep. At least if he was asleep, he was leaving her alone. The thought that he hadn't touched her was her only comfort.

It was a long night. As she lay there listening to his snoring, her arms had gone past the aching stage and now felt dead from being held above her head. She had no bed cover over her and although still clothed, her body felt cold.

Through the thin curtains she watched the dawn break. She had been handcuffed to the bed all through the night and was busting for the loo. Her hair smelt of his vomit. The room stank of it. It wasn't just her hair either, she was sure her clothes had also picked up his body odour. She had a headache from hell and her mouth felt dry.

Running her tongue along her teeth, she wasn't at all surprised that they were starting to feel mossy. She turned her head sideways; he was still lying next to her, but thankfully, facing away from her. He was clearly still in a bad way, and she had to use it to her advantage. 'Nick, I need to use the toilet.'

There was no response.

Arching her back, she raised her bottom up from the mattress as far as she could, then let it fall again. She did it several times, in the hope that it would stir him. Eventually he responded.

'What?' he answered groggily.

'The toilet, I need the toilet.'

With a groan and still looking like death warmed up, he slowly got up off the bed and stumbled across the room to get the keys to the cuffs to set her free. 'Hurry up.'

Once set free, she tried to flex her arms and found that she could hardly move them. The pain was excruciating, but there was no time to waste, she had to think on her feet.

She glanced over to the bed where, breathing heavily, Nick, having gone back to bed, lay curled up in a foetal-like position. By the sound of him he was still sleeping off the drugs and alcohol he'd consumed. She said a silent prayer, desperately hoping that he remained so out of it that he would leave her alone.

Tiptoeing across the room, she tried the door handle. She cursed under her breath, remembering he had locked the door. She tried the window; it too was locked.

Where was the door key? She picked up Nick's discarded trousers and searched the pockets but found nothing. Then she remembered, he had slipped the key into his shirt pocket. She wondered if she could roll him over onto his back, but as she approached him, he snorted loudly then started to stir. He was waking up. There was no way she could get at the key now. Even the gun was under his pillow. Thinking what to do, she had a change of plan. She would have to be nice to him, no matter how gut wrenchingly difficult. After all, she was an actress, and a good one too, so put on an act worthy of a BAFTA and get yourself out of captivity and out of this vile room, said the voice in her head.

There was no way he was going to get her on that bed again. Biding her time, she waited until he had fully woken up. She spoke softly. 'Nick, how about we get out of here and go for something to eat?'

He grunted.

'I thought I saw a little diner right next door,' she added hopefully.

'I suppose so. I've not eaten for a while, but any sign of the Feds and I'm gone,' he snapped, adding 'and I'll be taking you with me,' he tapped the gun now tucked back into his waistband.

The diner was empty. They found a table in the far corner. Nick studied the menu. 'I'll have ham, eggs, hash browns and a flat white.'

She pretended to look at the menu, all the while planning her next move. 'I'll have the same as you. It looks like we need to order our food at the counter. I'll go and do it.'

Nodding slightly, he looked her square in the eye. His pupils were like dots. 'If I get any funny business from you, I won't hesitate to use this.' As he patted the gun, sweat was running down his face and he seemed fidgety.

She could feel him watching her every move as she got up to order their food. He obviously wasn't of sound mind, if he was, she was certain that he wouldn't have let her leave the table. She was sure that he was still drunk and high on the drugs that he'd taken.

'Good morning ma-am, can we tempt you with some freshly made coffee and pancakes?' The young woman behind the counter, studied her face. 'Are you the lady from the UK, the nurse actress that's been on the TV looking for someone?'

'Yes,' she whispered. 'Please, please help me. I'm in danger,' her voice was almost drowned out by the sound of "All I Want for Christmas" blasting out over the radio. 'The guy with the beard, over at the corner table has a gun and is wanted by the Feds or something. He's abducted me. Can you call the police? The guy's name is Nick Curtis and he's also wanted by the UK police. He's extremely dangerous and unstable. He told me he's killed someone, and he's threatened me with his gun. Please, p-lease call the police straight away.' Then in a louder voice she ordered the food.

Returning to the table, she pulled out a chair and sat back down directly across from her ex.

'Food will be around twenty minutes Nick, but they will bring the coffee over in a minute.'

'They'd better hurry up or we're out of here,' he snarled. 'This bloody Christmas music is getting on my nerves; it's absolute crap.'

She noticed Nick's body shaking. As she sat there trying to drum up small talk, the shaking seemed to be getting worse and it was becoming increasingly harder to get any kind of a conversation out of him. Deciding to sit it out, she prayed that the lady behind the counter had already called for help.

The waitress came over and put their plates of food down in front of them without saying a word, then beat a hasty retreat.

Although it had been many hours since she had last eaten, she had no appetite for the food in front of her. She made a show of eating by moving the food around her plate and occasionally putting a tiny amount in her mouth. Nick on the other hand, was shoving his food into his mouth like there was no tomorrow and was completely oblivious to anything she was doing. Glancing across the table at the man she had stupidly left Joe for, she felt sickened at the sight of this dangerous and unstable person with egg yolk dribbling down his chin. How could she have left Joe for this man?

The door opened, and she saw two men wearing hoodies enter the diner. After placing their orders, they sat down at a nearby table. One of them was busily tapping away on his phone while the other one was keeping a sharp eye on Nick.

Belching loudly, Nick briefly looked up from his plate. Instantly his face twisted and paled in anger. 'Damn it,' he growled, glaring at the two men. Within seconds, he had thrown down his knife and fork and leapt up on to his feet. Reaching for his gun, he shakily pointed it at the two men and fired. But he was too slow, one of them opened fire first.

She watched in horror as Nick fell backwards, slumping over the seat where he'd been sitting. Screaming, she dived under the table. What happened next, she could only hear, but it sounded like there were multiple police sirens outside.

The next instant, the door of the diner was flung open, and the room was filled with the sound of pounding feet and low voices. One distinctive voice shouted out. 'Police. Drop your weapons and get face down on the floor NOW.'

Crouched down low and hidden from view, she could hear scuffling. Hardly daring to breathe, she peeped through the legs of the table. All she could see were the bodies of the two men in hoodies being forced down onto the floor. She watched two police officers bend down and handcuff the men before hauling them back up on their feet. Too scared to move, she saw the two men being led outside.

Still hiding under the table, she didn't know what to do.

'It's okay to come out now ma-am.' A uniformed police officer was peering under the table at her.

On all fours, she scrambled out. Gripping the edge of the table for support, she stood up, her legs wobbling like jelly.

'Here, sit down.' Another woman pulled a chair out. The woman opened her jacket, underneath she wore a black padded vest. The woman flashed her badge. 'FBI. We've been looking for these guys for quite a while. Are you alright? I take it you are the person who told the diner to call it in?'

'Y-yes, I am,' she stuttered, shaking like a leaf.

'We'll need to get a statement from you. We've been running checks and I believe you have raised a case with the UK police about him?' The FBI agent pointed to Nick who was slumped over with a bullet to his chest.

'Yes, he has been seriously harassing me back home and now, with a gun against my back, he has forcefully taken me from my hotel room, and held me captive in that place.' Sobbing, she pointed in the direction of the motel.

If the FBI agent was shocked by what Ally had just told her, she didn't show it. Instead, she said 'I think we need to get you checked out by a medic. We know why you are in the US; the local media has been buzzing with it. I guess they will have even more to buzz about after this,' she added wryly. 'When are you due to fly back to the UK?'

'Tomorrow night.' She looked over at Nick's slumped body. 'I-is h-he -d-dead?'

'Afraid so ma-am. We will need you to answer a few questions.'

She suddenly felt incredibly sick and light-headed and could feel herself slipping off the chair. She was caught just in time by the FBI agent.

'Call for the medics, she needs checking out.' The agent patted her around the cheeks attempting to keep her conscious. 'Someone, quickly bring her a glass of water.'

CHAPTER 24

Ally nervously waited to be interviewed. Being in a police station back home was bad enough, but this place was in another league. Glancing around her, she felt a sense of unease, for sitting alongside of her were people with obvious issues. All sorts of thoughts were swirling around in her head. What if they thought she was in cahoots with Nick and arrested her? Would she be left to languish in a US jail? The implications of it all were just too awful to contemplate. She tugged at the neck of her top, was it just her or was it hot in here? Finally, she heard her name being called. She followed the uniformed officer down a narrow corridor, preparing herself for the worst.

'Sit down,' the stony-faced officer said curtly, pointing to a table with two chairs one side and a single chair the other. She did as she was told and, once she was seated, the officer left the room.

She glanced around her. The small room had no natural light and felt airless. The walls, a dull beige, were completely bare. An internal window took up most of the far wall, but this appeared to be blacked out. Inhaling deeply, she hoped her self-help exercises would help her stem the anxiety that she could feel building inside her.

The door opened and she recognised the FBI agent who had spoken to her at the diner.

'Just a few questions Ally,' she said abruptly. 'This should not take long if you co-operate with us.' The agent began flicking through her notes. 'How long have you known Nick Curtis?' Her tone was matter of fact and far from friendly.

Ally explained how she had met Nick and how they had moved in together.

'You say that you didn't have any knowledge of Curtis's activities? Did you not meet any of his acquaintances? Did you not wonder where he was when he wasn't at home?' The agent barked out her questions.

'I was on set, working all hours on the tv show. Towards the end of our relationship Nick and I hardly saw each other, which as far as I was concerned, was a good thing. He spent a lot of time away. I have no idea where he went to, I was too frightened to ask. My work schedule was so hectic that I didn't have time to dwell on it. As far as I am aware, he didn't bring any friends or acquaintances to the flat. I never met any of them. I only socialised with people involved with the production company. All I know is that when Nick did come home, he was often extremely aggressive and violent towards me. I was never able to trust him, and he would turn very nasty if I challenged him in any way. I'm sorry, I know I sound a bit naive, but I had no idea of Nick's criminal activities until I had already left London, and then, it was only when he tracked me down and started vindictively harassing me and I filed a complaint against him, that the police told me that he was a person of interest to them and under investigation. Before then I had no idea.'

After what seemed like hours of questioning, the FBI agent seemed to become less hostile. She told Ally that they had interviewed the hotel staff, including the trainee receptionist who had handed Nick the key to her room. Apparently, it had been the trainee's first day on duty. Luckily, warning bells had been set off after the trainee had noticed Nick's unkept appearance and Ally's unhappy face and body language as she was being ushered off the premises by Nick. Knowing she'd done wrong and regretting her lapse of judgement, the trainee had quickly told the duty receptionist what she had done. The receptionist had immediately alerted the police.

As she stepped out into the fresh air, she breathed a sigh of relief. It had been hard going, but she knew she had told the truth and was reasonably sure the agent had believed her and was satisfied that she was not Nick's accomplice or involved in his criminal activities in any way. The agent had also mentioned that, although they knew Nick was in the area, they hadn't known exactly where he was. It wasn't until they had received the information from the member of staff at the diner, they had known Nick's whereabouts. Getting this information had enabled them to act quickly. The agent had praised her quick thinking, which had helped them apprehend two high profile and dangerous members of a crime syndicate.

After agreeing to let her go, the agent had stipulated that it was on the condition that she reported to the UK police once back home, something she was only too happy to do.

It was early evening by the time she was able to return to her hotel. She had been gripped by panic the minute she'd stepped into the elevator, and by the time she had reached the door to her room, her hands and knees were trembling like they had a life of their own. She took a deep breath. Why did Nick have to ruin everything, things had been going so well since coming here. Fishing frantically around in her coat pocket for her room key, she swore softly. Where was the blasted thing? She had to calm down. She had been feeling so content and festive the last time she had entered this room. That was before she had found Nick in there, waiting to waylay her. After that her contentment had shattered like a fragile glass bauble.

Her chest felt tight, and she was finding it hard to get her breath. She realised that she must be having a panic attack. Leaning against the wall outside her room, she willed herself to do slow breathing on repeat until the feeling passed. She had to accept that she was still in shock and coming to terms with what had happened, and that it would probably take her a long time to get over it.

With her breathing under control, and key found, she stood in the doorway to her room. As she glanced around, she was sure she could still smell Nick. Would she ever be able to forget the smell of him? Looking across at her bed, she realised that she didn't even want to sit down on it, let alone sleep in it. This room held such traumatic memories, and she knew that she would never again be completely at ease here.

Tentatively stepping inside the room, she reached for the light switch. She nervously looked around, then cautiously checked the bathroom, half expecting an intruder to be hiding in there. She wanted it to be alright, she really did, but suddenly it was all too much for her. She had a sudden flashback of Nick leaning against the bathroom door. Feeling the anxiety increasing and starting to take hold of her, she knew she had to get out. The voice of reason told her to get a grip. Nick was dead, gone, zilch and could no longer hurt her, but it was overridden by her fear.

Overwhelmed with panic, she ran out the room, down several flights of stairs to the reception. There was no way she could face using the elevator. The memory of Nick pushing her into it with a gun pressed into her back felt real.

'Are you alright Ally?' The receptionist looked concerned at the agitated and breathless woman looking at her from the other side of the desk.

'P-please, can you find me another room, just for tonight. I can't sleep in there. I can't deal with the elevator either. I'm sorry,' she added, feeling ashamed of her weakness.

'No worries, I completely understand. Let's see what I can find you.' The receptionist tapped away on her keyboard, then after a few seconds, looked up at Ally smiling. 'How about Suite 22? It's at the back of the hotel and overlooks the garden. It's on the ground floor too, so you won't need to go anywhere near the elevator. The suite is one of our best and is very comfortable.'

'Thank you.'

The receptionist handed Ally a key. 'I'll get someone to move all your belongings to your new room, so there will be no need to go back inside the old one.' She gave Ally a voucher. 'Here, take this. Go and get yourself something to eat and drink on us while we sort it all out.'

As she sat down on the beautifully dressed bed in her new room, she wished she was in a better place to appreciate the luxurious suite that she'd been given.

With her emotions all over the place, she still couldn't take in all what had happened and couldn't process the fact that Nick was no longer around to hurt her. The medics, after checking her out, had prescribed something to calm her down. She hadn't wanted to take it, but her nerves were so shot, she knew she had no choice. One minute she felt relief that Nick was dead, the next disbelief that he had finally gone. Then there was the trauma; the terror of being held at gunpoint and the revulsion she had felt when Nick had pushed her down onto the stinking motel bed. Then for some reason, which she couldn't explain, she had felt sorry for the man that Nick had become, his descent into drugs and crime, and how his life had ended. What was that all about? The man was a narcissistic bully who had made her life hell. Then there were the periods when she couldn't remember things, when her brain appeared to be shutting her out. What was the matter with her?

Despite being given a makeshift change of clothes and being allowed to shower and wash her hair at the police station, she decided a long soak in the bathtub might help her. If nothing else, it would help her get rid of the smell of Nick. Turning the bath taps on full, she tipped in a whole mini bottle of the hotel's high-end bath essence and sat on the edge of the bath watching the bubbles form. She might not sleep, but she would certainly smell good.

Although dog-tired through not having slept the night before, as she pulled back the bed cover, she doubted whether she would be able to sleep tonight either, even in this luxurious room which had its own comfortable lounge area with a sumptuous sofa. Emotionally drained and her nerves ragged, she absently plumped up the soft pillows. Desperately wanting to stop the appalling mind-traffic that was constantly running through her head, she searched for something positive to think about. The first thing that sprang to mind was the little village she now called home. Home, she felt a rush of affection for her home county. It felt a million miles away, and right now, she longed to be there.

She checked the clock on the tv panel for the umpteenth time; it was nearly midnight. Determined to concentrate on regulating her breathing, she closed her eyes, hoping she could stem the overwhelming tide of panic, which no matter how hard she tried, still broke through, taking control of her mind. Knowing she had to try harder to chase away the demons, she took a deep breath and willed herself to ditch any negative thoughts. She would dream she was back home, out in the fresh air, walking along the grassy clifftops and the wind rippling the waves as she looked down on the turquoise waters of the little coves below. Her thoughts drifted back to her younger years when she and the others had stood on their small sand and pebble beach watching Joe and Marco launch their little sailing boats into the frothy water and how happy they had all been.

Hot and sweaty, she tossed and turned. Kicking the duvet off to cool down, she lay there. Despite her best efforts, she had not managed to stop the horror of the recent events cutting in on her thoughts. After a few hours of watching the hours passing on the clock, she got out of bed, made

herself a coffee, wondering if she would ever be the
same again.

CHAPTER 25

She felt drained and devoid of any kind of emotion as she boarded the plane at JFK for her flight back to the UK.

Settling into her seat, she lay her head against the padded headrest and closed her eyes. The seats next to her were empty, something she was very grateful for. The last thing she wanted to do was make polite conversation with a stranger. She was still finding it hard to process everything. Whenever a painful memory surfaced, she had tried to push it aside. Sometimes it worked, sometimes it didn't. Her memory was selective. One minute it was blank, then out of the blue came the horrendous flashbacks. They came without warning, each one playing in her head like a bad movie - the heart stopping moment she discovered Nick hiding in her hotel room; the fear and revulsion she had felt at the seedy motel; the horror of the guns being fired in the diner, resulting in Nick's dead body slumped over the chair. Each episode had been replayed as vivid as the time it had happened and had ended in a panic attack so severe that she had found it hard to get her breath and which required all the willpower and determination she could muster to calm it.

The cabin crew had dimmed the lights. All was quiet. She felt almost jealous that most of her fellow passengers appeared to be blessed with sleep. She badly wanted to drift off too, but it just wasn't happening. She focused instead on the sanctuary of the cottage, where she would wrap herself up in her comfy fleecy blanket and lay her head down on the deep sofa cushions without the fear of Nick. She longed to be home, and hoped that once there, she would be able to release some of the trauma she was trying to blank out without anyone looking on or judging her. The medics had offered her counselling, but she had turned it down. All she had wanted was to be left alone. Maybe she should arrange for some when she got home, but there was no rush, she'd see how it went. She closed her eyes and hoped that the drone of the plane would eventually lull her into sleep.

When the plane landed, she felt anything but refreshed. As she waited for her luggage, she knew that she was in no fit state to undertake the long drive back to Cornwall. The one thing she needed to do before getting behind the wheel of her car was to get some proper sleep. She decided to book a room at a budget hotel, but first she needed a nice cup of proper English breakfast tea and a bacon sandwich. She headed over to one of the many food outlets dotted around the terminal. Once she'd had some food inside her, she would use her phone to check on-line for a hotel room.

Getting lucky with the last available room, she drove to the nearby no-frills hotel where she could hopefully get some sleep. The check-in went without a hitch, and clutching her room key, she wheeled her luggage down the long, carpeted corridor to her room. After placing her suitcase on the rack at the end of the bed, she looked around the room. It was basic but clean, just what she needed. She was just about climb into bed when she remembered that she hadn't phoned her mother. Picking up her phone she rang her mother's number. 'Hi Mum, I've just landed but have booked a hotel so I can get some sleep before the long drive home.'

'Good to hear from you Allegra and so relieved you have sensibly booked a room to get some rest. The weather here is awful, blizzard conditions, so please be careful and keep us posted on your journey. Have a safe journey love. Your dad and I are really looking forward to seeing you soon. I have some news to tell you, but it will keep until you get here.'

She wondered what her mother's news was but felt too weary to question her. 'Thanks Mum; don't worry I'll stay in touch. See you when I get home. I love you Mum, and Dad too.'

Unlocking her suitcase, she pulled out her wash bag and some fresh clothing to wear for her drive home, then peeled back the covers and climbed in between the cool bedsheets and slept like a log.

On waking, reaching for her phone, she checked the time and realised that she had been asleep for more than a few hours. Relieved that she was feeling a lot better, she had a quick shower to freshen up. On leaving the hotel, she was quite surprised to see that it had been snowing here too and that her car was coated in a thin white layer. After brushing off the soft snow from her windscreen, mirrors, and windows, she climbed into her car and turned on the ignition, relieved that it had started first time.

Knowing that she had a long drive ahead of her, she resolved to concentrate fully on the road and firmly pushed away any negative and panic inducing thoughts that entered her head. She needed to think of only the positive things in her life and not dwell on the past. Leaning forward, she switched on the car radio, some bouncy pop music would help.

As she drove along the M25, she was relieved that the snow was turning to sleet. She was feeling quite upbeat, almost like she had turned a corner. Maybe it was finally sinking in that Nick could no longer hurt her, and she could now start to enjoy her new life with no fear. It would be a fresh start.

She was so looking forward to seeing everyone again. What was the news her mother had mysteriously mentioned? She would find out after she'd given her both her parents a huge hug. She couldn't wait to have a relaxing coffee and chat with Kat and a good old natter and laugh with Millie. Then there was Ash's new baby. By all accounts, Ashna was loving being a mum to her gorgeous baby son. She had bought him a little US baseball team sleepsuit while in New York and couldn't wait to see him in it.

Oscar's photo and letters had been carefully packed in her suitcase and would be safely returned to him once she'd unpacked. She thought about her little cottage, she missed it, and for goodness sakes, she had even missed old Edna and her collection of stray animals next door, which is more than she could say about Edna's obnoxious son Darren, she thought wryly. Darren, who thought he was god's gift to women, which he certainly wasn't, obviously thought he was in with a chance with her. He had become a bit of a pest, for even while she was in America, he had phoned her. She had foolishly given her number to him in case his mother needed anything, something she now regretted, because she found out afterwards that he only turned up to visit his mother when he wanted something. The only reason she hadn't blocked him was because of Edna.

Deciding to avoid the small roads, she kept to the motorway which she hoped would be safer. After she'd been driving for a couple of hours, she could feel her stomach rumbling. She needed food and would pull into the next available services to buy a coffee and something to eat. Back in her car she nibbled on her warm pain au chocolate and sipped from the large full-fat latte she'd bought and hoped all the carbs would make her stomach feel better. Although it was a motorway, the journey was proving slow and quite treacherous. The weather seemed to be worsening the further west she drove, and she had already passed several stranded vehicles. With her eyes firmly on the road ahead, she tried hard to keep a good distance from the car in front.

Having stopped a few times for a break, she was finally on the last leg of her journey. She had now left the motorway and was driving along the more familiar Cornish A-roads.

When her mother had said the weather was awful, she hadn't been joking. Would it ever stop snowing? People often said that it was rare to get snow like this here in Cornwall. Cornwall had its own microclimate they boasted. Well, they were wrong! Even though the traffic was slow, her windscreen wipers were still not strong enough to clear away the driving snow which was pounding against her windscreen. The last thing she saw was a long, articulated lorry jack-knife and swerve in front of her, then it all went black.

Back in Truro, Joe looked out of the Police HQ window at the snow steadily falling, it was looking to be a whiteout. His phone pinged. His heart leapt when he saw it was a message from Ally's mother. True to her word, she had let him know that Ally had landed back in the UK. Although it hadn't been, it seemed a long time ago when she'd told him that Ally had left for America. He'd been counting the days ever since because he really wanted to talk to her and get what he was feeling off his chest, lay his cards on the table so to speak. She would probably knock him back, but it was a chance he had to take.

He heard the door open; it was his boss. 'Joe, we've had an update on that case, the one you passed on because you knew the woman. An old flame of yours, wasn't she?'

'Yes, she was, but a good few years ago. I hope that you're going to tell me they have put the obnoxious creep behind bars Guv.'

His boss nodded. 'Er, not quite, but he won't be giving her any more trouble. He was shot by a rival gang in the United States, it was fatal. I'm afraid your ex-girlfriend was there when it happened.'

'What! You mean he was in America all the time? What about Ally? Please tell me she's not been hurt?' Joe said hoarsely, his stomach somersaulting.

'Come into my office son, you look a bit shaken. Sit down and I'll tell you what I know.'

Joe followed his Inspector into the glass partitioned office. 'Shut the door Joe and take a seat. Now then, it looks like your ex has been through the mill a bit. It appears that the guy who was harassing her, I forget his name now, let me check.' The Inspector quickly leafed through his notes before continuing, 'Nick Curtis. According to the US police, he was on their watch list, him being a major player in organised crime and heavily into the drugs trade. Curtis had somehow found out where your ex was staying and conned his way into her hotel room, where, by all accounts, he held her at gunpoint before dragging her off to some seedy motel. Apparently, it was due to your ex's quick thinking that the US police were alerted. They arrived on the scene just in time to see Curtis get shot. They've got the perpetrators in custody, and, as far as I know your ex wasn't hurt.'

The colour drained from Joe's face. 'Oh my god, poor Ally. She had previously lived with the guy too. I hope they didn't think she was involved in any of his activities Guv.'

'No, as far as I am aware, her slate is clean. She was also one of the people who turned him in, although the FBI had been tailing him. Your Ally's tip-off certainly helped them to get on the scene a bit quicker.'

Joe couldn't get what had happened to Ally out of his head. He would go and see her as soon as he knew she was home to offer her some support. Knowing what she'd been through, it would be better to keep his feelings for her to himself for the time being though. Ally had enough on her plate without him declaring his undying love. It was later as he sat at his desk catching up on his crime reports that he saw a major incident alert flash up on his workstation. There had been a nasty RTA. Looked like a five-vehicle pile-up, a lorry had jack-knifed in the poor weather conditions. Joe shook his head, that's some poor sod's Christmas ruined. He hoped there were no fatalities. It was treacherous out there on the roads, even with the grit spreader lorries out doing their stuff.

That evening, he got a phone call he didn't expect. It was from Ally's mother; she was in bits. Ally had been badly hurt in a road traffic accident caused by a lorry jack-knifing. The police had phoned her, having retrieved her number from the contacts on Ally's phone, which they had found on the floor of her wrecked car. Ally had been taken to hospital.

CHAPTER 26

She was only slightly aware of the blue flashing lights, the sound of sirens, and the grinding and drilling of the equipment being used to free her from the wreckage of her car. She vaguely remembered someone speaking to her before being lifted onto what felt like a rigid board with straps being fastened tight across her body. She also remembered blocks being placed both sides of her head. Drifting in and out of consciousness, she realised they must have given her something to numb the pain, because she now couldn't feel a thing, not even her legs. A woman in a green uniform kept leaning over her telling her to stay awake. She felt a jolt as the vehicle suddenly braked after which she heard someone curse. Someone was talking about the treacherous road conditions. Above the sound of the voices, she could hear a siren. Was the siren for her? She slipped into unconsciousness.

Sometimes she could hear voices and sometimes not. Try as she might, she could not open her eyes. She could hear machines bleeping around her and was aware there was often someone next to her holding her hand and talking to her in a soft caring voice. The voices, there were more than one, were always kind. She knew the voices loved her because they kept telling her so. There was one voice, a male one, that seemed to be cutting through all the mind fog, a voice that was, for just a moment, vaguely familiar. Maybe she was dreaming. She wanted to let the voices know she was hearing them, and that she loved them too, but no matter how hard she tried, she just couldn't do it.

Day and night morphed into one. She could hear the voices around her talking about Christmas. Suddenly, in a moment of clarity, as well as the voices, she could hear music playing; it was always the same song. She loved that song, but she needed to sleep, the music faded. She realised it was her parents' voices she could hear; they were talking to the voice she couldn't place. She wanted to open her eyes but couldn't. She heard the nurses around her bed, talking about her as if she wasn't there. Why couldn't she open her eyes?

'Ally, can you hear me?' the voice said again, there was only one voice this time. 'Ally, it's Joe. Please wake up. I've never ever stopped loving you. Wake up my darling, please wake up.'

The voice was gentle and close to her ear. It was her Joe.

Joe thought he was imagining it when he felt Ally's fingers softly grip his. He leaned over and pressed the buzzer.

A duty nurse ran into the room. 'What's wrong?' The nurse anxiously went over to check Ally's monitor.

'I'm sure I just felt her fingers move.' Joe studied Ally's face and saw a slight flicker. 'I swear her eyelids just moved,' he said excitedly, gently squeezing Ally's hand. 'Come on Al, you can do it.'

The nurse took over, almost pushing Joe out of the way. Ally's hand moved again. The nurse beamed. 'I think she's coming around. I think playing her favourite song over and over and you constantly talking to her may have done the trick.'

She sat up in bed sipping a cup of tea that one of the nursing assistants had brought her. She had just had an emotional visit from her parents. Her mother had cried, and even her father's eyes had moistened, something he would never admit to.

Things were starting to come back to her. Her mother seemed really pleased that Joe had been there while she was regaining consciousness. Joe had told her mother that he was coming back to see her after his shift later. Her mother had obviously been keeping in touch with him. She wondered if she had dreamt what Joe had said while she had been drifting in and out of consciousness. Was it wishful thinking on her part? Besides, hadn't Kat said that Joe had a girlfriend who he was living with? It must be over ten years since she'd walked out on Joe to be with Nick, and she wondered what Joe looked like now. He had been so good looking back in the day. At senior school he always seemed to have loads of girls after him, he could have taken his pick, but instead he had remained loyal to her. Feeling herself getting emotional, she told herself not to be silly. To have Joe back as a friend had to be enough.

It was evening visiting time. She surreptitiously checked out every male visitor coming onto the ward, hoping one of them would be Joe. Would she even recognise him now? Half of her was looking forward to seeing him, the other half was feeling nervous. She was just about to give up when he came in holding a little teddy bear and a box of chocolates.

'Hi Ally.'

She looked at the tall handsome guy standing before her. Joe's wide grin hadn't changed. His face had filled out slightly, but it suited him. He had the same healthy glow about him that he had before moving to London. Her heart leapt. Joe was still gorgeous. She wiped her clammy palms on the bedsheet. Her mouth had gone dry. She managed a smile, while telling herself to hold it together.

'Joe…'

Joe, sensing her embarrassment, quickly presented her with the teddy and chocolates. 'Hey, it's so good to see you sitting up, last time I was here you were out for the count.'

She smiled. 'I could hear people talking, I think it was hearing voices that brought me round, and the song on repeat.'

He looked embarrassed. 'You heard all that?'

'Yes, it was lovely,' she said, her voice barely above a whisper.

'Glad all my efforts paid off then,' he said jokily.

For a moment there was silence.

'I'm so sorry Joe.'

He didn't answer. Instead, he studied her face for a moment. Then, dragging a chair over, he sat down next to the bed and took her hand gently in his. 'Still friends, right?' he asked softly.

She nodded, her eyes glistening.

CHAPTER 27

Joe had been a frequent visitor to the hospital, coming in to see her whenever his shifts had allowed. The little teddy bear, which hadn't left her bedside cabinet, had become her most prized possession. The doctor had told her she had been extremely lucky and had got off lightly. She was so relieved that she had the feeling in her legs back. She'd been told that she would only need some physio to get her walking again.

The daily trips down the corridor to Physiotherapy were pushing her to the limit, but she hadn't minded. She had obeyed their instructions to the letter, so keen was she to get back on her feet again. Each day there had been a marked improvement.

It was almost Christmas and there was an air of jollity on the ward. A twinkling Christmas tree had appeared behind the Nurses' Station and the staff had decorated the food and medication trolleys with tinsel. There were also mince pies on offer with the afternoon cup of tea to those patients who were allowed to have them. There had been a visit from a local school choir, who had sung carols, which she noticed had brought tears to the eyes of a couple of the more elderly patients on the ward.

The severity of her injuries had made her realise the importance of the present and how lucky she was to be alive. There had been a few panic-attacks, but the hospital staff had been on it straight away and had given her some useful tips on how to deal with them. Her sole aim was to be positive and not to dwell on the bad things that had happened, which at times seemed impossible, but was something she strived to overcome. She had mostly come to terms with what had happened to Nick and because he was no longer a threat, she was even going to start planning her future once she had returned home. Apart from the few random flashbacks, she was feeling far less anxious.

She had just been brought back to the ward after her daily physio session and they had told her that she was doing so well that there was every chance that she would be discharged soon. She was beyond pleased, for she had been dreaming of spending Christmas Day by the roaring fire in the sanctuary of her parents' living room. Her mother certainly did Christmas in style. Every year there was an enormous Nordmann fir tree loaded with fairy lights and decorations, beneath which were piles of beautifully wrapped presents. Her mother loved Christmas, always had done, and never missed the opportunity to put on a good show. She thought back to when she was younger and how Joe, CJ, Marco, and Kat used to love staying at her house for sleepovers. She smiled, and Tom, Joe's younger brother, he always came too. Tom had been such a cheeky little scamp back then. She thought back to the time of his first visit. She had shown him the cinema room and Joe told her he wouldn't stop talking about it afterwards. Then there were the summer pool parties, when Joe and all the others would be diving in and out of their swimming pool. Those were the days, lovely memories, but all that was in the past. She had to look to the future.

She and Joe had drifted back into their former friendship. She hoped Joe hadn't picked up on how she really felt. She was doing her best not to show him her true feelings. She often thought back to what he had told her while she had been semi-conscious and if he had meant it. She didn't think she would ever know for sure. Joe had been her childhood sweetheart and the true love of her life; that was before she had stupidly gone and ruined everything. His girlfriend was a lucky woman.

After numerous scans and x-rays, the doctors had finally told her that they thought she was well enough to go home but would need to have physiotherapy as an outpatient. The doctors had told her that Christmas Eve would be the day of her discharge.

She counted down the hours. Even though she had been supplied with crutches, she was still finding it quite difficult to walk. Her x-rays had shown that her ribs had also been fractured but was told they would mend. The doctors had said that she had had a lucky escape, something she already knew full well, because her car had been smashed to pieces and had been written off by her insurance company.

The day had come for her discharge, and although all the hospital staff had been brilliant, the day couldn't have come soon enough. She had begged to return to her cottage after Boxing Day, but the doctors had stood firm. They told her that unless she had someone to look after her, she wouldn't be allowed to leave the hospital. Her mother had been in her element on hearing this, and had gone into full nurse mode, even as far as moving her old bed downstairs into her father's study so she wouldn't have to go up the stairs.

She left the hospital in a wheelchair. As soon as she was wheeled into her makeshift bedroom, she saw the effort her mother and father had put in for her. The study, which had always been her father's beloved sanctum, had been cleared of all his books and his old mahogany desk replaced by an easy access armchair that she'd never seen before. 'Mum, Dad, you didn't have to do this for me.' Her mother smiled triumphantly. 'It's about time your father had a clear out of all his musty old books.'

'Ha, she thinks I've got rid of them,' her father chipped in, winking at Ally. 'Little does she know my books are all stacked up in the garage ready to come back in here when you have moved out.'

'You two will never change,' she giggled, easing herself down into the new chair, which was surprisingly comfortable. She was so grateful to be here.

She had got her wish for a Christmas Day spent in her childhood home. It was a few days later when she and her mother were basking in the cosy warmth of the living room fire, enjoying a girly chat about the good old days, that they heard the doorbell ring. They looked at each other in surprise.

'I'll get it,' said her mother, getting up from the sofa. 'I wonder who it could be, I'm not expecting anyone, are you?'

'No, sorry Mum, I haven't a clue.' She heard the puzzlement in her mother's voice as she addressed the person standing at the door. The person obviously wasn't known to her mother.

The living room door opened, and her mother came into the room, followed by a tall, slimly built, dark-haired woman who she had never seen before.

'Allegra, someone to see you.' Her mother stood aside to let the woman enter the room. 'I'll go and put the kettle on and leave you two to chat.'

'Oh, hello?' She did not recognise the sharp-featured woman who had just entered the room. Had the accident made her memory so bad that she couldn't remember? Why didn't she know who this frosty faced person standing before her was?

For a moment the woman didn't answer. The animosity radiating from her was palpable.

Who on earth was she? She was starting to feel uneasy. The woman obviously had an axe to grind. The next moment she found out.

'I'm Maxine, Joe's partner. I know he has been spending a lot of time with you and I wanted to find out what's going on,' said the woman aggressively.

Although she knew that she would find it painful, she reached for the crutches the hospital had given her and eased herself up from the sofa. Deciding to ignore the woman's bad manners, she offered her spare hand out to Maxine. 'Nice to meet you.' She spoke sympathetically, trying to diffuse the woman's antagonism. 'I'm afraid there is nothing going on. Joe is a childhood friend and has been supportive of me since the car accident, that's all.'

Maxine's aggression didn't lessen. 'It's not just that is it? I know you lived together, and he left Cornwall and went to London just for you. He told me how devastated he was when you walked out on him.'

She nodded, there was no point lying. 'Yes, but that is all in the past. What Joe and I have now is friendship, nothing more.'

Maxine's stance immediately softened. 'I'm sorry. Things have been strained between Joe and I lately. I don't want to lose him.'

Immediately she felt sorry for her. 'I hope things work out for you,' she said lamely.

Maxine stiffened. 'I doubt they will.' Looking disdainfully at her, she sniffed before saying, 'I'll go now but I want you to stay away from him.' With that she abruptly turned and left.

Standing there, she was both shocked and appalled at Maxine's rudeness. She heard the front door open then bang shut. Shortly afterwards her mother returned carrying a plate laden with mince pies and slices of Christmas cake.

'Oh, where's your friend gone?'

She shrugged, not knowing quite what to say. 'She's Joe's partner Mum. I think she was checking me out. She has just left. She was very antagonistic towards me, so I think calling her a friend might be stretching it a bit.'

'Oh dear. That's a bit odd, and you say she was checking you out, what does that mean?'

'I honestly don't know Mum,' she answered, shaking her head, and wondering what was going on with Joe and his girlfriend.

'Never mind, some folk are strange. Let's forget about her and have a cup of tea and demolish some of these cakes.' After setting the laden tray down on the coffee table, she went over to assist her daughter back to the sofa. 'How about a mince pie?'

Settled on the sofa Ally picked at her mince pie, then pushed the plate aside. Her appetite for it had just crumbled, along with any hope of getting back with Joe. She couldn't help feeling an overwhelming sense of guilt, even though she knew she had done no wrong, apart from still having feelings for Joe that is. After Maxine's visit, she was now even more determined to keep them under wraps. No way would she ever get in the way of Joe's relationship with his girlfriend. She decided she wouldn't tell Joe about Maxine's visit either in case it caused trouble for him.

CHAPTER 28

The Christmas break was now over. It had been spent quietly with just her parents, although Kat, bearing a huge box of her favourite chocolates, had surprised her with a visit. As they were sitting chatting, she had really wanted to ask her old friend about Joe's relationship with Maxine but thought it might give the show away. She did manage to ask Kat if she'd seen him though.

'Yes, Joe and Maxine came out for a drink with us on Christmas Eve. To be honest, the atmosphere felt a bit strained. I don't know if he and Maxine had had a tiff before they came out. Even CJ noticed it, and he never notices anything! I've always thought that Maxine was a bit of a strange one,' said Kat, shaking her head. 'To be honest Al, I've never really warmed to her, but because she is Joe's girlfriend, we just accepted her.'

Ally said nothing. Instead, kept her head bowed, making a show of tearing off the cellophane wrapper from the box of chocolates so that Kat wouldn't be able to read what she was feeling.

Joe was in turmoil. Maxine had been driving him nuts. They had both taken annual leave and her constant carping about getting engaged was getting him down. They had bickered non-stop during the Christmas period over almost everything, and he would be glad when he was back at work. It didn't help that he constantly thought about Ally. He didn't dare mention her name in front of Maxine, it was like a red rag to a bull.

It was now New Year's Day. It had started well enough; they had enjoyed a nice breakfast of smoked salmon and cream cheese bagels. It was after he had come back downstairs after his shower that he knew something was afoot.

'Sit down Joe, I have something to say.' It was then that Maxine had given him an ultimatum – get engaged now or we are finished.

He put his head in his hands, thinking what to say. He hadn't been expecting this. He decided to tell the truth. He stood up and took both Maxine's hands in his.

'I'm sorry. I can't marry you Max, I care for you, but I don't love you. It's not your fault, it's mine.'

'I thought as much! Don't try and be nice about it. You sound like one of those bloody romantic novels,' she sneered, snatching her hands away. 'What's that even supposed to mean? We've been together for three years now, it's a bit bloody late to say that now,' she spat. 'It's HER, isn't it? You've not been the same since she came back on the scene, running from her vile criminal lover.' She sat down on the sofa and started to cry.

Not denying it, he stood there feeling helpless. 'Max, I'm sorry.' He hated doing this to her.

Maxine's tear-streaked face looked up at him. 'Does *she* know that you have feelings for her?'

Joe shook his head. 'No, I don't think so. We are friends, we've known each other since we were kids, but other than that, no.'

It was a week later that Joe found himself back in his childhood home, in his old bedroom, which still had some of his teenage possessions piled up in the corner. He had agreed that Maxine keep their rented house and that he should be the one to move out. He hadn't said anything to Ally, or to anyone other than his parents and brother, about his split from Maxine, partly because he was feeling so guilty and partly because he needed time to think. Although he knew how he felt about Ally, he didn't know how she felt about him. Besides, he couldn't leave one relationship then go straight into another, it wouldn't seem right.

It was strange being back in his old home after all these years. Somehow his bedroom seemed smaller than it had done when he was younger. He had hung some of his clothes in the small wardrobe and had stashed a few of his things under the bed, but most of his belongings were still in his car, which was packed to the hilt. He had left all the furniture and fittings for Maxine. He really hoped she would get over the hurt that he'd caused, but knew, without doubt, that he had been true to himself and had done the right thing, and that he would have been living a lie if he'd gone ahead with an engagement.

It was a cold Saturday morning in mid-January. CJ was at a football match and Kat was getting ready to meet up with Ally. She would pick Ally up from her cottage then they would head over to have some lunch at Tom's place.

Tom, dressed in his chef's whites, gave them a wave as soon as they walked through the door. Ally waved back, smiling at him. He hadn't seen Ally face to face for years. He knew she'd been here before with Kat, but he hadn't seen her. He had always liked Ally; she had always had his back when they were kids. He had been gutted when she had left his brother. Considering all she'd been through she still looked good. 'Hi ya you two. Grab a seat and I'll be over in a jiff. First though, what can I get you?'

They both looked at the chalkboard menu. 'A latte and a toasted panini special with a side salad please,' said Ally.

'Same for me too please Tom; can I have extra cheese,' Kat added as an afterthought.

'Okey dokey. You've made an excellent choice there, ladies,' said Tom winking. 'I'll bring your food over as soon as it is ready.'

Once seated, Kat leaned forward and gently tapped Ally on the hand. 'Al, how are you and how are you coping with everything?'

'I'm muddling through Kat. I've been signed off at the hospital and I've moved back to the cottage. I'm even getting some auditions lined up. The only thing I haven't got is a car. Mine was written off in the accident. As soon as the insurance money has come through, Joe is coming with me to choose a new one.'

'Joe eh,' Kat raised her eyebrows and laughed.

'He's been such a good friend to me Kat, even though I don't deserve it.'

'Joe's a great bloke Al, but I think you already know that. I also know that he thought the world of you. Come to think of it, I don't really think he has ever got over you. CJ and I both think you were daft to leave him.'

'I know that now Kat. How I wish I could turn back the clock. It's too late though, Joe has a serious girlfriend, and I must accept that.' The memory of the awful visit she'd had from Maxine popped into her head. Struggling to keep her emotions in check, she was relieved when Tom turned up with their lunch order.

Tom put the plates of food down in front of them. 'Here you are ladies, a feast fit for a king.'

'It looks delicious Tom, thank you. How are you?'

'Fine thanks. Everything seems to be going well for me, thank goodness, which is more than I can say about my brother.'

Ally stiffened.

Kat looked surprised. 'Why what's happened with Joe?'

Tom shrugged. 'He's split up with that girlfriend of his, the one he was living with. He's now back in his old room at home. Our ma's not very happy with him being back, told him he's got to do his own washing and stuff.'

As soon as Tom had gone, Kat raised her eyebrows and smiled as she sipped her coffee. 'Well Al, that bit of news has put the cat among the pigeons hasn't it!'

Still reeling from Tom's news, she nodded. 'It certainly has. I wasn't expecting that. What the heck do I do now Kat?'

'Only you can decide that Al, but whatever your decision, I'll be there for you. Come on, eat up then I'll drive you home and you can think properly.'

After Kat had dropped her back at the cottage, she paced the floor thinking about what Tom had said. Should she tell Joe how she felt? Would it be too soon? She had to be sure and wouldn't want him on the re-bound. She decided to give him time.

Needing to take her mind off Joe, she decided to go and pay a visit to Oscar and Alice. She still had Frank's photo and the letters, which luckily had survived the accident. She hadn't seen them since she'd got back because she hadn't been well enough, but she had spoken to Oscar several times on the phone.

Oscar greeted her like an old friend, and she could tell that he was excited about something. 'Ally, I have had a few phone calls from Gertie.'

'That's brilliant Oscar. How is she?'

'She sounded wonderful. It is hard to believe that she is my aunt. We got on really well, she's very easy to talk to, isn't she?'

Remembering her long conversation with Gertie, she smiled. 'Yes, she's a lovely lady. She was very close to your dad. She told me that he was a good man, and it sounded to me like he was her favourite brother.'

Oscar nodded. 'Yes, she mentioned that to me too. Gertie told me all about my father. She said that she believed my mother had meant a lot to

Frank. She also said that if it hadn't been for his sick wife, Frank would probably have come back to my mother; especially if he had known my mother was pregnant with me.' He shook his head in disbelief. 'You know what Ally, all my life I've wondered about my father and if I had any other family knocking around. Now, thanks to you my dear, I feel as though I've found the missing piece in my life. Oh, and you'll never guess what - I have some more news to tell you.' Oscar grinned excitedly, 'Gertie's family, who I believe are quite well off, are going to make a sizeable donation to our village hall fund in my father's memory. Apparently, Frank wrote a letter just before he died asking the family to honour his last wish because he really loved his time here and never forgot about it.'

Ally beamed, her eyes twinkling. 'I know, Gertie mentioned it to me. I didn't want to say anything in case it didn't happen. I'm really pleased Gertie saw it through Oscar. It's a wonderful legacy which will benefit the whole village. Maybe they will put up a plaque or something in honour of Frank.'

'That would be wonderful,' said Oscar smiling, obviously liking the idea very much.

After popping upstairs to say hello to Alice, she walked back to the cottage feeling a warm glow that she had done something right. She was so pleased that Gertie had been true to her word because it had clearly made Oscar very happy. On hearing her phone vibrate, she checked her messages. Someone had left her a voice mail; it was her agent again. They kept missing each other's calls but the exchange of voice messages between them was getting slightly fractious. She knew that she needed to get back to work, not only to earn some money, but also for her self-esteem. When she had first contacted her agency, her longstanding agent Rebecca had promptly told her that she would do her best to get her some auditions but had warned her that most of the work was likely to be in London or other parts of the country not local to her. When she had stipulated that she didn't want to travel all over the place or go to London for work anymore, Rebecca had sounded a bit put out. Remaining adamant, she had told her agent that even if it meant losing out on the big money, she wasn't going to go back to her old life. She had paid the price of fame once and she wasn't about to do it again.

She stared at her reflection in the wardrobe mirror. Putting aside her concerns about Rebecca finding her work, she had made a special effort with her hair and makeup because she knew the rest of the day was going to be good. Her car insurance had paid out and Joe was going to pick her up soon and help her choose a new car. It had been a few weeks since Tom's bombshell news. She hadn't seen much of Joe, although they had been messaging each other. He had still not given her any indication that he had left Maxine.

Joe had cleaned his car specially for Ally. He wore his best jeans and a new jumper. The last couple of weeks he'd been in torment over what to do about her and after a sleepless night, he had finally reached the conclusion that he had to get over himself and tell her how he felt. He was a bundle of nerves as he pulled up outside Ally's cottage.

As they drove out of the village, heading towards town and the car dealership, she glanced sideways at Joe. Did he seem a bit quiet? Where was their usual banter and chat? Was it her imagination or did things seem a bit strained? She took a deep breath and decided to break the silence. 'Joe, I've been in touch with my agent about work, she's going to phone me back soon.'

'Oh, that's good news Al. What sort of work do you think it will be?'

'Well, I've told her I don't want the life I had before. I'm not hungry for fame anymore and I don't want to be driven to drink and prescription pills through stress again. Never again do I want to live like that, I don't want to be that person again Joe.'

'I understand. You have been through such a lot Al, and now you must do what feels right for you.'

'Thanks Joe,' she said softly. 'All I want is enough to pay the bills. A few low-key jobs, preferably here in Cornwall or nearby, would suit me fine. I don't want the highlife anymore; those days are well and truly gone.'

Joe smiled at Ally's words, how she had changed, and for the better too in his book. 'They are always filming around here; hopefully you might get lucky and land something decent.'

'Hope so. Anyway, enough about me. What have you been up to then?' she asked breezily, addressing the elephant in the room.

This was the time, Joe decided to go for it. 'I've split from Maxine.'

'How come?'

She felt her stomach knot as she waited for his reply.

'I didn't love her, she wanted more than I could give. It made me realise that I still l...'

'Oh damn, it's my agent. Sorry, I must get this Joe, she's already losing patience with me over my refusal to chase bigger roles.'

A few minutes later, after finishing her call, she lay her phone down in her lap, screen facing up. 'Sorry it took so long Joe. She's booked some auditions for me. I'll tell you about them later but first you must tell me about your split with Maxine. You said you didn't love her.'

'That's right. She kept pestering me for an engagement and gave me an ultimatum, engaged or it's over and I chose the latter. I knew I was living a lie because my feelings were elsewhere, always have been.'

Her heart flipped, did Joe mean herself or had he already got someone else? With the worst bad timing ever, her phone rang again. It was Edna's son Darren. She quickly pressed the red X on the screen to get rid of the call, he was the last person she wanted to talk to, especially right now.

Joe quickly glanced at the phone ringing on Ally's lap and saw it was an incoming call from someone named Darren. Saved by the bell, he had just been about to make a massive fool of himself. What was he thinking, of course Ally would have found someone else, there could be no other explanation for the way she had instantly abandoned Darren's phone call. She probably felt embarrassed about talking to a new boyfriend while she was sitting next to an old one. Ally was beautiful, he didn't stand a chance, guys would be queuing to go out with her.

She quickly shut her phone down, not wanting further interruptions. 'Sorry about that Joe. Bloody phone. There, I've switched it off. What were you saying?'

Joe gripped the steering wheel tightly. 'Oh, it was nothing Al, I'll tell you another time. Now then, where's that car place? I think it's around here somewhere.'

Her brief spurt of elation instantly deflated. She knew she had missed her chance. Blast Darren and his stupid phone call. She could have kicked herself for not having switched off her phone earlier.

It should have been a happy time when she and Joe came out of the car dealership, for she had bought herself a shiny red Mini Cooper. Instead, she had a dull ache in her chest and felt on the verge of tears when Joe gave her a perfunctory peck on the cheek before she got into her new car to drive it home.

CHAPTER 29

She hadn't seen or heard from Joe since she'd picked up her new car, apart from a few silly memes he'd forwarded to her that had been doing the rounds. She didn't know how to bridge the invisible gap that had sprung up between them, a gap that was causing her immense pain. She knew she had lost Joe's love but couldn't bear to lose him as a friend, and she didn't know what to do about it.

The winter days seemed never ending. She felt she needed to keep herself busy so she wouldn't think about Joe. The weather had been against her, it had been rainy for most of the week, which had put her off going out for a walk along the coast path in case it was slippery. She had driven to Truro to attend a couple of auditions and was waiting to hear back. Other than that, her days were spent running errands for Edna and catching up with her parents and her friends and helping Millie. Millie had offered her some paid work in the coffee shop, but instead she had given her services for free. She knew, it being winter, that customers were few and far between and that Millie couldn't really afford to pay her and was only doing it out of friendship. Besides, she wasn't on the breadline yet, she still had some savings.

Frank's legacy had caused great excitement in the village and there had been talks with the planners about building the new hall. Should it be built of brick or should they save money by building it in timber. The debate raged on, although brick seemed to be winning the vote, although they needed to do a bit more fund-raising first to cover the cost.

Out of the blue, she saw a message on her phone from Anne, her Psychic Medium friend. Anne had booked some engagements in the West Country and wondered if Ally was up for a visit. Immediately she brightened. A visit from Anne was just what she needed to take her mind off Joe. Straight away she messaged Anne back, inviting her to stay at the cottage for a couple of nights after she had finished her work commitments. As an afterthought, she had also asked Anne if she could do one of her sessions here in the village, to raise money for the new hall.

Straight away a reply pinged back.

Count me in. I will be more than happy Ally dear to help you raise some money for your village.

After putting the date of Anne's arrival in her diary, she raced up the stairs to check out the spare room. The bed itself looked fine, but she would need to buy a new duvet and bedding. Feeling buoyed up by Anne's impending visit, she spent the evening scrolling through her phone choosing new bed linen and other bits and bobs to make the spare room look nice.

The days passed quickly, and the day had finally arrived for Anne's visit. She heard the taxi pull up and rushed to answer the door. Smiling widely at the sight of the bundle of energy that was her psychic friend, she gave her a big hug, and after tipping the taxi driver, helped Anne bring in an assortment of bags and a large suitcase. Anne had only set foot inside the cottage a matter of minutes, when after a moment or two of silently looking around her, she announced, 'Ally dear, this place has a past, did you know?'

'Um, yes. I know a little. A lady named Mary lived here and she was tried as a witch and was hanged in the mid-1600s. One of her crimes was that she kept a pet crow. Her other alleged crimes were that a farmer's milk wouldn't churn and, also that a sick child died having taken one of her potions.'

'Ah, that explains what I'm picking up. Did you say she kept a crow?'

She nodded, wondering where this was leading.

'Back then they used to call them Familiars. Do you know what they are?'

'I know a bit, I was given an old book which mentions them.'

Anne nodded. 'All that seems a bit far-fetched now, but back in the day they took it very seriously indeed.'

'I've got a crow!'

Anne looked surprised.

'What I mean is that I often see a crow in the garden, I give it food, it's almost tame,' she explained, hoping she wasn't sounding too foolish.

'Ah, that's interesting. I think your Mary was probably a folk healer who practiced cunning craft, they were called Cunning Folk and were not malevolent witches at all, so don't worry about that. If anything, your crow is probably looking out for you.'

'That's reassuring Anne,' she murmured, not quite believing it, and wondering if it was all a load of old twaddle. Then she thought back to how the crow had been instrumental in her finding Frank and Alice's love-nest in the garden, which had led her to find their letters, and how it had been pecking at Nick's button and had dropped it at her feet after the storm. And, what about the noise in the fireplace and the disappearing crow footprints - could Anne be right?

While Anne was upstairs unpacking, she made a pot of tea and opened the bag of home baked scones she'd bought from Millie's earlier. Millie had even thrown in a carton of clotted cream and mini portions of jam. What a good friend she was.

Over numerous cups of tea, and several scones, she told Anne about Nick and Joe.

After listening carefully to what Ally had to say, Anne nodded slightly. 'As I told you before Ally, I believe you will have a rocky time of it at first then you will be happy. It sounds to me as if you have already been through the rocky bit.'

'Gosh I hope so Anne. It's taken me a while to come to terms with everything that has happened. I still get some flashbacks, but they seem to be getting less frequent. I could certainly do with something nice happening in my life.'

'It will Ally. I promise you; things will turn out wonderful for you.'

She smiled at this, wanting to ask Anne when exactly all this wonderfulness would happen but decided not to.

The conversation turned to the village hall and the psychic reading that Anne would be doing later.

'Will the village hall need some setting out Anne?'

'Just some tables and chairs dotted around that's all. Is there a stage of some kind there?'

'Yes, there is a sort of a stage. I must warn you though that it's not very grand.'

Anne smiled. 'I don't need grand Ally, just somewhere to sit so I can see everyone, that's all.'

Later that evening when she knocked on Edna's door to drive her down to the village hall, she had found it hard not to stare, for the elderly lady was almost unrecognisable. Edna had gone to great lengths to smarten up. Gone were the worn grubby clothes she normally wore, instead she had donned a smart navy knee length linen dress. Her unruly white hair had been kept in check by a headband covered in a paisley material which matched her scarf, which she had artfully arranged around her neck. Edna's ruddy cheeks had been powdered and she was wearing rose pink lipstick, and was that a hint of eyeshadow and mascara on her eyes too?

'Wow, Edna, you look lovely.'

Edna seemed to puff with pride. 'Thank you dear. Thought I'd better make a bit of an effort. I couldn't get me hands and nails clean though.' Edna held out her wrinkled, veiny gardener's hands, which were still showing signs of ingrained soil.

'Don't worry about them Edna, no one will notice.'

'Maybe I should sit on 'em,' Edna chuckled, as she surveyed her work worn hands.

'You'll be fine. Come on, get in the car.' She held the door open and helped Edna climb into the passenger seat.

As soon as they walked into the hall, she could see that the tables had been laid out café style and that most of them were occupied. It seemed like half the village had turned out for Anne's Psychic Medium reading.

She sat at a table with Edna and watched as Anne addressed her audience from the raised area that everyone called the stage but was in fact a set of huge wooden boxes which had been butted together, used by the local scout group to store their equipment. She wondered if Anne realised that half the people sitting before her hadn't a clue what a Psychic Medium was, and were only here out of curiosity, and to raise money for the new village hall.

The evening progressed. After a sip from her glass of water, Anne leaned forward and scanned the room. 'Are there two ladies in the audience who have lived here for many years?'

Betty and Edna both put their hands up and looked over at each other, looking worried, wondering what Anne was going to do to them.

'Something is coming through from a man named Bill. Bill tells me that he loved both ladies equally and asks that the two ladies make their peace with each other. Bill tells me that he still loves them both and watches over them.'

Both Betty and Edna sat bolt upright in their chairs, mouths agape. Then Edna nudged Ally. 'How did she know about Bill?'

She shook her head. What Anne had just announced was a surprise to her too. 'I really don't know Edna; all I can tell you is that Anne is well known for knowing about these things.'

After the reading, she led Edna over to a small table where Betty was sitting. 'Right ladies, I think it's time to make up for all those lost friendship years. Let's get you both a lovely cup of tea.'

CHAPTER 30

JOE

Joe squeezed his car into the narrow parking space allocated to his parents' cottage. Locking the car, he slipped the keys into his jacket. He glanced down at the inner harbour. The tide was in, and Pete Metcalfe's fishing boat was bobbing on the swell. He felt a pang of longing and spent several minutes taking in the warm colours of the setting sun, watching as it slowly disappeared into the horizon. He had missed all of this while he had been living with Maxine. He had always loved watching the sunset. Seeing it again reminded him of the years he had spent looking out over the sea from his bedroom window.

Looping the strap of his holdall over one shoulder, he walked down the alley to the back gate of his childhood home, part of an 18th century row of cottages built in thick Cornish granite to withstand the many ferocious storms that swept in from the sea. Today had been his last day on shift and he was so looking forward to tomorrow, which would be the first of his rest days. There would be no getting up at the crack of dawn for him either. He needed a break; work had been so busy. There had been a hint of Spring in the air all day and his thoughts had turned to his wooden dinghy that had been covered in tarpaulin all winter. One of his colleagues had told him that mackerel had been seen offshore. It was a bit early in the season for mackerel but hearing about it had stirred something in him, and he now had an urge to get his dinghy out of storage and attempt a bit of night fishing.

He needed to do something positive for he had been feeling so down after his discovery that Ally had another man. There had been no contact with her at all except for sending her a few funnies that came his way. So scared was he that he would show his true feelings for her if they met up, he had kept his distance. It was too late for him and Ally, there was no way he could show his hand now. A trip out in his little dinghy would probably do him good. He needed to get his act together and get his life back on track; he couldn't act like a love-sick fool forever.

After swapping his work clothes for jeans and a light grey hoodie, he went down to the quay to check out his dinghy, which he knew was getting past its sell-by date but which he couldn't bear to part with. Looking all around the little boat for signs of winter damage, he decided that it had fared quite well during its winter break. He would take it out tonight for its first sail of the season. It didn't matter if he got back late because he could have a lay-in tomorrow. He rummaged in his car boot and pulled out his life jacket for later and his fishing gear. First though he would get something to eat. He was too late for dinner and wondered if his ma had plated up some food for him. His dad would probably be in the Harbour Inn yarning with his mates and his ma would probably have her feet up, watching the tv.

Darkness fell. The harbour basin was quiet and the sea as black as treacle. After rowing to the outer harbour walls, Joe rested the oars and paused to listen to the gentle ripple of the waves splashing up the sides of the dinghy. It was good to be out here again. He looked back at the Harbour Inn which was set back from the quay and could see there were a few people sitting on the benches outside, a sure sign that it was starting to get busy again. He wasn't at all surprised, for the weather had turned mild for this time of year. At the first sign of good weather people descended on their historic harbour in droves. From here he had a good view of his parents' cottage. The living room curtains had not been drawn, revealing the flicker from the large television in the corner of the room. His ma always insisted on having no big lights on while watching the telly, and all these years later he still hadn't fathomed out whether it was the need to save money or, was just that in the evenings his ma liked their living room lit like a cinema.

Taking up the oars again, he rowed out into the open water of the bay, and it was only then that he noticed that there was something wrong with his navigation lights. In dismay, he watched as one light briefly flickered before going dead, followed by the other. Reaching over, he pressed the switches a few times and jiggled the wires, momentarily the lights sprang into life. The next minute they had plunged the dinghy back into darkness again. 'That's all I need,' he muttered under his breath. He would need to buy a new set and would order some when he got home, thankfully there were no other boats around.

He heard it before he saw it, like it came out of nowhere. It sounded like a speedboat, one that was driving at great speed too. He couldn't see any lights but by the sound of it, it was a powerful vessel and getting nearer and nearer to him by the second. By the time he saw the speedboat cutting through the dark night, it was almost on top of him. There was no way he could get out of its way in time. He braced himself for what was about to happen. There was an almighty bang, the next instant he felt his dinghy rise out of the water and despite holding on for dear life, he found himself being hurtled into the deep, cold sea. Something heavy came crashing down on him, then he knew no more.

Joe's dad was sitting at the bar, nursing his one and only half pint of ale of the night, while chatting to the landlord of the Inn. 'Our Joe's took his boat out in the bay tonight, thinks he can catch some mackerel,' he chortled.

'Mackerel? Isn't it a bit early in the season?'

'Aye, but you try telling him that.'

The landlord, while listening, had also been keeping a watchful eye on a young chap sitting in the corner, seemingly under the influence of something. He was just about to go over and have a word with him when the chap got up from his seat and walked unsteadily towards the door.

'Cor, that one's going have a bit of a sore head tomorrow by the looks of it. Hope he not be driving,' said Joe's dad.

'I'll go and check he's not heading for the car park; we don't want him driving home like that,' said the landlord, lifting the wooden counter flap.

'Has he gone?' Joe's dad asked, after the landlord returned.

'He has. He be walking up the hill I reckon.'

A few minutes later Pete Metcalfe came bursting through the door. 'Help! Some idiot has just taken off in a speedboat, no lights or anything. Drivin' like a bloody demon he was. Clipped the side of me fishing boat, nearly took it out he did.'

Joe's dad slammed down his glass. 'My son is out there in his dinghy. Quick. Raise the coastguard.'

Joe had no memory of what had happened and had spent the past week in hospital with head injuries, a fractured femur, bruised ribs, and multiple lacerations. He knew he'd been lucky not to have lost his life. Thank goodness for his dad and the pub landlord. He would be forever grateful that they had had the foresight to alert the coastguard. He had a vague memory of the loud whirl of the Air Ambulance and thought he remembered someone talking about loss of blood. He had woken to find he was in a side ward in the local hospital.

It was afternoon visiting hour and Joe knew his parents would be visiting later. He was not expecting any other visitors. Feeling drowsy, he closed his eyes in the hope he could get some sleep. Hospital wards were noisy at night, something he hadn't realised until now.

ALLY

After Anne had returned home, she had spent the last few weeks in torment. She had plunged into a black mood that she only managed to shake off by keeping busy. Her agent had secured her several voiceovers and she was also in the running for a decent role in a new police drama, set to be filmed here in Cornwall. She was keeping her fingers crossed that it would come off, as it would allow her to stay local and would keep her solvent. Never had she been more grateful to have her understanding agent.

Joe was constantly on her mind and when she heard her phone ringing, she had no idea of the awful news it would bring. It was Kat.

'I don't like being the bearer of bad news Al, but I've just been told that Joe has been in a boating accident. He's in hospital.'

She felt her legs go wobbly. 'I-is he going to be alright?'

'Think so, but he's got a head injury and a few broken bones and cuts. I'll message you the ward he's in.'

'Thanks Kat.' With that she jumped in her car and headed to the hospital.

She walked down the long hospital corridor mentally ticking off the names until she came to the ward Joe was in.

Hesitating, she stood outside the door. She was a bundle of nerves. Would Joe want to see her? Was she about to make a fool of herself? She wished that she had stopped off to buy him some grapes or a magazine. It would have given her a reason to be here. She needed to get a grip, she was here now, there was no going back. Placing her hand on the metal push plate, she entered the ward.

'Please can you tell me what bed Joe Tremayne is in?'

'Room 2, second room on the right,' answered the nurse after checking her notes.

As soon as she entered the little room, she had to fight back the tears. Joe was lying on the bed with a bandage around his head, tubes up his nose and his leg in plaster. Under his hospital gown she could see bandages. His eyes were shut, like he was asleep. There was no way she wanted to disturb him. Instead, moving as quietly as she could, she sat down in the chair right next to his bed and watched the gentle rise and fall of his chest. With tear filled eyes, she lightly caressed the top of his hand. With her voice barely above a whisper, she started to speak from the heart. 'Joe, I'm so sorry for the way I treated you. I was such a fool back then. Please forgive me for the hurt I've caused you. I love you and I've missed you terribly.'

Was he dreaming? He gradually became aware of a woman talking to him. Was she saying how much she loved him? He could feel her warm soft fingers on his hand. Straight away he knew who it was. Opening his eyes, he curled his fingers around hers.

'Ally?' his voice croaked with emotion.

'Yes,' she said softly, her stomach turning, knowing the time had come for her to tell him how she felt. Whether she would regret it afterwards, she didn't know. She took a deep breath. 'Joe, I need to tell you that I still love you and I'm so sorry for what I did. I'm not that person anymore, and no matter what happens next, or whatever you think of me, I want you to know that; even if you can never forgive me.' She gabbled her words, not pausing for breath.

He listened carefully, doing his best to absorb what she was saying.

The silence was unbearable. 'Joe, have I just made a fool of myself?'

After what seemed like an age, he looked up at her. 'No, Al,' he said tenderly, 'of course you haven't.' Even though he wasn't given to crying, he could feel his eyes starting to moisten. Taking both of her hands in his, he attempted to sit up, but a sharp stab of pain caught him. He lay back against the pillows. 'I can't believe you are here. I thought I had lost you to that other guy. It's not all those painkillers they've pumped into me giving me hallucinations is it, Al?' he rasped, wanting to talk despite the pain he was in.

Bursting with a mixture of happiness and relief, she bit back her tears. 'No Joe, it's not the painkillers.' Her voice wavered with emotion. 'I came as soon as Kat told me what had happened.' Pausing, she looked puzzled. 'What other guy Joe?' she asked softly.

'The guy that rang you in the car. I saw his name come up on your phone. I think his name was Darren or something like that,' he pressed further. He had to know for sure.

Smiling, she shook her head. 'Darren is Edna's son. The only reason he has my number is because of Edna. To be honest, he's a bit of a nuisance and not very nice and I was going to block him.' She looked startled as the penny dropped. 'Oh no. Joe, did you think I was seeing Darren?'

He gave a slight nod.

'I'm so sorry Joe. I promise you with all my heart, that there is no other man in my life. I don't want anyone else, only you.'

He blinked away a tear. 'All this time I've been thinking you had someone else. I had just been about to ask you if we could start over and put the bad stuff behind us. Then I saw his name come up on your phone.'

'Oh Joe, nothing could be further from the truth. I don't like Darren, never have.' More than anything, she wanted to put her arms around him, but not wanting to hurt him, she gently squeezed his hand. 'That call from Darren came at the worse possible moment ever,' she said softly. 'I wanted the same as you Joe and I had planned to tell you that, when for some reason, you seemed to go cold on me. After that, I thought I'd blown any chance I had. I was heartbroken and didn't know what to do. It was only when Kat told me you were in here that made me swallow my pride and come to see you. Even though you might not have wanted to see me, I had to take the chance. I had to tell you how I felt.'

He shook his head in disbelief. 'I've been such an idiot. How could I have got it so wrong? We have wasted all this time when we could have been together. I love you so much Al and have done for most of my life, probably from the very first moment I saw you at the Sailing Club.'

She smiled. 'That was such a long time ago. We could only have been about twelve. I thought you were the cutest thing on the planet.' Using the tips of her fingers, she gently wiped away the tear that wetted his cheek. 'Come to think of it, I still do,' she whispered.

Despite the pain he was in, his eyes crinkled into a smile. She could tell by the look of him that he clearly wasn't well. With a lump in her throat and wanting to stem her own tears that were threatening to fall, she said the first thing that came into her head. Husky with emotion, she whispered 'Sorry I didn't bring you any grapes.' As soon as the words came out of her mouth, she regretted them. She lowered her eyes, embarrassed.

Smiling, he very carefully leaned towards her. Cupping his hands gently around her face, he kissed her tenderly. Using his thumb, he wiped away one of her escaping tears. 'Who needs grapes. Can we start again Al? Please can we put everything that has happened behind us?'

'Yes,' she whispered. Despite her best intentions, tears of joy cascaded down her face.

THE END

EPILOGUE

Ally stood in the doorway and fondly watched Diesel and Indie, their newly acquired rescue cats. Diesel was raising his black paw to fastidiously wash behind his ears, and Indie was rolling over to bask in a shaft of sunlight. The cats had been a gift from Edna and were fast becoming their beloved fur babies. A feeling of contentment washed over her. She let her mind wander back over the past months and how her life had amazingly changed for the better. She knew that she couldn't be happier, even if she tried.

Once he was well enough to be discharged from hospital, Joe had become a frequent visitor, often staying over, and when he suggested they get a place of their own together, she had jumped at the chance. She loved the village, loved her friends, and for goodness sakes, even loved the crow, who was still hopping around. It seemed that he quite like her too, judging by the way he had hung around hoping for some crumbs whenever she had been in the garden. She would be sad to leave him behind but knew it was time to move on. She had accepted a leading role in a police drama, to be set in Cornwall. It was due to start filming soon, and she hoped it would run for a while. It would make her and Joe financially secure, secure enough to put a deposit down on a house with a bit of land. They would have to leave the village because the property prices here were ridiculous but hopefully, they would be able buy something near enough to visit friends and family and for Joe to continue sailing.

A year had passed. She and Joe now had a couple of new additions to their family of pets, another kitten called Toby and a mischievous golden red cocker spaniel named Ted. They were now living on the outskirts of the village, where property was more affordable. With a little help from her parents, they had been able to buy a house with a small parcel of land for Ted to run around. They planned to grow their own produce and plants and keep a few chickens. She was looking forward to the start of shooting the second series of the police drama which was due to start in a few weeks. She was still great friends with Ashna and Millie. Anne, her Psychic Medium friend had been right in her prediction. She had indeed survived the bumpy ride and found happiness with Joe. She would have to let Anne know and invite her to stay in their new home. Millie and Ashna often came over to see her. Millie with her cheeky cockapoo Charlie, who was best dog pals with Ted and Ashna, whose little boy was a delight.

Kat, CJ, and Tom were frequent visitors too, there being no elephant in the room now. Marco and his girlfriend popped in whenever their busy schedule allowed, which wasn't very often. When time allowed, she still popped in to see Edna, taking her a bar of her favourite chocolate.

Gertie's family had been true to their word and donated enough money to replace the old village hall. Plans had been passed for a new brick-built community hub and work would be starting shortly. Oscar had been proud as punch when the committee had agreed to put a plaque above the door in memory of his father Frank. Betty and Edna were friends again. Life was good.

I hope you enjoyed reading this book as much as I enjoyed writing it.
Thank you for taking the time to read Ally's story, and apologies for any bloopers or inaccuracies that may have slipped through the net.

Printed in Great Britain
by Amazon

30240368R00191